CW00555666

LOOK TO THE STARS

By

Wendy Howard

Look to the Stars

Copyright 2020 Wendy Howard

And
Woodrow Publishing

Woodrow Publishing
www.woodrowpublishing.com/

ISBN-9798653977695

CONTENTS

DEDICATIONS

This book is dedicated to

Stuart

They said it wouldn't last,
But we proved them all wrong

CHAPTER 1
NEW BEGINNINGS

She sat alone in the departure lounge at Manchester Airport. Although she held a book before her eyes she was unable to concentrate on the words written there. Jennifer Peters at forty-six looked ten years younger, sitting there in her pale pink and blue Dash tracksuit with Reebok trainers. An attractive woman with dark shoulder length hair cut in a fashionable bob, looking healthy with the remains of the tan she'd acquired when they'd taken an early break to the Canaries. She managed to retain her tan between holidays without resorting to salon sun beds by spending as much time as possible in the garden, or out exercising the dogs on the moors above their home.

Realising she'd read the same paragraph several times, she put away the book and sauntered to the duty free shop to pass a little more time before her journey. 'No need to buy cigarettes' she thought sadly, and then quickly moved on through the spirits section, where she glanced at the bottles of Pernod. She'd always liked the aniseed taste. It was that liking that had first attracted her to the traditional Greek drink, Ouzo, and very soon it would be Ouzo she'd be enjoying. She carried on to the perfume section and picked up a bottle of Chanel for her and a bottle of Coco for one of her many Greek friends.

Her husband had always objected to going into the perfume section, insisting that it gave him headache! She wondered if it had been the prices or her wish to purchase that had been the real headache. She shivered a little as if someone had walked over her grave, then hastily paid for the perfumes and made her way back to the seating area.

Very soon the singsong voice would ask passengers to go to the relevant gate, in readiness for departure. There would be a rush of people, all jostling for what they perceived to be the best position. Once at the gate area they would have to remain there for several more minutes before the details regarding boarding were made. Their rush would have been pointless, but everybody always did it. Today would be no exception. She remembered for a brief moment how it always amused her husband that they called the smoking rows forward first to board the plane. There would be no such call today.

She looked around at the passengers waiting to board, families with small children already fractious with waiting, some running wild and unchecked, much to the annoyance of other travellers, some tucking into crisps and sweets, their sticky hands touching seats and tables and pulling on their parents clothing to divert their attention from the newspapers they were trying to read. There were groups of young boys and girls clutching oversized hi-fis and wearing t-shirts announcing their availability, with intentions for this forthcoming holiday. She could see couples sitting close with arms entwined, whispering sweet nothings to each other, older married couples constantly checking that they had their tickets and passports in the flap of their flight bag, or rushing off to the toilet "Just in case they called them." Everyone seemed to belong to someone, except her. A wave of sadness washed over her momentarily. She thought how she should have been with someone and how fate had robbed her of that pleasure.

Not wishing to lose her composure she took out the book she'd been trying to read previously and looked for distraction in its fantasy world, but after a few paragraphs her mind began to wander. It had been almost ten years since her first trip to the Greek islands, when she'd fallen in love with them at first sight.

What a wonderful holiday that first time in Greece had been - Like a second honeymoon. Their first holiday without the children, when they'd acted like children themselves! They'd spent hours doing just what they wanted, laughing and joking all day, bathing their bodies in the hot sun and cooling down by splashing in the icy cold sea, making love every afternoon, staying late in the bars drinking endless bottles of wine and Ouzos and chatting about everything and nothing. They had fallen in love all over again. She sighed deeply and felt a prickle in the corner of her eye. Yes, it had been very special, their first holiday without the children

Not that those holidays with the children had been unpleasant. There had been fun filled holidays in the early years, visiting Wales and Cornwall. Then when the children were old enough, they'd taken them for their first holiday abroad, and what a success that had been.

Before she could reminisce anymore the public address system interrupted her, requesting that passengers for the flight to Kos go to gate thirty-six. It would not be long now before they would be boarding the plane, and in a matter of four hours she would be stepping out onto the tarmac at Kos airport to begin a new chapter in her life. She took a sharp intake of breath at the thought of this.

"Don't worry, its quite safe to fly these days," the reassuring voice of a fellow passenger was heard to say. "You'll be okay once we've taken off." She nodded to the woman who'd spoken to her but thought how frightened the woman actually looked herself. Jenny knew from her own past experience of flying that helping to comfort others often went a long way to comforting your own self.

Clutching her 'Jean Shilton' bag, which held the valuable documents she needed later today, as well as the essential travel wipes and barley sugars for take-off. She thought how the bag didn't really go with her outfit today, dressed as she was for comfort, knowing how crumpled she'd be at the end of four hours in the cramped seat on this holiday flight. Her friends had suggested she take a charter, but it seemed unnecessary at this stage. Also, she felt more at home and less conspicuous in the hubbub created by holiday travellers.

She reached inside her bag to retrieve the boarding pass she'd replaced after making her duty free purchases. It was strange to have to remember everything for herself instead of relying on someone else. The public address system announced that passports would be required and she delved once more into the bottomless bag. As she pulled out her passport, an old photograph fell to the floor. The woman who'd offered her comfort, reached down to retrieve it.

"A very handsome man, is it your husband?" she said approvingly, glancing at Jenny's wedding finger. Jenny nodded. Not wanting to get into lengthy explanations with a complete stranger, she thanked the woman.

As she went to replace the photograph in her bag she glanced at it, making her heart skip a beat. Yes he was a very handsome man sitting outside a tavern in the photograph, looking extremely tanned and at total peace with the world, a glass of beer in one hand, a cigarette in the other. Many of her photographs of him were in that poise, beer and cigarettes, the two items which had been so much a part of him ever since they first met all those years ago.

She was sixteen, he was a year older. Now twenty-seven years later, he was still the only man she'd ever really loved. She tucked the photograph back in the side pocket of her bag and took her place in the long queue in front of gate thirty-six.

Boarding the plane was the usual scramble, with the airhostesses making their polite greetings to everyone, even the noisy youngsters who, filled with holiday spirit, mostly acquired at the bar, would make the journey a bit of an ordeal for them.

Jenny took her place next to the window on row twenty-three, placing her bag beneath her seat so as not to disturb her fellow passengers during the flight by needing to retrieve it from the overhead lockers. She clipped her seat belt around her trim waist, having to adjust it considerably before it was secure. The extra weight she'd lost recently had been an asset to her, although she still felt that she looked a little weary and drawn, especially around the eyes. Still, a few weeks in the sun would remedy that.

Slowly the plane filled up and everyone took their seats, having put their overweight hand luggage in every space available. The airhostess handed out the fruit drops for take-off. The plane trundled laboriously along the outer road leading to the main runway whilst the airhostess stressed the importance of watching the video being played, telling of in-flight safety and emergency procedures. She wondered how many people were actually listening to this, remembering how at one time this would have had her full attention. As she glanced round now, a few rows behind she could see the woman who'd comforted her earlier. She was watching the safety drill intently, so as not to miss a single detail. Jenny had been right; she was a nervous passenger herself.

The plane meandered along, coming at last to its spot at the end of the main runway, which Jenny considered to be the point of no return - the pause before actual take off. With the engines revving to screaming pitch and building to a terrific crescendo, the pilot finally released the brakes and catapulted the plane at break neck speed along the rutted runway to eventually break into flight, at what always seemed the last minute before the runway merged with the surrounding fields. It was funny that even the noisiest of passengers seemed to be silenced at this time, as if holding their breath would help ensure that the plane would be successful in its transition from the ground to the air.

After an initial steep incline, the plane banked heavily to the west. Seconds later, the seat belt sign was switched off, the take off was completed.

No longer was there the familiar sound of matches being struck or lighters clicking followed the long intake of breath filling the lungs of the smokers who appeared so relieved at being able to smoke, even though it was only minutes before when they'd extinguished their cigarettes in readiness for boarding. All flights were now non-smoking.

Next came the rush to use the too few toilets onboard. Each one in the queue wishing they'd not had that 'last one' before take-off.

Next it was the time for the clattering of the trolleys, with polite hostesses offering refreshments of the liquid variety and encouraging customers to order any wine for their meal. Jenny ordered Vodka and fresh orange and a half bottle of red, which she hoped would not be too dry, as too often it was on flights. You certainly needed something to wash down the plastic food which would be served shortly.

Picking up the in-flight magazine she saw that the film to be shown was the same as the previous flight she'd taken. Well perhaps she'd sleep instead.

The food arrived hot and with an aroma that promised to delight the palate, but as often with promises, they never really match up to your expectations. She toyed with the salad in Marie Rose sauce and searched for the non-existent prawns that she felt should have been there. She had a couple of mouthfuls of the Chicken Chasseur, but left the sweet and the cheese with biscuits.

It seemed sacrilegious to eat the cheese and biscuits even now. She'd always given these to her husband who would devour them in place of the main course and sweet, which he never even attempted to eat.

She was just finishing the last sips of her wine as the hostess came to remove the finished tray. She settled herself with her head resting on her discarded tracksuit top, placed against the window so as to soften any knocks that may occur with turbulence.

The monotonous whirring of the engine acted as a lullaby and, helped by the wine, she fell into a somewhat disturbed slumber. She'd had a lot of vivid dreams recently, often waking in the middle of the night drenched in sweat and calling out for someone to help her. The calls, even if help had really been necessary would have been in vain, since there was no one there. She was alone, really alone for the first time in her adult life.

During her sleep recently, in an attempt to overcome this feeling of loneliness she'd searched for happy memories, returning many times to the distant past, as if trying to ensure every detail could recalled if necessary, and that no one moment of her past could be lost. It was to these early years that her mind now wandered.

CHAPTER 2
THE EARLY YEARS

It was the May Bank holiday weekend and as usual the fair had come to Ashtown. The rides and sideshows were strewn all over an area which became the town's football pitches in the winter season. There was always something exciting about the fair with its noise, hustle and bustle, bright lights with loud music and mingling smells of hot potatoes, donuts and candy floss. The entire inhabitants of the town seemed to visit at sometime over the fleeting three days it was there.

It was the place where families with young children would visit with dads showing their expertise at darts, throwing to win a goldfish which then required the purchase of a goldfish bowl, but would probably be dead before they reached home.

Courting couples holding hands and walking round clutching overstuffed, grotesque looking teddy bears that had been costly to win but showed how much they loved each other, hoping now to sneak a quick kiss concealed by the canopy that flicked momentarily over the passengers on the fast moving caterpillar ride.

Youths with leather jackets showing their prowess at riding the speedway, their hands never touching the safety bars, glancing round all the time to see how many young girls may be watching them perform this dangerous act.

It was the place to go, and Jenny was determined not to miss it. At sixteen she'd progressed through the clumsy early stages of puberty and had turned into an attractive young woman with a pretty face and a good figure, although she would have disagreed about the description of a good figure, since having the largest bust in her class at grammar school had made her the target of childish remarks. She would have gladly exchanged places with those girls whose development was way behind hers, girls who looked as if they would never have anything more than tiny mounds to bother them.

Jenny's hair was worn to help conceal some of her embarrassment at a length which when brushed forward, covered the contours of her bust and fell in loose waves just above the waist. It was dark brown with red hi-lights and always shining, since she rose early to wash it every morning. It certainly was eye catching, parted in the middle and left to hang loose. Her mother always said it looked like a pair of curtains.

It was the era of the miniskirt and Jenny liked to be 'in fashion.' Today she'd chosen to wear a white sleeveless polo neck sweater with a broad black belt, a red skirt - only a little wider than the belt - and her newly acquired white stretch PVC boots - the very latest in fashion. She brushed her hair and put on just the traces of mascara so as not to upset her mother, whom she knew would object to the minuscule skirt she was wearing.

She glanced at herself in the mirror. 'Not too bad;' she thought, then picked up her white shoulder bag which she'd bought to match the boots with last week's wages from her Saturday job at the local boutique. She checked the contents. Lipstick to apply once she was out of sight of Mum, tissues to clean it off before arriving home, a bottle of perfume bought from the Avon lady and a purse with several key rings attached. She didn't even own a key, but it was 'in' to collect key rings and it certainly stopped you losing your purse with all those noisy attachments.

She checked the money in the purse, change for the bus fare into town, (the bus conductors always complained if you didn't have the right amount in change,) bus fare back, although she didn't mind walking down the road from town, it was just the uphill walk she didn't like. Mum always said it would help her figure to walk more. What help did her figure need? It seemed to be doing too well enough without her help.

"Bye" she shouted, quickly passing the entrance to the lounge where her mother was busy cleaning the windows, hoping not to be stopped and have to listen yet again to the lecture about indecent skirt lengths and how common it was to wear too much make-up at that age. Fortunately today Mum was pre-occupied with her chores and only paused to call out a warning about speaking to strangers and curfew time – ten-thirty! Jenny heaved a sigh of relief.

Checking again that her purse was in her bag, she walked briskly to the bus stop. She saw one older lady glance at her, raise her eyebrows and sigh. She presumed this was a comment on her attire and smiled to herself, thinking that she might get a more pleasurable reaction from any boys they may meet at the fair.

She'd arranged to meet Sue outside the butchers at the end of the street leading to the fairground. Why the butchers shop, she couldn't understand, as it wasn't the sort of shop window you could gaze into whilst waiting. At least the ironmongers window was jam packed with all sorts of everything, and you could pass time guessing what some of the contraptions were actually for. Still, she shouldn't have to wait long as Sue's bus was due to arrive at the same time as hers.

The bus came and she boarded it quickly, pulling down her skirt a little so as not to upset the guy following her up the stairs. She always went upstairs, even for the shortest of journeys. You were more likely to meet people of your own age up there, as it was too much of a struggle for mums with kids or older people. She positioned herself next to the window, adjusted her skirt once again, flicked her hair behind her ear and glanced around the people occupying the other seats. There was no one there who she knew. She spent the rest of the journey looking out the window, hoping that the few grey clouds would blow away and leave a warm sunny day.

Nearing her stop she rose carefully, descended the stairs and glanced in the mirror at the top to check her appearance, only to see her distorted reflection peering back at her. From the moment she stepped down from the bus she could sense the atmosphere of the fair. She could hear the cacophony of noise coming from the playing fields and was immediately engulfed by the crowds coming and going. She caught sight of Sue outside the butchers shop. Her friend was wearing a short; almost see through white mini, a peasant blouse and a black crocheted waistcoat, about three inches longer than her skirt. She too wore the fashionable PVC knee high boots, but hers were black to match the waistcoat.

Sue waved frantically in case Jenny couldn't see her and then smiled when she realised she had. They linked arms and began to make their way to the fairground, heads together, chatting and laughing loudly as they went. They crunched over the cinders that had been laid at the entrance to the fields, checked their boots for damage and then suddenly they were there, in the mad frenzy of the fair.

Where to go first? The speedway to look at the talent, the big wheel with its wonderful vantage point, the waltzer, where the best music was always played, or the candy floss stall?

"Let's start at the waltzer," Sue suggested. "I think we should have candy floss after that ride, not before."

In agreement, Jenny followed her friend and pushed through the crowds to the waltzer where attendants, having positioned themselves at carriages full of young girls, spun them round and round evoking ear piercing screams from the riders.

As the ride slowed down and spewed out the occupants, Jenny and Sue rushed to find a carriage of their own. Pulling the bar down on top of their legs, they declared their ownership of this particular carriage for the duration of the ride. The carousel soon filled up with a mixture of riders. There were couples huddling close together, dads taking hesitant children for their first adult ride, and young boys out to prove they were brave by riding without the bar down.

Just before the ride began, two youths pulled at the bar and without waiting for a reply to their, "Do you mind if we join you?" they leapt into the carriage either side of Jenny and Sue, placed their arms over the back of the carriage in a sort of semi-nonchalant poise, broad smiles on their faces as if they'd accomplished what they'd set out to do. Jenny knew that this meant the attendant, who she'd noticed was quite a dish would not spin their carriage, since it would appear to them that they were already with someone and not available for them to make their advances.

The ride began without any words spoken. It gradually gained speed and the carriages spun first one way and then the other. They were bounced around from one side of to the other, constantly coming into contact with the body of the boy seated next to them. Then after what seemed only a matter of seconds, it was over. The boys got off first, turning as if to say something to the girls but then losing the courage, they disappeared into the crowds.

Embarrassed at their closeness on the ride, Jenny had not looked at the boy whose arm had hung so closely to her shoulders, but now she glanced after them. At that very same moment 'he' turned to catch a last look at the girls they'd shared the ride with.

As their eyes met, Jenny felt a strange churning in the pit of her stomach, a dull ache accompanied by butterflies. She'd never experienced such strength of feeling before. Catching her breath, she looked away and looked back, but to her disappointment she saw he was gone and the moment had passed.

Sue led Jenny around the fair, the big wheel, speedway and the cyclone. Glancing in her purse, Jenny found she still had enough money left for a couple more rides. In fact, if she didn't take the bus home she could buy a bag of chips to share with Sue as they walked.

"Dodgems," Sue suggested.

"Why not," replied Jenny, not wanting to miss out on anything.

As they approached the dodgems, Jenny had the funny sensation that she was being watched. As she looked up at the ride, would-be riders gathered around the ride to watch, leaning or sitting on the wooden fencing surrounding it.

Jenny glanced at the faces and suddenly met a pair of eyes staring back at her. Her heart skipped a beat as she realised it was the same boy from the waltzer. His green-brown eyes, which lowered momentarily in embarrassment at having been caught, were compelled to return again to look at her face. Jenny didn't know whether to look away, rush off and pull her tongue out at him, or what! All sorts of unusual feelings were racing through her body.

Without her consciously wanting it to, a little smile broke out on her face, followed by a sudden rush off red to her cheeks when she realised 'he'd smiled back.

It was too late now to make a hasty exit, as he was coming towards her. What should she do, what should she say, was her hair right, should she pull down her skirt? Just at that moment the other boy pushed forward, swaggered across and, much more confident than his partner in crime, said to Sue those immortal words" Do you come here often?"

Instantly pleased with the attention, Sue put her hand on her hip in a somewhat provocative poise and replied "Only when there is a 'Y' in the day."

Happy that his approach had not been rebuffed he positioned himself on the rail next to Sue. "Do you fancy a ride?" he asked.

Sue tittered at the double meaning, "Yeah okay," she replied, to which he smiled.

As the cars came to a halt the boy grabbed the upright pole and bowing low, announced to Sue, "Your carriage awaits, My Lady." Another fit of giggles came from Sue as she held out her hand to be assisted onboard.

Jenny felt a little abandoned but she was used to this. Sue was always quicker at making friends, always choosing the best looking guy and leaving the other to Jenny. She always found someone, whilst Jenny was not always so lucky.

Jenny smiled and waved as the cars lurched into motion, then feeling someone's presence she turned to her right to find that 'he' was there.

"He always manages to pick up the birds. He has the gift of the gab. Could sell sand to the Arabs," 'he' said. Jenny only smiled in reply.

Why was she feeling this way? She felt as if she was as red as a beetroot. There was a long pregnant pause. Should she say something? Would he say something? Was he just making conversation whilst his friend chatted up Sue? Was he trying to chat her up and did she want him to?

"Weather's kept fine" he muttered, looking down at his shoes. Why could he never think of the right things to say? She didn't seem to want to talk to him. Was she just being polite, not telling him to shove off? Why was he feeling so strange standing so close to this girl he'd only just met? He'd felt okay sitting close to her on the waltzer, but once she'd met his gaze as they left the ride he'd been overwhelmed with the desire to speak to her, to be close to her, to touch her.

Jenny nodded agreement about the weather and looked down at her boots. 'Come on,' she thought. 'Say something to him. You want to get to know him don't you?' She glanced up to see the dodgem cars coming to a stop and Sue and her new boy alighting, arms around each other laughing. Oh how she wished this other boy would put his arm around her waist in that fashion.

"We're going on the caterpillar," Sue announced. "See you back here in five minutes okay?"

"Sure," Jenny replied.

The girls had an understanding when it came to blokes; at least Sue had made the understanding quite clear. If you clicked with a lad the other girl would take a back seat, providing an arrangement was made to meet before going home.

The pair hurried off laughing with their heads together in similar fashion to how Sue and Jenny were when they'd arrived at the fair.

Jenny decided to buy a candyfloss. Looking round she saw that 'he' had made his escape and was no longer in view. She felt a pang of disappointment, then shrugged her shoulders and made her way to the candy floss stall. As she turned with her sticky purchase in hand, she came face to face with him

"Sorry," he said breathlessly. "I just went to get some cigs and when I turned round you'd gone. I er I er," Jenny thought he was losing his nerve again.

"Do you want to go on the dodgems?" he questioned.

"No thanks," came back Jenny's reply a little too quickly. She instantly saw the disappointment in his eyes. He did have such lovely eyes. "Er I have just bought this," she added, quickly holding up the candyfloss. "It would be a bit of a mess trying to steer and eat this at the same time." She saw the relief on his face. She didn't say no because she didn't want to be with him, just because of the candyfloss.

"Want to walk around until the others are back?" she asked.

"Yea" he said, almost too readily and stepped forward to take her by the hand. Then as if thinking this may be regarded as too forward, he dropped the hand loosely at his side and took another step back.

They walked around about a foot apart at first, then Jenny suddenly realised that from time to time their hands or shoulders brushed momentarily as they pushed through the crowds. It would be so easy to take hold of his hand she thought, but that would be terribly forward for a girl to do.

They found themselves back at the dodgems. Sue and her beau, bright eyed and red faced called to them.

"Mind if we just try the big wheel?" Sue asked. "You seem to be doing okay." She smiled a knowing smile at Jenny, who immediately positioned herself a more comfortable foot away from her new acquaintance.

"Get stuck in there mate!" Sue's lad shouted to his pal.

"Get lost Pete!" his friend replied, obviously embarrassed.

'So Sue's boy was named, Pete, I wonder what this guy's name is?' Jenny thought to herself.

As the pair hurried away, Jenny turned and was just about gathering up the courage to ask for a name when "he" took the initiative.

"I'm John. What's your name?"

"Jenny."

"Pleased to meet you, Jenny," John said, offering a hand to shake but then snatching it back, as he felt a little silly doing something regarded as so formal.

"Do you fancy that ride now?"

"Okay."

They walked closely but not quite touching, up the steps to the awaiting cars. John stood next to the car to let Jenny get in first, but didn't feel able to offer a helping hand as Pete had done for Sue. The seats in the cars were quite small and John had to press against Jenny quite strongly to get into the car. Jenny felt a rush of heat through her body at this closeness.

"Sorry," John apologised.

"It's okay," Jenny reassured. It seemed their conversation was only ever a couple of words followed by silence.

John steered the car expertly around the enclosure, avoiding as many collisions as he could to protect Jenny from the bumps and bangs. They rode in silence, as if the closeness was too much.

John stood as the cars came to a stop, and with a new found courage he offered his hand to help Jenny out. As their hands touched, both he and Jenny felt a kind of electric between them, and both retracted their hands quickly. John pushed his in his pockets and Jenny hastily repositioned the shoulder strap of her handbag. Sue and Pete were there to meet them.

"Getting on okay?" Pete asked. John and Jenny looked at each other, smiled in agreement and nodded.

"Pete says he'll walk us to the bus stop if you like," Sue announced looking at her watch. Jenny nodded, wondering if John would offer to do the same. Sue and Pete set off arm in arm, with Jenny and John shuffling along behind them.

At the bus shelter, Pete spun Sue around to face him. Leaning on the small wall he pulled her toward him, standing her between his legs. He put his arms around her waist and began to kiss her. Jenny looked away, only to see John looking away as well.

John lit a cigarette and offered the packet to Jenny, who shook her head. She'd tried smoking once but half choked herself to death, so she didn't want to try it again now. John lit up and took a long hard drag on the cigarette, as the bus came round the corner.

"Sue," Jenny said, interrupting the clinch. The bus came to a halt but John did not move. Jenny grabbed hold of Sue's arm.

"Come on," she said, "the bus won't wait."

"Bye Pete, see you Monday," Sue said, reluctantly releasing herself from his hold, "Outside Bob's." Jenny looked at John who said nothing, and felt a pang of disappointment. She stepped aboard the single-decker bus first and sat next to the window. Sue followed and was just about to start to tell of her exciting evening when there was a heavy hammering on the window. It was John. Jenny's heart missed a beat.

"Are you coming too?" he asked, looking as if he expected her to decline his invitation.

"If you like," Jenny replied.

"Right then, see you Monday," he added with obvious excitement.

The bus pulled away and Jenny could feel her heart beating hard in her chest, and felt a warm glow of satisfaction spreading over her body.

"Well?" asked Sue

"Well what?

"What's he like?"

Jenny wanted to say that she found him exciting, good looking, nice to be close too - all the things she was feeling inside. But to avoid too much ridicule from her friend she just replied, "Okay I guess."

"Pete's just fantastic," Sue began. "He's got a motor bike at home. He lives in a big house in Tilbury and says he can get tickets for the Faces concert next month and......." Jenny stopped listening.

Sue always had this surge of enthusiasm when she met a new boy and Jenny wondered just how long this particular relationship would last. Instead of listening, her thoughts went back to the moment their eyes had met and the wonderful feeling she'd experienced deep inside and the electricity felt when their hands touched. She'd certainly never ever felt that way before.

She thought about his eyes, the way they sparkled and laughed as he spoke, making his entire face light up. She could sense he was as nervous as she was, and this made him even more attractive to her. And now he'd asked to see her again. Her reverie was interrupted.

"What are you smiling at?" asked Sue.

"What? Oh nothing," Jenny stuttered, embarrassed at having been caught out.

Sue got up from her seat. It was her stop.

"I'll meet you at the corner shop on Monday. I'll be wearing blue, okay?" Jenny nodded and Sue was gone.

Wearing blue meant that Jenny had to avoid that colour, since wearing the same was seen to be juvenile. She wondered what she might wear instead, but had tomorrow to think about that. Now she was going home to dream about John, who she'd only met a couple of hours ago, yet she felt she'd met her partner for life, someone to marry maybe, have children and grow old with. She laughed out loud at the stupidity of such thoughts.

Leaving the bus, she hurried down the road to ensure that she reached home before curfew –ten-thirty.

"Is that you?" she heard her mother call as she opened the front door.

"Yea, it's me," she replied.

"Had a good time?"

"Okay" was her nonchalant reply. However, 'Super, wonderful, fantastic, out of this world' was what she thought

"Meet anybody nice?" Mum asked. Jenny's heart skipped a beat at the thought of John.

"No not really," she lied. "I'm going straight to bed." 'To dream and dream,' she thought to herself.

Sunday came, a nothing day, family tea with a visit from Grandma and Granddad. Jenny's brother, Mark was a pain as usual, whilst her younger sister, still the baby of the family, threw the usual tantrums when she didn't get her own way. But tomorrow was Monday and she was seeing John, so it didn't matter how boring Sunday had been.

Sue had agreed to meet Pete outside Bob's at two. Bob's was a sort of shop come café that played popular music in the back room, where you could sit for hours with just one drink, usually hot vimto. At Bob's, no one would hurry you to leave.

It was the place where most youngsters met. The meeting being at two, Jenny had agreed to meet Sue at the corner shop at one-thirty. It was only ten in the morning, but she couldn't wait to get ready.

The night before she'd raided her wardrobe, extracting virtually all her clothes and then sorting them into definite, maybes and "no chances." Amongst the definites were a multi-coloured tent dress with long sleeves and a large ringed zip, down the front, a pale blue cheese cloth dress, recently shortened without her mum knowing, and a white lace shirtdress.

Jenny looked down at all three items as they lay on her bed. First to be discarded was the tent dress, as it didn't go with her boots. Sue had said she was wearing blue, so the cheesecloth was out. It had to be the white lace.

The dress was very short with long sleeves and buttons all the way down the front. She dressed it up with a gold chain belt fastened tightly at the waist, with the remains of the chain left to dangle at the side. She'd carefully chosen her finest white underwear before having a bath and washing and conditioning her hair.

"What's the big occasion?" Dad had asked when she'd taken so long in the bathroom. If only he knew.

She slowly dried her hair, ensuring that every last lock lay perfectly straight and brushed it until it shone. She meticulously applied the minimum of makeup, just in case Mum noticed. She pulled on her white boots and surveyed herself in the mirror. If only she was a little taller and had a smaller bust and her hair was a little longer, and the spot she could feel beginning to erupt on her chin wouldn't appear, and, and, and....

She looked at her watch. Even though she'd taken as long as possible in the bathroom it was still only twelve-thirty, another hour before she was due to meet Sue, another hour and a half before she was due to meet John.

There it was again, that funny feeling in the pit of her stomach, a combination of ache and butterflies. What if he didn't come? Please, please, let him come. What would she do if he didn't turn up?

She brushed her hair again and put away the remains of her make-up, then straightened the covers on her bed, picked up her handbag, checked the contents and deciding she was ready, went downstairs.

"Where are you off to then?" questioned Dad

"Nowhere special," Jenny replied.

"You look pretty dolled up for nowhere special," Dad remarked, as he went back to reading his newspaper.

As ever, Mum came in with her warning not to speak to strangers, to be home by five o'clock if she wanted tea, or by ten-thirty if she didn't want to be grounded for the rest of the week.

"Can I come, Jenny?" her little sister pleaded.

"Not today, Lizzie."

"Oooer why not? Please, pleeeease. I want to go with Jenny. It's not fair, she never takes me anywhere. I want to go too."

'Here comes the tantrum,' thought Jenny, hoping Mum wouldn't take her side and insist she took Elizabeth with her. How embarrassing that would be. However, Mum seemed to sense that today, Jenny did not want a baby sister tagging along.

"Come on Lizzie, we'll make some cakes for tea," offered Mum to compensate for the missed outing.

"Yes, well I want to do all the weighing and the mixing," Lizzie added, in an 'I've won anyway' voice.'

Mum thought of the mess her younger daughter would create and wished she hadn't been so quick to offer this solution, but it was too late now. She took Lizzie by the hand and led into the kitchen. Jenny smiled with relief, shouted a goodbye to all and left quickly before there were any more problems to overcome. Mum had said nothing about her dress length or the mascara she was wearing. She wondered if Mum knew she had a date. She probably did, as she seemed to know most things.

The altercation with Lizzie had only taken a few minutes, but now she felt that if she didn't hurry she might be late. Walking up the road she could see Sue leaning against the post box outside the corner shop. Although she'd said she was going to wear blue, she was actually dressed in red. Jenny thought she could have worn the blue cheesecloth after all, but it was too late now.

Linked arm in arm as usual, the girls walked up the road to Bob's. As they neared the meeting place, Jenny was filled with all sorts of distressing thoughts. What if he wasn't there, wouldn't she look a fool? What if he wasn't like she remembered him? It had been quite dark that evening at the fair and the lights from the carousels changed people's looks.

As they neared the meeting place, she could make out the silhouette of one boy but could see it was Pete. John was nowhere to be seen, making Jenny's heart sink.

Sue started to walk with an exaggerated wiggle, obviously to ensure that Pete would still fancy her. The young man, realising that it was Sue, stepped forward to greet her with a quick peck on the cheek. Jenny crossed her arms and felt extremely foolish. It looked like she would be playing gooseberry again.

"Are you looking for John?" Pete asked. "He's not coming."

Jenny fought back the tears of disappointment. Shuffling from one foot to the other, she stared down at the floor.

"Only kidding," Pete smiled, then seeing how disappointed she looked, he continued. , "He's just gone for cigarettes."

At that moment, John appeared from round the corner, cigarette in one hand and the other in his pocket. He was wearing a pair of faded Levi jeans and a plain white T-shirt with white trainers. Jenny's heart skipped a beat. She was sure everybody saw her gasp and was overcome not only with the fact that he looked so good dressed that way, but the smile which radiated from his face showed that he was extremely pleased to see her.

"I didn't think you'd come," he said in a whispered tone as he approached her.

"Pete said you weren't coming when I got here," Jenny explained.

"Pratt" he said laughingly.

"Right, drink here first then we'll go down to the park," Pete said taking charge. "There's a bit going on there with it being Bank Holiday. We'll see how things go."

They went into Bob's. The shop part of the establishment sold sweets, newspapers and cigarettes, whilst the back room was furnished with odd tables and chairs and with a juke box. On the walls were old posters with torn edges, advertising last year's pop concerts. This room was always filled with people, noise and cigarette smoke. Sometimes it was so smoky that it stung your eyes and burnt your throat. Today it was reasonably empty.

A group of four lads sat at one table, dressed in black leather biker's gear, smoking heavily and sharing a bottle of coke between the four of them. As long as someone bought a drink, Bob didn't normally mind how many sat and watched. Two girls sat in the far corner, heads together chatting furiously. No one looked up when the four of them entered. No one was interested in anyone else's business at Bob's, which was what made it so popular. There was never any hassle, because everybody minded his or her own business.

Pete sidled into a corner bench seat next to the wall and Sue cuddled up close to him. John let Jenny sit down and then sat beside her.

"What'll it be?" Bob called from the kitchen.

"Four cokes," Pete answered, not stopping to ask anyone if they wanted anything else.

"Four cokes it is," called Bob. He brought them through on a tray, "Glasses or straws?"

"Just straws," confirmed Pete, again taking the decision for everyone else.

Bob put the cokes on the table and placed two straws in each bottle. Pete passed the drinks around and then put his arm round Sue and began to whisper to her. Jenny sipped her coke a little uneasily. John appeared to be doing the same. It was a bit awkward sitting next to each other on the bench. They couldn't look at each other and if they looked straight ahead, all they could see were Pete and Sue canoodling!

They finished their cokes in silence. Pete and Sue hadn't even begun to drink theirs as they were too engrossed in each other.

"Want to walk down to the park?" John asked Jenny almost apologetically. Jenny nodded

"See you two by the bandstand. That is if you manage to make it down there," John said, getting up from the bench and allowing Jenny to get out. Pete raised his arm to show he'd heard, but didn't move from his clinch with Sue.

"Sorry, but I couldn't watch them any longer. I just had to get out," John said, once outside

"Me too," agreed Jenny.

They ran across the road like two children who'd been let out to play after being kept inside for hours, and then walked down the road leading to the park. Although they didn't speak, there was a spring in their step and a closeness which made conversation unnecessary.

"I reckon they'll be at least an hour before they come here," John aid as they reached the park gates. "Do you fancy a game of putting?" Jenny looked at what she was wearing and felt a little overdressed for putting, but nodded never the less. At least it was away from Sue and Pete.

They went to the kiosk, paid their money and were each issued with a putting iron and two golf balls. John positioned himself at the first Tee with legs slightly apart. He rocked his hips whilst bringing the club to almost touch the ball on three occasions before striking it. The ball was carried down the length of the rough grass and onto the smooth turf surrounding the hole. He smiled, satisfied with his performance. Jenny took her place at the tee. She couldn't bend very far because of the length of her dress, so went down on one knee to place the ball on the ground. Taking an almighty sweep, more in keeping with her own sport of hockey than of golf, she missed the ball completely.

'What an idiot!' she thought.

"Try again," John said encouragingly. She did, and missed the ball again!

He positioned himself behind her, putting his arms around her and holding her hands on the club. Jenny's pulse began to race. Rocking her from side to side he controlled her striking of the ball. As soon as the shot was made he released her from his grip.

"You'll soon get the hang of it," he called, as he made his way down to the hole to take his second shot with Jenny following. Hole by hole, her confidence grew. It was obvious that John was an accomplished player, and although they didn't keep the score, Jenny knew the difference between them was formidable.

John didn't take hold of her again during the game, even when she missed the ball or played very bad shots. When the game was over, they returned the irons to the kiosk.

"What now?" he asked. Jenny shrugged her shoulders. "Want to walk?"

"Okay."

They made their way away from the putting green, past the tennis courts and Bowling Green, which were alive with activity and down the path which led to the rose gardens. Couples quite often went here because it was a little more secluded than the main park. Jenny had never been in there before. A group of four of five lads were walking towards them. Suddenly Jenny felt John's arm around her shoulder, pulling her close to him.

"Hi John," one of the lads called. "Who is this?" he added, looking appreciatively at Jenny. The grip on her shoulder tightened momentarily

"Jenny," John announced proudly.

"How come you've got such a dishy bird?" asked another of the lads.

"Some of us have what it takes, some of you don't," John replied in a cocky voice.

"Where are you off to?" enquired the first lad.

"To the rose garden for a bit" John replied.

"And do you think you'll get a bit?" added one lad, with a dirty laugh.

"You bet!" called back John. And then taking Jenny completely by surprise, he pulled her roughly towards him and planted a kiss firmly on her lips. Jenny blushed bright red as the lads went away laughing.

As soon as they were out of view, John released his hold on her, but instead of stepping away he dropped his hand down to take hold of hers and looked apologetically at her.

"Sorry for that," he said. "You know what lads are like. Call you a puff if you haven't, well you know, if you haven't." Jenny nodded, not sure she knew what he meant but deciding it was best not to question him. She felt relieved that it had just been a show put on for the lads. At least he was holding her hand now and that was a step in the right direction. She wondered how things might progress in the rose garden.

They sat on a bench, surprised at how empty the garden was today. Perhaps the activities currently taking place around the park were more interesting than sitting in the peace and quiet of the rose garden.

John turned to Jenny and looked straight into her eyes. Her heartbeat increased immediately and the red glow returned to her cheeks. She wanted to look away to hide her embarrassment, but found she was somehow locked into his gaze.

"I want to tell you something," he said, taking hold of both of her hands. "You may think I am absolutely stupid and may not want to see me after I have told you this, but I am still going to tell you." Jenny wondered what on earth he was going to divulge to her. "You know at the fair, when I was walking away from the waltzer and turned to look at you and you were looking at me?" Jenny nodded, still held in his gaze. He did have such beautiful eyes. "Well I knew from that moment that I fancied you something rotten. I even thought about what it might be like marrying you and having children. There, I've told you. Do you think I am mad?" Jenny wanted to tell him she felt the same way but couldn't, as she continued to look directly into his eyes. He gave her a little smile, as if acknowledging the fact that by not saying he was mad, it was okay to feel the way he did.

He leaned forward towards Jenny and she didn't pull away. He knew inside what he wanted to do next. Plucking up all the courage he could muster, he pulled Jenny towards him and kissed her on the lips. This time the kiss was gentle and full of feeling and she felt her body responding immediately. The kiss lasted only a brief number of seconds, but in those seconds a bond was formed between them. They belonged to each other and whatever life had in store for them, they knew they would never leave each other.

CHAPTER 3
OH SO YOUNG

"It's not you that I am fed up with; it's just the way things are at the moment. I want some fun," Jenny tried to explain.

"You mean I'm not fun," John asked, feeling hurt.

"Well no, not really," Jenny was finding this very difficult.

"Great!" John said, beginning to get annoyed. "What do you want me to do - cartwheels?"

"John, please," Jenny pleaded. "I just think it's time we split up for a while and take a break from each other, see how things go. We might find that it's better for both of us."

"It won't be better for me," added John. "I think things are fine as they are. You know I care about you."

"It isn't about caring, it's about enjoying life," Jenny observed. "We are much too young to be settling down, and still have lots of things to see and do with our lives."

"I don't want to do anything else. I just want to be with you. I have always wanted to be with you. I love you. I have always loved you since the day we met. I will never stop loving you."

Jenny could tell that his voice was getting shakier as he forced himself not to break down in tears. She really didn't want to hurt him, but things had got too heavy lately. She seemed to be missing out on a lot of the fun her female friends were having. She'd been so tied up with John that she'd lost contact with a lot of them, and after the party at Jan's last week, she'd begun to think about what she was missing. She still cared about John; in fact she probably still loved him, but was just bored with the routines.

Pete and Sue had only remained together for about four months. Jenny and John had been together nine months. She'd enjoyed most of that time together, but John seemed to only be able to make decisions if Pete was involved. It always seemed to be more about what Pete wanted to do with his latest girlfriend and not really what she and John wanted. John was forever in Pete's shadow and Jenny had grown to resent it of late.

"You need to stand up for yourself," she was always saying. "Can't you do anything without Pete?" If anything, this was the real reason for the split.

Pete had had several different girlfriends during their time together, sometimes more than one at a time. Jenny had grown fed up making up stories to tell to one girlfriend whilst Pete was out with the other.

John always defended Pete saying, "He's been my mate for a long time. We have grown up together and I can't walk out on him."

Jenny had tried to explain on more than one occasion that she didn't want him to walk out on Pete, just spend less time with him. But things hadn't changed, and that was why she was now in this difficult situation of trying to get John to agree to them having a trial separation.

"You said you would never leave me," John said, now close to tears.

"I know, and at the time I meant it," Jenny said, her voice beginning to waiver. "Perhaps I still mean it, but I need some time on my own."

She wondered if she was doing the right thing, knowing that deep down inside she still had very strong feelings for him but she really did need some space, time to get her mind straight and time to have fun, to do silly things again. She was only seventeen for god's sake, no age to be considering settling down and getting engaged. Too young to be thinking about buying a house and planning a life together, although she knew that John was the type of bloke she would like to eventually do those things with, but not yet. No she must make the break now, as difficult as it might be.

"Can we talk about this tomorrow?" John asked, looking for any opportunity to still see her.

"I can't, John, I've already agreed to meet Sue and Jan," Jenny divulged.

"Oh those two prick teasers!" John reacted badly. "You'll enjoy yourself with them, won't you," he smirked, trying to hurt her in an attempt to stop the hurt that he himself was feeling at her rejection of him.

"There's no need for that!" Jenny demanded, visibly hurt that he was categorising her with them. She would never have the confidence to behave like them nor did she want to, since neither of them had a particularly good name locally. Or perhaps she did want to be like them. They were always having a good time meeting new people and going places that she would never dream of going.

"No John, we have to give it a chance. See what it's like without seeing each other all the time"

"What if I call you at the weekend?"

"John - please"

"Okay-okay, I give up! You obviously don't want me anymore. I know I still want you, but you'd rather have someone else. Okay. I'll go."

Seeing the tears welling up in John's eyes, she almost reached out to tell him to stay, but didn't. He walked through the door and down the front path and out of her life without turning around.

It was over. The ordeal of finishing with John was over. It was what she'd wanted, yet why was she feeling so desolate watching him walk away with his head down, not even turning to see if she was watching.

It was for the best. Sue had said she would come alive again once she'd split with John, but she was beginning to have doubts already. Perhaps she'd ring him tomorrow to see how he was. She really did care whether he was okay or not, as she really did still love him.

She turned on the radio and heard one of those really sad songs and felt tears pricking in the corner of her eye. She switched the radio off and went to her room, thankful that the house was empty and she didn't need to speak to anyone. She picked up a magazine. 'How to Chuck Your Fella' was one of the sections advertised on the front cover. A little ironic, she thought.

She thought back to when they'd met at the fair. How striking their first touch had been. How much fun they seemed to have at the beginning, but now things had turned a little sour over the past few weeks. She tried not to think about how downtrodden John had looked when he'd walked away and tried to squash the guilty feelings she now had at hurting him, along with the strange longing to run after him, put her arm around him and tell him what a mistake she'd made.

The telephone ringing downstairs interrupted her guilt trip. It couldn't be John, as he wouldn't have gotten home yet. It must be Sue.

"Hallo?" she said questioningly.

"Hi, it's me," It was Sue. "Have you done the dirty deed yet?" she asked laughing. Jenny felt annoyed. She hadn't found it funny at all. It had been an awful experience.

"Well?" Sue pushed, when Jenny did not answer.

"Yes," Jenny heard herself saying. She'd ended a relationship which until recently had been the most fulfilling relationship of her life, and Sue thought it was a joke.

"Right, then as a single woman you'll want to meet some groovy blokes then won't you?" Sue suggested.

"Well I don't know whether I want to just yet," Jenny said, trying to put her friend off a little. The last thing she really wanted was to fall into another long-term relationship.

"Don't want to. Don't want to. You must be joking," Sue taunted. "It's just what you need, a little fun in your life. Be ready at eight and we'll pick you up. Wear something sexy. Not blue, I'm wearing blue."

There she was, calling the shots already. Taking control of her life and laying down the rules. Jenny didn't stop to think of who 'we' might be who'd be picking her up, she just said okay and put down the phone.

Had she done the right thing finishing with John? Sue had said it was the right thing, but did she think so herself. He was a lovely guy and she did care for him, and he did look so hurt today.

'Stop it!' she told herself. She went back upstairs and opened the wardrobe door and looked for, 'Something sexy but not blue.' She moved dresses along the rail scrutinising them and then moving on to the next. She finally came across the white shirtdress she'd worn on her first date with John. He'd said she looked sexy in it, but that was John. It would seem wrong to wear that on her first outing after finishing with him. She moved along the rail - Black lace - That colour was more in keeping with her mood.

The dress itself was short, with a low scoop neckline which showed the roundness of her breasts. It had short sleeves and four or five little mother of pearl buttons up the front, and went well with her black strappy high-heeled sandals. Having made the decision to wear this, she searched for dark stockings and underwear. Having done this she ran a bath, poured a large amount of bubble bath in it and soaked herself for ages, as if trying to wash off the past. She carefully dried her hair.

It was whilst she was doing this that she realised she'd not really spent time getting ready to go out for ages. When it was John it didn't really matter, as he liked her just as she was. She tried to remember when she'd last bothered about how she looked, but couldn't.

She fastened her hair up in a loose knot and left wispy bits dangling over her ears and down the back of her neck, so that it didn't appear too severe. She added pearl earrings and necklace. Mum wasn't going to see her so she added a little more makeup than normal, and then surveyed the result in the full-length mirror. She wondered if Sue would think this outfit was sexy, knowing the outfits she wore lately. Still, she felt good, apart from that little nagging conscience which kept asking her why she hadn't dressed up like this for John lately, and wondered if it might have changed things if she had.

The doorbell rang. There was no mum calling out about speaking to strangers or curfew time. They wouldn't be back until the early hours of the morning since they'd gone over to Sheffield to a cousin's wedding. She could stay out until 4 in the morning if she liked and no one would know.

She opened the front door and there was Sue, who looked her up and down but said nothing.

"Your carriage awaits my lady." (Hadn't those been some of Pete's first words to Sue?)

Jenny could see the blue Ford Anglia parked outside. The guy in the driver's seat looked about twenty-one and Jenny could see there was another person in the back seat. The passenger door was flung open and a deep voice called out.

"Wow! Sex on legs! Come on in."

"Do you mind," protested Sue. "You're supposed to be taking me out. Keep your eyes off her!"

"Hey don't get so uptight," the boy, or rather man told her. "Room for one in the back."

The car seat was pulled forward and Jenny got in with difficulty, trying not to display stocking tops beneath her short black dress. She didn't' look at the person sitting next to her, but could feel he was inspecting her down to the very last detail of her shoes. She felt very uneasy. John had sat closer to her than this on the waltzer when they'd first met, but she hadn't felt as uneasy as this.

"Jenny this is Mike. Mike this is Jenny," Sue announced, leaning over the chair in front. "Jenny needs to have some fun Mike, do you think you could oblige?"

"Could I!" he leered, having completed his inspection of her and liking what he'd seen.

35

"Jenny is twenty, like me," Sue added, nodding at Jenny to ensure she took in this piece of information.

"Good," said Sue's partner from the driving seat, "then we should have no problems."

Jenny wondered what this meant but didn't dare ask. She certainly felt uneasy, wishing she were with John, sitting in front of the television eating crisps and mars bars as they'd done so often over the past few weeks.

"Sean is taking us to a club in town," Sue told Jenny.

"Oh," was the only response Jenny could muster.

Most of the journey was in silence, but Jenny couldn't help noticing that Mick had the habit of putting his hand on his knee and letting it slip onto hers with the movement of the car. She was unsure whether this was accidental or intentional. She hoped it was the former, but couldn't help thinking it was the latter.

When they arrived in town, Sean explained that he would drop them off at the front door, speak to the doorman, and then he'd park the car down a nearby side street. They all got out of the car and Sean led them to a small door next to a department store. The entrance was very dimly lit and a large bouncer filled up most of the door space.

"Hi Sean," the doorman smiled, recognising him immediately. "How many?"

"Me, Mick, and the two birds."

How Jenny hated that word, 'birds.' It was a degrading term. She felt an arm go round her waist and jumped!

"Steady girl, I ain't going to hurt you," Mike said, putting his other arm around Sue's waist and escorting them inside the club.

Once inside, there was a flight of steps leading down into a smoke filled room. The smell of stale beer and mild body odour mingled with the smoke, and the bar area was very badly lit. Jenny could see that through an archway to the left was a dance floor, and to the right was a series of alcoves with two-seater settees, occupied by couples.

"Drink?" Mike asked.

Jenny was about to say coke, when Sue said, "We both drink Brandy and Babycham."

"You would," said Mike disapprovingly. "Give the ladies a B & B each and two pints of bitter," he said to the barman.

Jenny looked at Sue. "Brandy and Babycham?" she mouthed so that Mike couldn't hear.

"Of course," mouthed Sue. Jenny raised her eyebrows. She must have been out of things for a while.

Mike placed the glasses and bottles on a table and motioned for them to sit down. As they did, Sean appeared and took his place next to Sue. Mike pushed in beside Jenny, immediately putting his arm around her. She remembered how long it had taken John to even hold her hand, and here was a man she hadn't even spoken to with his arm around her. She felt very uneasy again.

"Well Jenny, what do you do?" asked Mike.

Sue quickly turned round and said, "She is a hairdresser like me." Why on earth was Sue telling all these lies?

"Oh well, then you'll have to have a go at mine," Mike grinned, making Jenny look up at him for the first time.

She could see that his hair was shoulder length and dark brown. He also had a small moustache. She wondered how old he was, guessing that both men must be in their twenties since Sue had made such a fuss about them both being twenty and working.

Sue looked at Jenny, "Are you coming to the loo?" she asked in a way that meant, 'Come with me now.' Jenny stood and followed her friend towards the conveniences.

"Don't be too long," Mike said, and patted Jenny's bottom as she left the table.

'Damn cheek! Who does he think he is!' she angrily thought.

Once inside the ladies, Sue turned to Jenny and said, "Sorry I couldn't brief you beforehand, there wasn't time. Sean works at the bank with Mick and they are both twenty-four. Great isn't it?" Jenny wondered what was great about it. "I mean they've got money to spend on a girl, haven't they?"

"But what about the hair dressing?" Jenny quizzed.

"Just say we work at 'Hair-Raising' in town, they will never check. Anyway, what does that matter? What do you think of Mick?"

"He's a bit forward," Jenny replied.

"A bit forward," Sue Queried, "Why, what has he done?"

"He put is arm round me."

"Oh come on, Jenny, you really have been out of it too long. I get you a good-looking bloke and you complain when he puts his arm round you. Are you serious?"

'No just not used to this,' thought Jenny.

"Come on, let's have some fun," encouraged Sue, putting the finishing touches to her lips.

When they returned, Jenny noticed that Sean and Mike were on their second pint, and there were two more 'B & B's' waiting for them.

"Cheers," Sue said, raising her glass high in the air and almost emptying it in one gulp. Jenny sipped at hers.

"Come on, down the hatch," Sean encouraged Jenny. She finished the rest of the drink in one mouthful. Mike pushed the other across the table and then put his arm round her again. She took a sip.

"Do you want to dance?" asked Mike. Jenny shrugged her shoulders. "Come on then."

He took her by the hand and led her to the dance floor. The DJ was playing some slow, smoochy numbers. Mike pulled Jenny close to him and placed his arm tightly around her waist. She placed her arms a little reluctantly onto his shoulders.

"Relax and enjoy it," Mike encouraged. The drink was beginning to take effect and she began to relax a little.

After a couple of records, Mike lifted his hand up to Jenny's face and turned it towards his and then pushed his lips roughly on hers. She could smell the beers on his breath, and his moustache felt rough against her skin. She wanted to pull away but found she couldn't, as Mike was holding her head so tightly. He finally released her and she gasped for air.

"I always have that effect on women," he said, thinking the gasp was in appreciation of his kissing skills.

"Can we sit down?" Jenny asked.

"Sure," Mike however did not lead her back to the table were Sue and Sean were sitting, but to one of the shady alcoves with the two seat settees.

Immediately after they'd sat down, Mike wrapped his arm around her and again pushed his lips roughly on hers. Jenny was certainly not enjoying this. The more she tried to pull away, the stronger he kissed her. Now he was pushing his tongue against her lips, intent on making her open them and let his tongue reach deep inside. She struggled and opened her mouth to let out an objection, but Mike saw this as an invitation and pushed his tongue deep inside her mouth, touching the roof of it and licking her tongue furiously. Jenny pulled away.

"You are some hot girl," Mike told her. She certainly felt hot, but not in the way he meant.

The drink was making her feel a little light-headed and she found it harder to prevent Mike from kissing her. He pressed his body hard against her now as he kissed her. She suddenly felt a hand on her left breast and gasped! Mike took this to be a sigh of pleasure and pulled at the small, mother of pearl buttons at the neck of her dress.

"No!" she demanded.

"Okay." Mike protested, "I can wait." He took her by the hand and led her back towards the table where Sue and Sean had been.

"Looks like they've already gone," Mike announced. "Come on, I'll take you home."

They walked up the stairs towards the exit and Jenny wobbled a little as she negotiated the stairs. Once outside, the evening air began sobering her up a little.

"I'll get you a taxi," Mike said. Jenny wondered if he meant to put her in a taxi or go with her. She also wondered if she'd be expected to pay for it. If so, she hoped she had enough money in her purse.

Mike hailed a taxi, helped her inside and climbed in beside her. "Tilbury town centre," he instructed the driver. He put his arm round Jenny, "Alright now?" he asked.

"Fine" replied Jenny, although she didn't really feel fine.

He began to kiss her again, his hand returning to the buttons at the front of her dress and he expertly undid them in a matter of seconds. She tried to object, but he just kissed her harder and pushed his tongue deep inside her mouth. He looked down at the lace edging Jenny's bra that he'd now exposed and admired the firmness of the curves secreted inside. There was no gentleness when he squeezed her breast, his hand moving swiftly from one to the other. Jenny finally managed to break free from his kiss and forced his hand away.

"I really don't think you should do that," she managed to spurt out.

"You don't think I should do that, but I do!" he reacted. "I've paid for you to go into a club and bought you drinks all night. You have been giving me the come on, but you don't think I should do that! What a prick teaser you are turning out to be. I thought at your age you'd be past those games."

"At my age!" she retaliated. "I am seventeen, and no amount of drinks gives you the right to push yourself on me!"

"You must be joking!" he returned, looking shocked. "You're more than seventeen. Dressed like that with a figure like that. At seventeen you should still be in school uniform, not wearing stockings and suspenders! I thought you said you worked as a hairdresser."

"No," she replied. "Sue said I worked as a hairdresser. I'm actually at college doing a degree."

"Shit!" said Mike. "I thought you were really up for it. Sue said you wanted some fun, so I thought, well you know what I thought. Shit!"

"I'm sorry Sue misled you," Jenney informed the young man. "I've just finished with my boyfriend and Sue thought I needed cheering up. I didn't expect this tonight."

"Well he must be mad finishing with you, you are one good looking bird," Jenny winced at the word bird, as he continued. "I'm sorry that you are only seventeen. What about Sue?"

"The same," Jenny instructed.

"Shit! I wonder if Sean knows. He's only been seeing Sue for a few weeks. He's had a fall out with his missus and Sue has been keeping him amused. God if he knew she was only seventeen."

"He's married?" Jenny asked shocked. "Does Sue Know?"

"I doubt it," John confessed. "It's not something you talk about when you are trying to pull a bird."

"She'll be devastated when she finds out."

"Please forget I ever said anything about Sean being married. If he wants to tell Sue, he will do. If he doesn't, he won't. It's not up to you or me. The pair of them caused enough bother roping you and me together."

Jenny began to feel a little sorry for Mike. Perhaps she'd looked older wearing the makeup with her hair up on top. Mum always said it made her look older, and her dress was quite short and revealing. Perhaps it hadn't entirely been Mike's fault.

They were nearly at Tilbury when Mike asked, "Shall I give the taxi driver your address to take you straight home, or do you want to walk the drink off a bit?" Feeling a little more relaxed with him, she agreed a walk would be advisable. Mike asked the driver to drop them off and paid the fare.

"How much do I owe you for the taxi?" Jenny asked.

"It's okay. Seeing I'm working and you are just a college girl with no income, I'll pay." He took hold of her hand. "I promise no heavy stuff." Jenny looked at him and smiled. For the first time she looked at his face properly and could see he was quite good looking. When he smiled, he looked much younger than his twenty-four years.

They walked hand in hand down the road He asked about her college subjects, she asked about his work at the bank. He questioned her about her break up with John, but Jenny said she preferred not to discuss it. He said he understood, since he himself had been in a long-term relationship that had recently come to an end. In fact, that was why he was out tonight with Sean.

Soon they came to Jenny's street. She wondered if he would expect to be asked in for coffee. It was only one-thirty and she knew the house would be empty, but it could put her in a very dangerous situation if he knew that and reverted to previous behaviour.

She looked at him now. He was no longer the threat he'd been earlier. He was now just a normal guy chatting to a girl, a girl quite a few years younger than him, but never the less a normal guy.

"Want to come in for a coffee?" she asked, happy to risk it now.

"I don't think so, do you? Looking the way you do and me feeling the way I do, I don't think it would be a good idea." Jenny felt a little disappointed. "But before I go," he said turning her towards him and taking hold of both her hands, "let me tell you something. You are a stunner. I don't know what you are doing hanging about with that Sue, she's simply not in your class. You have a fabulous body, a body which men will find irresistible, as I did. You certainly turn a bloke on. But Jenny, listen, and I mean this. If you go to clubs like we have tonight, with blokes like me, then expect to get more than you can handle. Don't put yourself in this situation again.

God I must be mad. You invited me in and I can see there is no one home. You are standing there looking like that and everything about me says 'grab it while you can!' Yet here I am giving advice, when all I would like to normally do is screw you. Sorry about that, but this is just how I feel now. Get in there quick before I change my mind!" He turned her round and smacked her on her bottom, as you would a child.

"Thanks," she said, turning to face him. "Thanks very much. You'll make someone one hell of a husband one day."

He caught hold of her and pulled her to him. This time the kiss was gentle. He did not try to force his tongue into her mouth, but gently brushed her lips with it. He heaved a big sigh and pushed her away.

"Go," he said, and Jenny started to walk up the path to the front door, all the time feeling Mike was still watching her.

She turned round and called cheekily, "Your body ain't too bad either."

"See you around," were his parting words. Jenny unlocked the front door, pushed inside and closed it firmly behind her.

What a night that had been. What a day it had been. All she wanted to do now was sleep. She went straight upstairs, undressed and got into bed. Within minutes she was fast asleep.

Mike walked slowly into town to catch a taxi back home. As he did so, he pondered on the evening. Had he known she was only seventeen, would he have acted differently? He decided he would, and felt ashamed at the way he'd behaved. Sean had said this girl Sue was bringing needed a good seeing to, and he thought that that was he was meant to do.

Had he handled it in a different way they may have enjoyed each other's company and got to know each other, instead he was intent on getting a leg over. She sure was a sexy girl, especially since she was only seventeen. He felt an ache inside that he knew could not be satisfied.

Jenny woke in the early hours of the morning when she heard the bedroom door open. It was Mum.

"Just checking you're okay," she said.

'If only you knew,' Jenny thought, remembering the events of the night before. 'I will never ever get myself in a situation like that again.

Jenny woke early the next day, shivering at the thought of the happenings of the day before and wondering what today would bring. She listened to the sounds coming from downstairs. She could hear Mum up already dusting and cleaning. That was usual, but she could hear her humming to herself as, and that was unusual. Putting on a housecoat, she ventured downstairs.

"Morning," Mum called, flicking the duster over the bookshelf.

"Hi Mum, you seem happy this morning," Jenny commented and waited for an explanation.

"I am," her mother revealed. "Your dad has won a bit of money on the pools and we're going to have a holiday - in

Cornwall," she added quickly, before her daughter could speculate on a holiday abroad. "We are all going - You too."

Jenny was about to protest that she didn't really want to go away with her parents anymore, but suddenly had second thoughts. It would be change, a chance to get away from the upset of John, and the controlling way that Sue was trying to run her life. Yes it would be good to get away, she decided.

"Super," she said, with real enthusiasm.

"I didn't think you would want to come with us," her mum admitted. "You can ask Sue if you like."

"No thanks," added Jenny quickly. "I want some peace and quiet."

"Do you think you will get that with Lizzie?" Mum laughed.

Lizzie had talked of nothing else all the way back from Sheffield the night before. She was probably dreaming of it right now! Mum had left her in bed, as they'd arrived home in the early hours and Lizzie needed her sleep. She was trouble enough without being overtired as well.

"When do we go?" asked Jenny, now genuinely interested.

"In a fortnight, we'll travel down overnight and stay at a little guesthouse near Helston. Margaret has been there before and says it's really nice and the food is good, which should please your dad." Mum laughed as she said this. It was nice to see her laughing. She didn't laugh an awful lot. Jenny thought that she herself hadn't laughed a lot lately. She was in a rut, but now she was getting out of it. Still, she had something to look forward to now. There would be clothes to sort out, perhaps new ones to buy and cases to find from the loft. Yes she was quite pleased with the idea of two weeks in Cornwall. She must phone Sue and tell her.

The phone rang for some time before Sue finally answered. Jenny realised why, when she heard Sue's sleepy voice on the other end of the line.

"Hallo, who is it?" Sue asked, as if she didn't care who it was, as long as they would soon let her return to her bed.

"It's me - Jen," Jenny said. It was only with Sue that she ever shortened her name to Jen and she'd noticed that John had started to call her that too.

"Yes?" questioned Sue, wanting to know the emergency making it necessary for her friend to ring her at such an early hour on a Sunday!

"I'm going away on holiday," announced Jenny.

"Who with?" Sue asked, anxious to find out if this was anything to do with the night before, because Sean had mentioned that he was planning a trip to Mallorca. Surely Mike hadn't asked Jenny.

"My mum and dad," Jenny paused, "with Mark and Lizzie, of course." Sue felt relieved.

"Some holiday," she retorted to Jenny.

"Oh I don't know. I'm quite looking forward to it."

"You're looking forward to a holiday with your mum and dad?" enquired Sue in disbelief. It was just not the done thing.

"Yes, it's like you said, I need a change, a chance to get out of the routine," confirmed Jenny.

"That's not quite what I was thinking," Sue stated. "What about Mike?"

"What about him?" Jenny questioned.

"Aren't you going to see him again?" Sue queried. "He's quite tasty isn't he?

'Tasty!' Jenny remembered last night when his tongue had invaded her mouth, with the taste of beer and cigarettes on his breath. There was nothing pleasant about that.

"I don't think so, he's not my type," Jenny said, and meant it.

"Not your type?" Sue guffawed. "What is your type? Boring old John, who doesn't take you anywhere and doesn't have a mind of his own, forever sucking up to Pete. Great, well if that's your type you're welcome to him!"

"Sue!" Jenny pleaded.

"Don't come asking me to find you someone else," Sue continued with her rampage. "Sean and I did you a favour arranging for Mike to take you out last night, and this is the thanks we get. Well anyway, I'm going to Mallorca with Sean and I bet I have more fun than you do in Cornwall." Sue sounded very spiteful as she said this and Jenny felt a little hurt that her so called friend was turning on her in this way. She also remembered that Mike had told her that Sean was married.

"But..." she began to say, but then thought better of it. "Are you sure you want to go away with Sean?"

"Bit of a daft question isn't it? Of course I do. We will have a great time and come back with a fabulous tan. I bet you won't get that in Cornwall."

"Oh, I don't know, the weather down there can be quite good at this time of year and…." Jenny was interrupted mid sentence by Sue.

"Anyway," she said, "if that's all you wanted me for, I've got a terrific hangover and need some more sleep. Sean is taking me bowling this afternoon. I guess you and Mike won't be joining us, since he's not your type," she said this mimicking Jenny's voice. "I'll ring you later in the week. See ya." Sue put down the receiver before Jenny could say anything else.

Jenny thought how nasty her friend had turned when she'd said she didn't want to see Mike, and it had hurt Jenny when Sue had said that John was boring. Perhaps he was a little at times, but at least he was a nice lad. But Sue didn't like nice lads, she wanted exciting lads with money, who were prepared to lavish it on her and take her on holidays to Mallorca.

Jenny wondered when Sue would find out that Sean had a wife, maybe kids at home. She thought for a brief moment how John had said he wanted to settle down with her and have kids and how from time to time she'd thought herself how it might be nice to do that. Still she'd called a halt to that relationship and come the twenty-fourth of June, she would be starting a new chapter in her life. John and Mike were the past. The holiday in Cornwall was going to be new beginning for her.

She cheered up and went upstairs to examine the contents of her wardrobe and plan what to take with her.

CHAPTER 4
THE CRUEL SEA

The car was full to bursting, with not a square inch of space available. Jenny took her place besides Lizzie and Mark in the back whilst Mum settled in the front seat, complete with flask of coffee to keep Dad awake through the night, along with a collection of maps, just in case they were unsure of the way.

"I hope we've got everything," Mum said. (She was a born worrier!)

"Well if we haven't, it doesn't matter because we couldn't fit it in the car anyway," chortled Dad, feeling a little worried about the effect this amount of weight might have on his back axle.

It was nine o'clock on Friday evening and they had roughly a twelve-hour journey ahead of them. Dad planned to drive until around eleven-thirty and then stop at a service station for supper and a drink. Mum hoped that after this the children would sleep and she would spend her time ensuring Dad didn't.

Now they were on their way, everyone seemed to be in a good mood. Even Lizzie hadn't moaned once!

Jenny was hoping this would be a good holiday. She loved the sun and hoped that they would be fortunate enough to get plenty. She leant against the window of the car and watched as they passed through the town and on to join the motorway which would carry them a long way, on their journey to Cornwall.

She wondered about Sue. She'd be catching a plane tomorrow morning that would take her to Mallorca in only two hours, and. she smiled at the thought that it would take them twelve hours to get to Cornwall. However, she was glad she wasn't going with her friend, as she'd found out that there were five men going with Sue, including Sean and Mike. A bit of a funny set up, she thought to herself.

Dad stopped as planned at the service station about midnight. The three kids in the back snuggled under the blanket and dreamed of what was to come. Lizzie dreamt of sandcastles and ice creams, Mark of surfboarding, and Jenny about endless sunshine.

It was only just coming light when Jenny opened her eyes and stretched a little to relieve the stiffness in her neck. She'd slept fitfully whilst leaning on the window, unable to move because Lizzie had lay full length across the back of the car, with her head on Jenny's lap and her feet on Mark. Although the smallest, Lizzie had taken up the most room. Both Jenny and Mark had uncomfortable positions to put up with.

Glancing out of the window she could see they were travelling down the narrow winding lanes, typical of Cornwall.

"How much further?" she whispered, so as not to wake Lizzie.

"About twenty minutes," replied Dad, half turning to her so that he didn't need to raise his voice. It was far easier driving without Lizzie making a noise in the back of the car and he knew she would be bad tempered when she woke.

Jenny settled back as best she could in the seat to enjoy the last twenty minutes of the journey. The lane they were now going along was becoming increasingly narrower.

"Are you sure this is the right road?" Dad asked, doing his best to avoid the trees and shrubbery that threatened to scratch his precious car.

"Quite sure," said Mum with her finger on the map, carefully tracing every inch of the journey. "The road will swing to the right shortly and then it's about two hundred yards to the guest house." Moments later, the road lurched to the right as Mum predicted, and Jenny could see the guesthouse perched precariously on the cliffs, only yards from the sea. Dad brought the car to a halt outside the gate in the wall which surrounded the grey stone house.

"Are we there yet?" Lizzie asked, stirring sleepily.

"Yes, we're here," reassured Mum. "Now remember Lizzie, best behaviour or its back home for you."

"I know, I Know," remarked Lizzie, wriggling and stretching. "Come on Jenny, hurry up and get out. I want to get out."

'Here it comes, the bad mood,' thought Dad.

Jenny stretched her arms high into the air and took a deep breath. The air was sweet and slightly moist. It smelt of damp grass and bales of hay, and with the faint aroma of fish and seaweed.

Mum went to the front door and knocked, hoping they weren't too early. Almost immediately the door opened and Mum was met with a broad, welcoming smile.

"Mrs Mitchell? Hello, come on in, I expect you are ready for some breakfast?" Everyone smiled. It was just what they needed.

The aroma wafting from the kitchen told them that the landlady had been up early baking fresh rolls to accompany the newly laid eggs and the bacon sizzling on the AGA in the kitchen.

The house was very old and had in fact once been a sort of coastguard station. With Cornwall having been rife with smugglers, there were many such houses perched on the cliffs giving good vantage points of the coves below.

Their first breakfast was to be taken in the kitchen, but later meals would be served in the dining room their host informed them. They were seated around an old pine table, scrubbed clean hundreds of times over the years. There were red and white checked napkins at each place, with shiny plates and cutlery. A large jug in the centre contained fresh milk, as not only was this a guesthouse it was also a working farm, with cattle, sheep and hens in the surrounding courtyard and fields.

The breakfast was well received by all, eggs, bacon, sausage, mushrooms, tomatoes, fried bread with fresh bread rolls and homemade Jam, all washed down with freshly brewed, hot coffee. Margaret had been right when she said the food was good. Dad sat back in his chair and folded up his napkin.

"That was just grand," he announced to which everyone agreed, even Lizzie.

"I'll show you to your rooms" their host said after breakfast. They all followed her through the house and up the stairs to a long corridor stretched out at the top. There were mirrors on the walls and, to Lizzie's horror; stag's heads were mounted on the walls at intervals along the corridor. The mirrors made the effect worse, which to Lizzie, it seemed as though the house was full of staring eyes and giant antlers.

"I don't like it," she complained. Mum took hold of her hand.

"Shush" she said, and Lizzie clung onto her hand.

Mrs Callow opened the door of the first bedroom, "This be yours, Mrs Mitchell," motioning for them to go in. "Follow me," she said to Jenny, Mark and Lizzie. "This one is for you two," she motioned to Lizzie and Mark, "and if you would follow me I will show you yours," she said smiling at Jenny.

Another narrow flight of stairs ran up from the corner of the corridor and Jenny followed behind Mrs Callow. At the top of the stairs was a small landing where just one door lay off. Mrs Callow threw open the door and allowed Jenny to push past her and into the room which was hers for the next fortnight.

"I thought being a bit older, you might like a bit of privacy," she told Jenny. "I'll leave you to it then." Mrs Callow was gone before Jenny could even thank her.

She looked around the room. The floor was bleached pine with rugs scattered here and there. There was a pine double bed with a patchwork counterpane thrown over it. The bedside cabinet and dressing table were the same bleached pine as the floor. There was a large window in the corner of the room and Jenny realised that this room must be in the roof space, since the ceiling sloped quite dramatically down. She looked out the window and the view took her breath away! She could see the whole of the bay from here, the black cliffs encompassing the bay, gave way to soft yellow sand which sloped down to the sea, the sight of which Jenny felt she would never ever be able to describe. The dark green, almost black swell of the waves seemed to heave and then explode into a boiling bubbling mass of white, forcing its way up the shore and covering the yellow sand so rapidly with foam and then, as if afraid to linger on the shore, rushed back again, lost beneath another onslaught.

She couldn't take her eyes off it. It was magnificent. She would never forget this sight as long as she lived, and was held by the view for some time.

'If ever I buy my own house, I will ensure that it has a magnificent view like this,' she told herself.

After daydreaming a little while longer, she heard someone behind her and turned to see Lizzie coming into the room, complete with bucket and spade.

"We're going to the beach. Are you coming?" she asked excitedly.

"I haven't unpacked yet," replied Jenny.

"What have you been doing? You've been here ages," Lizzie complained indignantly. "Well I'm not waiting for you. Bye." she said, and was gone.

Jenny realised she must have been looking out through the window for a lot longer than she'd thought. Opening the doors of the pine wardrobe, she hung up her clothes. She opened the drawers of the dressing table and smiled to see scented drawer liners in each of them. These little touches made it so special. She placed her underwear and swimming costumes in the top drawer, shorts and t-shirts in the bottom, and placed her shoes and sandals under the wardrobe.

Taking her wash bag and towels out of the case, she wondered where the bathroom might be. Looking around, she noticed another door in the room and slowly opened it. She was delighted to find a tiny bathroom with a deep cast iron bath which almost filled the room, with a washbasin and toilet almost touching. The walls had white and flowered tiles scattered at irregular intervals. A tiny window let in a little natural light, and the room was heavily scented with potpourri in a basket on the little window ledge.

'Wonderful,' she thought. 'No need to share.'

It looked like she was going to enjoy her stay here in Cornwall. 'I bet Sue hasn't got a room like this in Spain!'

The task of unpacking completed, Jenny changed into shorts and t-shirt, with her swimsuit underneath. She put on her trainers and, closing the bedroom door behind her she left to explore.

The narrow lane they'd originally come down continued past a field belonging to the farm and then to the cove itself. As she approached the cove she could hear the pounding of the waves on the rocks and could feel the spray on her face. To the left of the cove hidden behind an outcrop of rocks, she was surprised to see a tiny Church. The grey stone of the building was covered in green moss, like the rocks surrounding it. She could see it was very old and imagined fishermen's wives quietly praying here for the safe return of their kinsfolk, and the farmers and their families thanking God for the harvest. She thought about smugglers wives praying their husbands would not be caught by the coastguards.

She promised herself a visit inside the church during her stay but not today, the weather was just too good to be spending time inside and the English climate was so unpredictable, unlike Spain, where Sue would probably be enjoying uninterrupted sunshine

Jenny walked across the small row of pebbles and onto the soft yellow sand. At the far side of the cove she could see Dad and Lizzie hunting in the tiny rock pools for crabs. She looked for her mum, but decided she'd still be back at the guesthouse finishing the unpacking for everyone. She saw her brother Mark perched on a rock at the edge of the sea, throwing stones into the waves. She wondered why people always felt compelled to throw stones into any water they came across. She decided not to join her family, but waved to let them know she'd seen them and walked further up the beach, which apart from her dad and siblings, was deserted at this early hour.

Once on the grass at the top of the beach she followed a little track which took her onto the cliffs, and could see that this would eventually lead to the next cove, and decided to carry on. The track was probably used by sheep and goats as it was narrow, and Jenny sometimes had to half straddle to stay on it. It eventually dropped dramatically and she had to scramble down the side, holding onto clumps of rough grass and sea pinks that clung to the sides. Once down in the cove she looked up. The sheerness of the cliffs took her breath away and she wondered whether it would be as easy to get back to the top. The sun was not yet high enough to warm this tiny cove and Jenny shuddered a little with the dampness of the air. Maybe a sweatshirt would have been great at this moment.

The waves broke ferociously on the cliffs and rocks, and the sound of their pounding filled the whole cove. Jenny noticed the sand was whiter here than in the bigger cove. She stood for a while just looking out to sea, watching the relentless pounding of the breakers and being mesmerised by the sheer force of the waves.

She visualised cargo ships heavily laden with merchandise, lured by the lights of the wreckers, finding themselves in mortal danger as the waves threw them against the perilous rocks. She wondered how many people had lost their lives in that way on this stretch of shoreline. She shivered at the thought of how cruel the sea could be, and people too.

She turned her back on the sea and began the scramble back up the cliff to the path. It was not too difficult and she was soon in the sunshine on the grassy top. Her clothes and hair were damp from the spray. She walked back along the track and as she looked down into the big cove, she could see that Mum had now joined the others on the beach. She walked slowly down to where they were seated on brightly coloured beach towels, surrounded by sand pies and a large sand castle, expertly crafted by Dad.

Mrs Callow had prepared a picnic for them and although they'd had a good breakfast, Jenny felt a pang of hunger deep in her stomach. She wondered what delights were inside the large wicker hamper. It seemed everybody was feeling a little peckish so Mum laid out the coloured tablecloth and proceeded to empty the contents on it. There were bread rolls with home cooked ham, freshly baked sausage rolls and tiny Cornish pasties, home grown tomatoes, and to complete the feast, scones and jam. There was a flask of piping hot coffee, and although the day was beginning to hot up, Jenny was glad of the coffee to rid her of the dampness.

Appetites duly satisfied, each member of the family spread out their beach towels and lay down, taking in the warmth of the sun's rays. Lulled by the sound of the sea, they soon fell into a pleasant sleep. A little later, Jenny woke refreshed and looked around the cove. She could see that other couples and families had now positioned themselves a comfortable distance away from each other along the beach.

The sun was becoming quite fierce now and she reached inside her pockets for her sunglasses. She removed her t- shirt and shorts to reveal her blue and white spotted swimsuit and positioned herself on the towel. Propped up on her elbows, she could watch the happenings on the beach. The sun warmed her body and she began to relax, forgetting about the unhappy time she'd had with John, along with the awful experience with Mike! It felt good to be alive. This was going to be a good holiday, she told herself.

She watched the children splashing at the edge of the water, others building walls of sand in an effort to prevent the sea from destroying the castles they'd carefully created. She saw older children with buckets trying to hit each other with the cold seawater, racing about the beach and shrieking.

There were couples holding hands, walking along the edge of the beach whilst others a little braver, waded slowly into the waves and finally lowering their shoulders under the water.

There were a couple of guys who ran into the sea and dived immediately into the waves, hoping to impress any watching females. Jenny smiled at this and thought to herself, 'Why did the male of the species always have to show off?'

Jenny saw that Mum had brought a collection of magazines to the beach so she selected one and started to read stories of holiday romances and unrequited love, of sibling rivalry and teenage pregnancies. She flicked idly through the pages.

Suddenly she heard a shrill whistle and turned to look up the beach. A group of eight youths, all wearing identical swimming trunks were being drilled by an older man. Jenny was intrigued.

"They're lifeguards, Jenny," Dad informed her. Her interest in them increased.

She could see they ranged in age from about sixteen to twenty, and all had quite muscular bodies. She watched as they carried a large surfboard down to the water's edge.

The group huddled together for a moment, almost like a rugby scrum. Then, as if a decision had been made, one of the group ran into the sea, swam out a short distance and began to tread water. After a few moments he raised his arm in the air and waved frantically. As he waved to the group on the shore a whistle was blown and the youths sprung into action. A rope was attached to the waist of one boy who picked up the surfboard, plunged into the water and began to paddle towards the boy in the sea. Three others stood in line and fed the rope over their heads, allowing the 'rescuer' to pull it behind him. As the rescuer reached the boy in the water, he helped him onto the surfboard. The rescuer gave a signal and the boys on the beach began to pull the rope and brought the surfboard and riders back to the shore. The 'victim' was then laid on the beach and a mock mouth-to-mouth resuscitation was acted out. The victim and rescuer both then stood up. All the occupants of the beach, who had like Jenny, been totally pre-occupied with watching the event, began to clap and cheer.

'I wouldn't mind being saved by them,' Jenny daydreamed, probably with many other females on the beach sharing her thoughts. She wondered if they'd repeat this performance tomorrow, and made a mental note to position herself a little nearer to the lads if they did.

She protected her eyes with her hand as the sun shone fiercely through the curtains. She reached for her yellow swimsuit from the perfumed drawers of the dresser, took out the matching beach robe and slipped them on, adding flip-flop sandals to the attire. After washing and brushing her hair she arranged it in a large tortoise clip, on the top of her head. Guided by the wonderful aroma of fresh bread and grilled bacon, she made her way down to the dining room. The rest of the family had not yet arrived. Mrs Callow entered the room wearing a hand-embroidered apron, carrying a basket of fresh bread rolls.

"You can have yours now if you like," she said. "The others don't appear to be stirring yet. Are you always an early riser?"

"Not usually," Jenny said shaking her head. It would take several calls and even threats from Mum to get her up at home.

After drinking a glass of ice-cold orange juice she helped herself to bacon and tomatoes from the tray, with a fresh roll from the basket. Everything tasted so delicious here. Having eaten her fill, she thanked Mrs Callow and asked her to pass on a message to her mum.

"Can you tell her I'm going for a walk along the cliff path?" she said, and then went out into the bright sunlight of the early morning.

As she walked, she thought to herself that this was the sort of morning that might inspire a poet to write, or an artist to paint a wonderful picture, a wonderful day to be alive. Forgotten were the bad days that had proceeded the trip and she felt happy again. She walked along with a real spring in her step and soon found herself overlooking the little cove she'd visited the day before. Again the breakers lashed against the rocks and the air was filled with salty spray.

Today, Jenny did not clamber down the steep cliff side, but carried on walking along the cliff path. The path became virtually non-existent and the bracken grew taller and taller. Gorse bushes, deformed and misshaped by the constant battering of the sea winds, reached out to the scratchy branches like knurled fingers trying to catch hold of her legs as she walked.

Within fifty yards, the path came to a sudden halt and she faced a sheer drop into another isolated cove. The rocks in this cove were smooth and black from the constant washing by the waves, and driftwood was strewn along the tide line. Jenny peered over the edge, feeling sure she'd be able to climb down if she was careful, but wishing she'd chosen trainers and not flip-flops for her walk today.

It was too far to go back and the cove seemed so inviting, so holding onto clumps of sea pinks, she carefully made her way down the side of the cliff and into the black rocks below. Some of the rocks were slippery with seaweed, and limpets were clinging to the sides. They were sharp, and Jenny was only too aware of the nasty scratches they could give.

Once on the sand she shook her hair loose and gazed up at the clear blue sky. The crashing of the breakers echoed all around, with spray from the sea filling the air. Today didn't seem as cold as yesterday. She revelled at the power of the sea and the feeling of oneness with nature. Sue would not be getting this experience in the smooth waters of the Mediterranean Sea.

She picked up a few pieces of driftwood and marvelled at the contorted shapes but then discarded them after inspection, keeping only one long straight piece to move the seaweed around whilst combing the beach for treasure.

Having walked the length of this tiny cove several times and finding nothing of great interest amongst the empty bottles, food cartons and pieces of rope and wood, her eyes were drawn again to the sea. A few moments later, something caught her eye.

About thirty yards from shore she could see someone swimming or at least they were trying to swim. The waves were high and strong outside the confines of the cove. The swimmer raised an arm in the air and Jenny was unsure if this was to get her attention or just playing a game in the waves. Then she heard a faint cry over the crashing of the waves and the arm was raised again. Were they in difficulty? She felt her heart sink as she realised the swimmer was definitely struggling in the water. Forgetting everything she'd ever been told about attempting to save people, she ran swiftly to the sea.

The first wave covered her waist, as she pushed forward a bit more. The next wave lifted her feet from the sand. She would have to swim from here, but luckily she was a strong swimmer, actually winning medals for it. The sea was strong and she was being thrown this way and that. She tried to dive under the waves whilst trying to keep her eye on the struggling swimmer, now about fifteen feet away, whom she realised was a young woman.

"Help me - help me," she cried.

"I'm trying to get to you," Jenny cried back. "Try and tread water."

"The current is pulling me out!"

Jenny tried to reach out to the woman and felt like her hand could almost touch her, but the next wave drove them apart again and the woman was pulled several yards further out with the back flow of the tide.

Jenny suddenly realised that she herself was no longer in control. The sea was pulling her out and around the rocks of the cove. She frantically tried to return to the shore, but all her efforts were getting her nowhere. She looked over her shoulder and could no longer see the other woman, hoping that she'd perhaps managed to swim against the strong tide. Jenny's arms and legs began to ache and the water felt much colder than at first. Each wave seemed more difficult to cope with and she began coughing and spluttering.

Fear began to grip her. What if she couldn't get back to shore? No one knew where she was. She tried to shout for help, but instead she just swallowed several mouthfuls of salty water! This was hopeless. She felt tired. Her arms were heavy and her legs were stiff and would not kick anymore. She felt herself slide under the waves. It was cold and dark. She bobbed up again. The shore was such a long way away now. She sank again. This time it was much longer before she surfaced and she was weary and cold! She began to sink below the waves again. It was too much effort to struggle. Her body felt so numb, not painful. As she sank further under the water, she was beginning to lose consciousness. 'This must be what it is like to die,' she thought, too exhausted now to care.

Suddenly there was a great amount of splashing and a rough hand grabbed her arm and shoulder. Was it Mick? Was he trying to tear off her swimsuit? She fought back with every last ounce of strength, lashing out at whoever was handling her so roughly but realised someone was trying to save her.

"Don't save me," she demanded. "There's another woman farther out than me. Save her first."

She tried to escape from the clutches of her rescuer, but her fight was in vain. He was a strong man and he gripped her tightly, flipping her onto her back and swimming strongly across the width of the bay rather than towards shore. She gave up the struggle and momentarily lost consciousness. The next thing she knew was being pulled onto the beach by two other young men. It wasn't the beach of the cove she'd departed from but the main beach, where only yesterday she'd watched these very same young men practising the life saving activities. They sat her on the sand and wrapped a towel around her shoulders. She coughed and spluttered a little.

"How are you now?" asked one of the lifeguards.

"I'm alive," whispered Jenny. She looked out to sea and could see a group of lifeguards letting out the line to two more swimming in the sea.

"Where is the woman?" Jenny asked, but no one replied. "Are they looking for her?" The lifeguard sitting near her on the sand only nodded his head, but said nothing.

"I think you should go to hospital and get checked out," another lifeguard said as an ambulance came onto the pebbles of the beach.

"I'm fine now," said Jenny. "Please, I don't like fuss."

"Are you sure?"

"Yes, sure," Jenny confirmed looking out to sea. The lifeguards were still searching.

Suddenly an arm went up and the lifeguards on the sand began to pull the line in. After what seemed an eternity, one lifeguard stumbled ashore carrying the limp body of the woman. The paramedics from the ambulance ran down to meet them. Jenny couldn't see what happened next because the lifeguards surrounded the paramedics. The lifeguard who'd been sitting with Jenny turned to her.

"Are you here alone, or with your parents?" he questioned.

"I'm here with my family."

"Come on then, I'll take you to them."

As she stood up, Jenny felt a strong arm round her shoulders. It felt very comforting as she walked up the sandy beach to the pebbled area. Suddenly she saw Mum and Dad running towards her, followed at a distance by Mark and Lizzie running hand in hand. The lifeguard released his hold on her shoulders. As he did, her legs suddenly became very wobbly, almost incapable of keeping her upright. Dad threw his arms around her and pulled her head onto his chest. This was really unusual of Dad. He was never very demonstrative when it came to love, kisses and hugs.

"What on earth happened?" he asked, almost crying.

Mum had now arrived and she questioned the young man, who told her how Jenny had been pulled from the sea by another lifeguard.

"There was a strong rip current that affected the coves," he explained to Mum. "Your daughter was caught in it, and dragged quite a distance."

"There was a woman in the sea," Jenny interrupted.

Mum looked up at the lifeguards face to question him. He shook his head.

"There was," protested Jenny, thinking he was contradicting her account. Then it dawned on her that he was shaking his head to tell Mum that the other woman hadn't been as lucky as she'd been.

"She didn't make it," he conformed sadly. Jenny fell to the floor and sobbed convulsively.

"I nearly reached her," she sobbed. "I nearly got there. I shouldn't have given up. I should have tried harder!"

"You tried very hard," another lifeguard said upon his arrival. "Have you seen the state of my arms?" Jenny looked up to see deep gouge marks on the arms and chest of this young man. "You would not let me save you. You kept fighting me off saying don't save me, save the other girl. It was a real struggle to bring you ashore."

"Yes but…." began Jenny.

"Yes but nothing" interrupted the lifeguard. "Although we advise people never to try to save others, you made a very brave attempt to save her. In no way should you feel guilty"

Sadly, Jenny felt very guilty that she'd made it and the other girl had not. The guilt she felt that day would stay with her throughout the rest of her life.

After a restless night Jenny was woken by a knock on her bedroom door. Mrs Callow popped her head round.

"A couple of lads are here to see you Jenny," she told her. "Can you come down?"

"Sure, just give me a minute," Jenny replied.

"They said to put on a swimming costume and bring a towel," Mrs Callow added.

Jenny was a little confused but this, but quickly pulled on a black costume and covered in with an orange sweatshirt. She put on black shorts and her old Reebok trainers and then hurried down the stairs. Mrs Callow directed her into the front room, where two young men were waiting, both turned to face her as she entered the room. She instantly recognised the lifeguard that had shown her his scars the day before, but the other youth she did not as yet know.

"Hi, remember me?" asked the one she recognised. "This here is Simon. He was involved in the incident yesterday." Jenny nodded in acknowledgement of the introduction.

"Without wishing to be rude, why are you here?" Jenny queried.

"We have to take you back in the sea," the lads said in unison.

"Er no thanks," Jenny replied, turning to walk away.

"Sorry, but we won't take no for an answer," Jenny opened her mouth to protest, but was told. "It's the rules. It's very important that you get back in the water as soon as possible. If you persist in refusing, I will get hold of you like I did yesterday. A few more scars won't make much difference," he added with a laugh.

"I'm sorry for that," Jenny blushed, "I didn't mean to, I mean….."

"No explanation needed, just follow us," she was ordered.

Before she knew it she was on her way to the beach, escorted either side by the lifeguards. She wondered what Sue would have made of this, her being escorted to the beach by two hunky young men.

They soon reached the beach and both the boys discarded their top clothes to reveal muscular, sun-tanned bodies in black swimming trunks. Jenny slowly removed her sweatshirt. As she did so, she could tell that both of the lads were admiring her body and she began to feel embarrassed. She glanced around the beach to see they were alone. The sun was shining but there was a chill in the air, and she had no idea what the time was.

"Ready?" asked Simon.

"For what?" asked Jenny, a little nervously.

"Take Jamie's hand," instructed Simon. Jenny did as she was told and turned to look at Jamie. Until now she'd not really taken in his rugged good looks and firm muscular body. He had short dark hair that curled slightly, with dark brown eyes. Jenny imagined he was nineteen or twenty. Simon in contrast was blond and a little taller than Jamie.

Simon led the way, whilst Jenny went hand in hand with Jamie and walked slowly down the beach and water's edge. Her toes felt the first cold ripples of the sea. She froze, feeling an icy chill creep through her. Instantly she dug her heels into the sand as a feeling of absolute terror filled her body.

Jamie tugged at her hand, "Come on its okay," he encouraged.

"I don't think I can," Jenny admitted, her voice beginning to tremble while her arms and legs began to shake terribly.

She'd always loved the sea. It had held a special fascination for her and she'd marvelled at its power, yet now it filled her with fear, a fear she was unable to control. She remembered how the waves had covered and dragged her down and it made her want to scream! She remembered how the salt water had filled her mouth and stung her nostrils. The last thing she wanted to do now was to go back in and risk her life again.

Seeing her pain, Simon took her hand and smiled at her to comfort and encourage her. She didn't feel any easier about it and was still filled with terror. Helped and encouraged by the two lads she walked a step at a time, pausing momentarily with each wave that splashed her body, filling her with fear. The lads both knew from experience how difficult this was for her. It was imperative they did not rush her.

The water now reached her thighs, with each wave presenting a new threat. To Jenny, it was more terrifying than having a gun pointed at her head.

The water was now past her waist and each wave lifted her feet from the sand. She felt the strong, reassuring arms around her.

"You should try to swim now, Jenny," said Jamie. "We are here, so just grab us if you need to."

"I can't, I can't," she screamed hysterically. "Take me out. Please take me out," she pleaded.

"Soon, very soon," Jamie coaxed. "Come on Jenny, please try. I'm here, and I won't let anything happen to you, I promise."

She tried a few strokes but quickly put her feet back on the sand.

"Shall we go out a little further?" suggested Simon.

"I'm too frightened," Jenny pleaded. "Please don't make me go out of my depth." She felt as though she might faint if they made her do this, such was her feeling of absolute terror.

"It's okay, we understand," reassured Jamie. "You've done tremendously. Shall we go back now?"

"Please, oh yes please," she cried, like a frightened child.

They turned and waded slowly back to the beach. When she reached the soft sand, her legs gave way and she collapsed onto her knees. She began to sob. Jamie put his hand gently on her shoulder and she felt relief that the ordeal was over, but was filled with so many other emotions that all she could do was to let it all out through her tears. The lifeguards stood close to her, experiencing this reaction from others they'd rescued.

It was several minutes before Jenny regained her composure. She looked up at the two young men who stood either side of her. They both offered her a hand to help her up. She brushed the sand from her body and began to walk up the beach to where they'd left the towels. It seemed like an eternity since they'd left them. All three began to rub themselves dry and put on their clothes in silence. Jenny now felt a little better and had stopped shaking.

As they walked up the beach, Jamie took hold of Jenny's hand, pulled her towards him and planted a kiss firmly on her lips, making her jump back.

"Sorry," Jamie said apologetically. "I just wanted to show you how proud I am of you for going in today."

"And the rest," Simon laughed. "He hasn't stopped talking about you since yesterday. He's smitten with you." Jamie's face reddened and Jenny felt her cheeks beginning to glow.

"Thanks mate," Jamie reacted sarcastically, aiming his comment at Simon. He then turned to Jenny and said, "Please excuse Simon, he can't keep his mouth shut!" Jenny looked at him and he smiled back at her. He looked like he was going to say something else, but didn't.

"Shall we walk you back to the house?" Simon asked.

"No thanks, I think I'm okay now," replied Jenny, needing to be alone. Jamie looked up again as if to say something, but didn't.

"Thanks for everything," she called as she walked away, although right now she didn't really mean it. She took another couple of steps when she heard Simon's voice.

"Hey, Jamie wants to know if you'd like to join us at the barbecue tonight, eight o'clock on the beach," Simon suggested.

"I can speak for myself if you don't mind," added Jamie, pushing Simon on the shoulder. Jenny thought the idea of spending time with Jamie might be fun.

"Sure," she called. "See you later."

"We'll be on the beach this afternoon," called Jamie.

"Might see you then," Jenny shouted as she waved and walked away.

She walked slowly back to the house, calming herself as she went. She tried to push out of her mind the picture of the lifeguard the day before carrying the limp body of the woman who'd not been as lucky as she'd been. The image would stay with her for the rest of her life and would often haunt her thoughts and dreams.

It was about one-thirty in the afternoon when Jenny strolled back to the beach. Unlike her earlier visit, it was now quite crowded. She scanned the length and breadth of the cove and caught sight of Mum and Dad sitting on bright towels, with Lizzie playing on the sand nearby. Mark was flying a kite, supposedly for Lizzie's amusement, but looking totally engrossed with the task in hand. Jenny did not intend to join them as she was looking for Jamie. She couldn't see him amongst the many families and felt a little disappointed. It was he who'd told her he'd be on the beach this afternoon.

She found a vacant spot on the sand, spread her towel and sat cross-legged looking out to sea. The waves were big today and they rose and fell, then exploded into boiling foam of white as they raced up the beach.

There was no one swimming today, only a few children paddling at the edge watched anxiously by their mothers. The sea was so beautiful, so engrossing, so dangerous, giving life and taking it away! As she sat contemplating, two hands covered her eyes.

"Guess who?" a soft voice was heard to say. She shrugged her shoulders, although she thought it was Jamie and really hoped it was. He took away his hands and moved in front of her.

"Been here long?" he questioned.

"No. I've only just arrived," she replied.

"Sorry I wasn't here to meet you, I had to deliver the bread rolls for tonight's barbecue," Jamie revealed. "But I'm here now." He placed his towel next to Jenny's and sat down, drawing his knees up and wrapping his arms around them.

"Rough today," he said, pointing to the sea. "It puts people, off, thank goodness. We shouldn't have to go in after anyone today."

"Are you always on duty?" asked Jenny.

"If I'm here I'm on standby, we are all volunteers."

"You mean you don't get paid for risking your life?"

"No. But we're hoping that the Parish Council will see fit to appoint a full time lifeguard in the near future and I'm hoping that I might get the job."

"Good Luck, if that's what you want," Jenny said.

She could feel that Jamie was looking at her, but she didn't meet his gaze. She took up the same pose as Jamie with her arms around her knees and gazed out to sea once more. They sat in silence for a few moments until Jenny broke the silence.

"I bet you get to meet lots of girls down here," she suggested.

"I hope you don't think I am trying to play a fast one with you," Jamie laughed. "I don't find it particularly easy to, well you know, to chat up a girl. Simon does. He has a different girl every week."

Jamie suddenly reminded Jenny of John and Pete on the fair. She smiled to herself at the recollection.

"Care to share the joke?" asked Jamie, seeing the smile.

"Oh its nothing," she told him. "You just reminded me of someone I know."

"A boyfriend?" questioned Jamie.

"Yes."

"Right, you don't mind me being here. I mean if you'd like me to leave you alone, I will." Jamie stood up and was ready to leave.

"It was an ex-boyfriend. Please don't go," Jenny pleaded. "I'm really enjoying your company." Jamie sat down again, pleased at this announcement.

They chatted about anything and everything that afternoon, soaking up the sun and thoroughly enjoying being together, with the time passing too quickly.

Mum and dad passed close by as they left the beach and gestured to Jenny to let her know they were leaving, but did not want to disturb her as she seemed to be very involved with the good looking young lifeguard. Mum could see she was smiling a lot and thought it was just the tonic she needed to get over yesterday and the split with John. Jenny hadn't spoken to them about it, but they knew it was over. Both her parents missed seeing John, he was a nice lad, the kind you'd like for a son-in-law. But that wasn't going to be.

A few minutes later Jenny turned to Jamie. "Look," she said, "if I am coming to the barbecue tonight, I need to go home to change."

"Of course, yes, er I'll walk you back to the house, if that's okay with you?" Jamie said, a little scared that if he wasn't careful he might spoil things between them.

"Thanks," Jenny smiled, which reassured him.

They picked up their beach towels and as they began to walk, Jamie took her hand. Somehow it was different to when he'd held her hand that morning to walk her into the sea. This time it was because he wanted to, and not because he had to. Jenny couldn't explain the feeling any other way than it felt right.

When they arrived at the gate, Jamie gave her a quick peck on the cheek and then walked off.

"I'll call for you at around seven, okay?" he asked, to which Jenny nodded. She turned and walked up the path to the guesthouse. Once inside, Jenny told her parents about Jamie and that she was going to the barbecue.

"I want to come too," whined Lizzie.

"Not tonight, Lizzie," Mum said quickly. "Jenny wants to go on her own tonight. You can go another time."

"It's not fair." Lizzie moaned.

"I'll give you not fair," called Dad. "Come here Lizzie and leave Jenny alone." Dad looked at Jenny and nodded, "You alright Jenny?" She could tell this was genuine concern for her well-being.

"Fine thanks Dad," she said smiling.

"Good," he said firmly, happy that his daughter was okay. He'd been worried about her.

Jenny went to her room and ran a bath and soaked for a while. The heat of the water made her realise she must have caught the sun that afternoon. She stepped out of the bath and wrapped the big bath towel around her, beginning to dry her hair with the smaller hand towel.

Glancing through the window she could see it was beginning to go dark and could see that lights had been erected around the canopy of the beach hut, and that the barbecue coals were glowing. A few people were already beginning to gather near the hut. It was six-thirty and Jamie would be here in half an hour, so she finished drying her hair. The red hi-lights looked particularly beautiful, possibly affected by the afternoon sun.

She opted for knee length white shorts and a white cricket jumper, white socks and comfy trainers. She applied only the minimum of makeup to tone down the glow that the sun had added to her cheeks and nose.

Looking at her reflection in the mirror, she liked what she saw. She looked terrific. There was no need to wear sexy low cut dresses to make her attractive. She was definitely a natural beauty, although she didn't think so. Throwing a long handled crochet bag over her shoulder, she was ready.

'Five to seven,' she said to herself. 'Jamie will be here in five minutes.' She felt a few butterflies in her stomach. She wondered if Jamie would kiss her properly tonight, really hoping he would.

Walking downstairs she heard a knock at the front door, and Mrs Callow answered.

"Er I've, I've come to call for Jenny," Jamie was heard to stammer.

"Okay Mrs Callow, I'm here," she announced.

"And very nice you look too," Mrs Callow said. Jamie also smiled in approval. He didn't take her hand until they were down the lane, but then he squeezed it hard.

"Ouch!" Jenny cried.

"Sorry, I just wanted to make sure you were real," Jamie complemented. "I cannot believe how beautiful you look tonight." Jenny smiled to acknowledge the compliment, and the butterflies fluttered in her stomach again.

Soon they were in the crowd around the barbecue. The music was banging and people were dancing on the wooden platform in front of the beach hut.

"Drink?" asked Jamie. Jenny nodded. "Would you like punch or orange?"

"I think I'll stick to orange, thanks," Jenny replied thoughtfully.

"Me too," added Jamie. Simon caught sight of them and came to join them, complete with a female companion.

"Hi, this is Jamie and Jenny," Simon said to the blond on his arm, "and this is Mandy." Introductions completed and acknowledged, they wandered to the barbecue where they sampled the burgers and hotdogs. They chatted together, all four of them, for some time. Then Simon excused him and Mandy.

"A walk on the beach," Simon said winking. Jamie raised his eyebrows.

"I know where he's going," he whispered in Jenny's ear, "and I know what for!"

"What?" Jenny asked in a mock innocent voice, to which they both laughed.

The music had slowed down and Jamie asked, "Would you like to dance?" Jenny nodded, and they walked hand in hand onto the makeshift dance floor. Jamie's arms slipped easily around her waist. She lifted her arms and placed them on his shoulders and lent her head gently on his chest. It felt so comfortable, so right.

As they danced, Jamie held her closer and she could feel the muscular frame of his body encircling hers. She could hear his heart beat thumping strongly in his chest, and could feel his breath as he nuzzled into her neck. She felt so happy and contented.

There were only two or three couples left on the dance floor when Jenny looked round. She'd been gazing into Jamie's eyes for such a long time, with is deep brown eyes holding her spellbound. They'd moved slowly around the make shift dance floor oblivious to everyone else, not really hearing the music at all. Now the evening was coming to an end, Jenny wished it could go on forever.

She felt so safe in Jamie's arms. He'd saved her from certain death the day before, but it wasn't gratitude that made her want to be with him. She found him very attractive, comfortable to be with, and totally lovely!

Jamie also thought Jenny was wonderful. She looked great, smelt delicious, and was fun to be with. He'd never met anyone like her before. He felt so at ease with her, not lost for words like he was with other girls. With Jenny he could just be himself.

He'd enjoyed every minute spent with her and wished so much that the evening would not come to an end. The DJ finally announced the last dance and it brought Jenny and Jamie out of their reverie. They clung to each other until the very last note. He put his arm around her shoulder and escorted her off the floor.

"Is it too late to go for a walk?" Jamie asked, hoping against hope that Jenny would say it wasn't.

"It just depends what you mean by a walk," she teased.

Jamie went pink. "I just thought we could stroll along the beach and look at the sea and the stars," he stammered painfully. Jenny smiled. He really was lovely. She wrapped her arm around his waist.

"Come on then," she smiled, "show me the stars."

They left the lights of the barbecue and strolled down the beach, arm in arm. The sea was inky black and the moon painted silver streaks upon it. It was surprising just how much light the moon provided. Although the cliffs that surrounded the beach looked black and menacing, the sea looked serene and beautiful.

"I bet it's wonderful to swim now in the moonlight," whispered Jenny.

"It's magical," replied Jamie. "It's my favourite time. Would you like to go in with me now?" Jenny felt butterflies in her stomach, but wasn't sure if it was fear of the sea or excitement at the prospect of being with Jamie. She turned and looked up the beach. All the lights had now been extinguished and they were quite alone.

"Well?" Jamie asked.

"What about costumes?" she questioned.

Jamie shrugged his shoulders and began discarding his clothes. Jenny only hesitated for a moment, but then began to remove hers. She'd never done anything like this before.

Jamie was now almost naked. He turned slightly away from her as she removed her bra. No one had seen her without clothes before, but funnily enough it just seemed right. She'd always been embarrassed about her bust before, but now it didn't matter. She slipped out of her panties and looked nervously at Jamie. He smiled so sweetly at her that she forgot she was standing there naked. She took hold of his hand and they walked slowly into the sea.

The cold water caressed their naked bodies, but this time Jenny felt no fear. When they'd waded just past waist deep, Jamie pulled her to him, put his arms tightly round her and kissed her firmly but gently. The kiss seemed to go on forever. Standing, as they were, naked together in the cold sea, Jenny could feel his body pressed against hers. She'd never before experienced anything like this and it was wonderful. She felt a stirring inside that was totally new to her, and could tell by their closeness that Jamie too was aroused by the experience.

They clung to each other, neither wishing to release the hold they had on the other and kissed for what seemed an eternity, breaking only momentarily to catch their breath. Jenny felt Jamie's hand on her breast. She moaned quietly. So gentle was his touch, not at all like the roughness of Mick. She shivered, more from excitement than from cold.

Jamie pulled away and looked at her. She was so beautiful, so completely his, here in his domain of the sea. Yesterday it had tried to take her from him, but he'd won that battle. He shivered, perhaps more from emotion than from the cold of the sea, but they had been in there for quite some time.

"Time to go back?" he suggested reluctantly.

"I suppose so," Jenny agreed sadly.

Jamie kissed her once more, took her by the hand and led her ashore. They found their clothes and quickly pulled them on with difficulty. Their bodies were cold and wet, but their hearts were aglow.

Once dressed, they kissed. The intimacy they'd just shared had formed a special bond between them. They smiled at each other.

"Race you back up the beach then?" Jenny laughed.

"Want a bet?" Jamie joked and set off running, closely followed by Jenny. They raced up the beach laughing and shrieking. As they reached the beach hut, Jamie caught sight of Simon and Mandy looking a little dishevelled.

"Looks like you've had a nice walk too," Simon said in an all-knowing voice.

Jamie looked down at his sweatshirt, it was inside out. He looked at Jenny to see her white shorts displayed telltale damp patches where she'd pulled them on hastily over her wet body. What a sight they must have looked. They both burst out laughing and Simon looked puzzled, but Jenny didn't give a damn about what he thought they'd been doing, it had been a wonderful experience.

She felt totally cleansed by her bathe in the sea with Jamie and wondered what might have happened if they'd stayed longer. She felt disappointed but also relieved that it had ended when it did, but wondered what the rest of the holiday would bring.

Arriving at the guesthouse Jamie kissed her gently, but with a great amount of affection.

"See you tomorrow?" he asked.

"Maybe," Jenny teased.

For the rest of the holiday they met each day on the beach, and spent every evening together. Jenny acquired a deep golden tan and looked and felt terrific. She laughed a lot and there was a renewed sparkle in her eyes. With Jamie's help and encouragement, she learnt to swim again. By day they lay on the sun drenched beach holding hands and talking, relating tales of the past and discussing their aspirations for the future, comfortable to relate their innermost thoughts to each other. By night they strolled along the beach and visited other coves. They kissed passionately, but never again did they experience the sense of intimacy they'd shared in the sea.

Although Jamie's kisses aroused deep feelings in them both, he never again touched Jenny breasts. She didn't know why he hadn't and at times she wished he would have, so she could again experience that deep surge of excitement in the pit of her stomach. However, feeling so comfortable with him she didn't feel disappointed, she just enjoyed the closeness between them.

Time flew by and suddenly it was their last evening together. Jenny had carefully a chosen a yellow mini dress, which showed off her tan and her figure beautifully. She wrapped a white cardigan around her shoulders and went down the stairs to meet Jamie. He smiled as she entered the room. His heart pounded, she was such a beautiful girl. These two weeks had been the most wonderful days of his life.

Tonight he took hold of her hand straight away, not wanting to waste a precious second of time. He led her out of the house and down the lane towards the beach. With their arms around each other, they were totally relaxed and contented. The only thing that spoilt is was the thought that after tonight they may never see each other again. They would write, as holiday lovers often promise to do, but long distance love affairs were hard to maintain. They both knew this but at this moment they were together, and it was now that mattered. They would enjoy every last second together and walked down to the sand hand in hand.

It was pitch black tonight. The clouds were hiding the moon and only occasionally did it break through to add silver tinges to the black sea. They sat in the darkness, the sound of the breakers filled the night. Jenny shivered and Jamie quickly put his arm around her.

"Cold?" he asked with concern.

"Not really, just thinking," she returned.

"About what?" Jamie questioned.

"About us," she said honestly. "This is our last night together and I'm wondering if I'll ever see you again."

"Don't think about it," he said.

He pulled her to him and kissed her with a passion that took her breath away. She felt her body respond to his kisses in a way that she'd never experienced before. At that moment she felt she could have given herself to him totally, in every sense of the word. She felt his heart beating and wondered if he was feeling the same way as her. He cradled her in his arms and they sat for a long time in silence. At that moment the moon broke through the clouds. Jenny looked up at Jamie to see tears running down his face.

"Please, don't cry," she pleaded.

"Sorry," Jamie said apologetically. "I'm just so happy, but so sad at the same time. This has been a wonderful two weeks for me and I don't want it to end."

"It has been very special for me too," Jenny confirmed. "I will never forget what we've had together - Never ever." He squeezed her so tight it took the breath out of her and she gasped.

"Sorry," Jamie said. "It's just, well, it's just that I love you and want to keep you here. But I know I can't and......" his voice gave way. He was so full of emotion that he could no longer speak. Jenny grabbed hold and kissed him, with tears now running down both their faces.

Again the moon broke through the clouds. "Look," said Jamie. "Look at the sea." Jenny looked as he continued. "If ever you find yourself looking at the sea, anywhere, anytime, I will be there. If ever you need help, just call to the sea and I'll come running. Jenny, I promise I will always be there to rescue you from whatever happens to you." She looked at him through bleary eyes.

They kissed and momentarily she felt Jamie's hand close to her breast. Her heart skipped a beat as he put his hand on her shoulders. The intimacy they had shared in the sea should not be spoilt by careless caresses. He would never forget that time in the sea and neither would she.

It was very late when Jamie walked Jenny back to the house. He would not see her tomorrow, since Dad was planning to get away early to avoid traffic. These were their last moments together. They clung to each other outside the house, neither cared if anyone was watching, they needed to hold each other close for as long as possible. This was their goodbye, the end of a very special time for them both.

She stood at the door and watched as Jamie walked away with his head hanging down. For a brief second it reminded her of when John had left following their split. She knew Jamie was crying, she was crying too. This holiday would be remembered forever, and she would remember Jamie forever. Jenny knew the promise that Jamie had made about always being there was a real promise, a very special promise. It was also a promise he would have to keep.

CHAPTER 5
FRIENDS AND RELATIONSHIPS

When she awoke, the realisation hit her. She was home, the idyllic holiday was over. She could hear Lizzie shrieking downstairs and Mum shouting at her. Gone was the singing. Dad had been left to rest in bed, as he had driven all the way home the day before and was exhausted.

Jenny reached for the telephone; she had so much to tell Sue. She dialled the number and Sue's Mum answered.

"Hi, this is Jenny. Is Sue there?" There was a long pause. Sue's mum sounded dreadful when she finally spoke.

"Oh Jenny, I'm so glad you're home," she responded. "I cannot get through to Susan. She just stays in her room all the time. I don't know what's wrong with her. Perhaps she'll speak to you. Could you come round?"

"Of course, I'll be round in about half an hour," Jenny replied, then replaced the receiver. Sue's mum seemed really worried, so Jenny dressed quickly, called to Mum to say she'd be back soon and rushed off to Sue's house, where Sue's mum let her in.

"I've never seen her like this," she said, shaking her head in disbelief. "She came back from holiday on Thursday and I don't think I've had more than two words from her since. Go on up, she's in her room." Jenny went up the stairs and knocked hesitantly on the door of Sue's room.

"What do you want now?" was the sharp response to the knocking.

"It's me, Jenny, can I come in?"

"If you must," she heard her friend say.

Jenny opened the door and went in to see Sue lying on the bed. The room was a mess, but nothing like the mess her friend was in. It looked as if she hadn't washed her hair in days, her cheeks were streaked with black eye makeup and er eyes were red from crying. However, the strangest thing was, although she'd holidayed in Spain she hardly had any tan at all.

"I suppose you've come to gloat," Sue said, with such bitterness in her voice. "You there with your English Riviera sun tan!"

"Whatever's wrong with you, Sue?" asked Jenny, really worried. She went towards the bed, tripping over discarded clothing as she went and sat down close to Sue, but her friend gave her the cold shoulder. "I'm not going until you tell me what's wrong," she stated.

"Please yourself!"

"Come on Sue, it can't be that bad," Jenny volunteered.

"How the hell do you know how bad it is, you weren't there! You weren't there when they," she turned, ashen faced towards Jenny and began to sob.

"When they what, Sue, and when who did what?" Jenny demanded with all sorts of things running through her mind. "Please tell me." It took a few minutes for Sue to pull herself together.

"It was great the first few days," she began. "Sean and I went down to the beach on our own each day and out on our own at night. Although we shared a bed, he didn't try anything. I was really enjoying myself and we got on so well. Then one evening he really surprised me by telling me he was bored. He said he needed some fun and wanted to spend more time with the lads. I thought he was dumping me. I only wish that was what he had meant."

"So what happened?" asked an attentive Jenny, and Sue continued.

"That evening, he left me alone in the apartment and went out with the lads. I went down to the bar and had a few drinks to drown my sorrows, well, quite a lot of drinks. With difficulty, I made my way back up to the apartment and went to bed in the room Sean and I were sharing. The drink must have sent me to sleep because it was quite a bit later when he came back with the others. I could hear them shouting and swearing, but that was usual for them after a few drinks. The next thing I knew, the door was flung open and Sean swayed in."

"Hum..." was all Jenny could say. Sue took a deep breath and Jenny put her arms around her friend as if to support her.

"Sean was obviously really drunk. When he came in he shouted, 'Come on sexy. Let's see what you look like!' and he flung back the sheet covering me. I had bought a little sexy nightdress which I thought would impress him. It hardly covered anything. He pulled me roughly off the bed demanding, 'Come on, come and see the boys. Let's show them what a fun bird you are.' He dragged me into the lounge area where the other lads were sitting and drinking. It was obvious they were all paralytically drunk. I tried to hide behind Sean, but he wouldn't let me and threw me into the middle of the room. I was unsteady on my feet because of the amount of drink I'd had earlier and I fell over onto one of the lad's knees. He grabbed hold of me and kissed me really hard. He smelt of stale beer, but what was worse was that Sean just stood there and laughed."

"Oh lord," Jenny sighed. "What happened next?"

"Sean grabbed hold of me and pulled me to the centre of the room. He tore off my nightdress and shouted,' Come on girl, get your tits out for the lads.' The others joined in with the chant. Jenny, it was terrible." Jenny could see the tears streaming down Sue's cheeks.

"There I was, completely naked in a room full of men. I tried to get to the door, but Sean blocked my way and pushed me onto the floor. 'Now lady, you have done your prick-teasing once too often,' he jeered. I watched in terror as he knelt down, pushing me flat onto my back and positioning himself between my legs. I tried to fight him off, but two of the others held my shoulders to the floor as he undid his trousers and took 'IT' out!"

Sue stopped talking but Jenny did not speak. She just held her friend tight in her arms and comforted her. She couldn't begin to know what she'd had gone through.

"He pushed his manhood inside me," Sue continued eventually. "It hurt so much! I could feel his hands on my body, pushing and squeezing me. But what was worse was that he was laughing and telling the lads to get a good look at me. I think I must have passed out at this point and don't know what else he did to me, or what any of the others did.

The next thing I knew was Mick giving me his T-shirt, picking me up off the floor and carrying me into the bedroom. The other lads were all asleep, unconscious from the drink. Mick placed me gently on the bed and covered me with the sheet. He didn't speak, but just walked out and closed the door.

The next morning, when I woke the lads were still in the lounge. I was afraid to even go into the toilet, so I crept past them and locked myself in the bathroom. I stood in the shower and scrubbed until my skin was red raw, trying to wash Sean and the lads from my body. After the shower, I dressed and went out without waking anybody and walked for hours.

When I finally returned, the boys were awake. I didn't know whether to go in or not, terrified of what might happen, but didn't have enough money to go anywhere else.

They all looked rather sheepish, with nobody speaking. I spent the rest of the holiday on my own. Even Sean never spoke to me. He never came into the room again and totally ignored me."

Sue started to sob again and Jenny hugged her, feeling tears in her own eyes. It was heartbreaking to see her best friend in this state and was horrified to hear what had happened to her. Not knowing what to say, she just kept on hugging her until suddenly her friend sat upright.

"You mustn't tell Mum," she pleaded, frantically. "You mustn't tell anyone what I've told you," she commanded.

"I won't," assured Jenny. "But shouldn't you go to the police?"

"No!" came the emphatic answer.

"But you must see a doctor, you could be pregnant" Jenny saw the horror on Sue's face. It was obvious she hadn't considered this prospect. The rape had been the most hideous experience she'd ever had, but the thought she could be pregnant was just too much to comprehend.

"We'll phone the doctor and make an appointment," Jenny said, taking control. "You can tell your mum you've got a bit of a stomach bug. I'll come with you if you want. We need to get it sorted straight away."

It was usually Sue who called the shots, but she was in no way able to think clearly at the moment, so it was down to Jenny. They discussed how they would handle it. Jenny hugged Sue again and the hug said it all. It said thanks for helping, thanks for listening, and thanks for being here. Most of all it said, thank you for being my friend.

"Did Sue have a good holiday?" Mum called as Jenny arrived home. "Did you tell her about your little adventure?"

Jenny offered no answer to her mum and went to her room, where she mulled over what Sue had just told her and tried to take it all in but felt drained. She wished that John or even Jamie were there to put their arms around and comfort her.

It was a dreadful ordeal for Sue at the doctors. She explained that she'd had sex with her boyfriend and that there was a chance she may be pregnant, but left out all the other details. The doctor gave her a lecture about her careless attitude to sex. It was the last thing Sue needed. He prescribed some tablets and told her to come back if she didn't get her period within the next few days.

The waiting was terrible, but much to the relief of both of them, Sue's period came as normal. It had been a very difficult time for Sue and she spent most of her time in her room. When her mum had asked Jenny what the problem was, Jenny had said, "it was boyfriend trouble."

"What a lot of fuss about nothing," her mum kept saying, not knowing the real reason. "Plenty more fish in the sea."

Jenny 'half' kept her promise to Sue not to tell anyone of her friend's predicament. Since she'd been back from her own holiday she'd written to Jamie twice a week and confided to him the events of Mallorca. He was totally disgusted at what had happened to Sue and asked constantly about how she was. He really was such a nice boy and she missed him. She missed John too, but didn't like to admit that.

Taking care of Sue was keeping her very busy and she had little time to think of her own enjoyment. It therefore came as a pleasant surprise when she was invited to stay at a friend's house in Manchester. Although she felt she couldn't leave Sue, it would be her last chance before college started again.

Mum had noticed that Jenny had been very quiet lately and wondered if she was missing Jamie. She thought this trip to Manchester would do her good. Jenny told Sue about the invite.

"You must go," Sue told her. "Don't turn down the invitation because of me. I'm fine now - really." Jenny knew otherwise, but her friend continued. "I will be very angry if you don't go."

"Then it's settled," said Jenny.

She telephoned her friend in Manchester and made arrangements to go two days later. Jenny was really looking forward to seeing Michelle. They'd been friends since primary school. She'd moved away about a year ago and Jenny had only seen her once since then. It would be good to catch up on the gossip.

She took the early morning train to Manchester. As she alighted she could see Michelle waiting at the far end of the platform. She waved frantically and Jenny almost ran along the platform before falling into Michelle's outstretched arms.

"It's so good to see you," exclaimed Jenny.

"You too," came the reply. They hugged for a moment, linked arms and walked out of the station into the busy streets of Manchester.

"Would you like to go for a coffee?" Michelle asked, and Jenny said she would. It had been a while since she'd had that early morning 'cuppa' brought in by Dad before he left for work.

Michelle headed for a coffee bar she knew. It was frequented by students from the university and Art College. Michelle spent a lot of time in there, skipping lectures to meet up with fellow students and putting the world to right in heated discussions.

It was quite crowded today. Michelle pushed her way through to an empty table in the corner, followed closely by Jenny. They ordered cappuccinos and toasted teacakes, looked at each other and laughed.

"Jenny you have a fantastic suntan, where have you been? Some exotic place no doubt."

"Cornwall, actually," Jenny confessed.

"No way!"

"Honestly, Cornwall."

"Well you look terrific."

"You look great too, Michelle. You have a wicked twinkle in your eye. Has something happened that I don't know about?"

"Just wait till I tell you," her friend divulged. "You won't believe it, but I'm getting married next month!"

"Married, next month?" Jenny queried in disbelief. Michelle had always said she would never get married. She was so Women's Lib - So independent.

"He must be someone extra special to make you change your convictions," Jenny offered.

"He is, he really is," Michelle replied. "He's called Donald, don't laugh." Jenny had never thought of laughing, she was just intrigued to know about this special guy. "He's at the university and he's wonderful," her friend went on. Jenny could see that Michelle was besotted with this guy.

"Well, come on, tell me more" she pushed.

"I've been seeing him for about six months and he asked me to marry him. I said yes."

"Is that it?"

"Isn't that enough?"

"But why so soon?"

"Well there's a bit of a complication, I'm pregnant!" Michelle announced, stunning her friend. Jenny was unsure whether to congratulate, or commiserate her.

"What a surprise," were the only words she could find at that moment.

"Donald is thrilled. He's always wanted children."

"And what about you?"

"Well I didn't really expect to have children so soon, but it's happened and that's that."

Jenny was not totally convinced that Michelle was happy about being pregnant, but she could see that she was happy about marrying Donald.

"Jenny, there is something I want to ask you," Michelle said with a mischievous grin on her face. "Will you be my chief bridesmaid?"

"I'd love that," Jenny replied, giving the impending bride a quick hug.

"That's sorted then," Michelle smiled. ""We'll go and look for a dress tomorrow. I'll introduce you to Donald later."

They chatted for quite some time whilst having refills of cappuccino to keep them going. When asked about her holiday, Jenny told of how she'd met a nice boy and had spent most of the holiday with him. She didn't say anymore about it, as it didn't seem the right time. Michelle was so full of wedding plans and tales of how wonderful Donald was that it was difficult to get a word in, let alone relate the story of her ordeal in the sea. She would talk about some other time.

Leaving the cafe, Michelle led the way to the university. Manchester colleges always started back two weeks before other colleges and the surrounding area was bustling with people.

"How come you're not back?" asked Jenny.

"Oh I've dropped out, what with the baby and everything."

Jenny remembered what a first class student Michelle had been and thought it was a great waste.

"Donald should be here any moment," Michelle announced, "He's just about to finish his lecture."

Jenny was looking forward to meeting her friend's future husband, Donald. At that moment, the door opened and a group of students emerged from the classroom. Jenny tried to guess which one was the man himself. Their lecturer followed the students and Michelle rushed forward and flung her arms around his neck.

"Not here my sweet," he said, shaking himself free from the embrace.

"Jenny, this is Donald," Michelle announced.

Jenny was stunned! Before her stood a man of about forty with receding hair greying at the temples. He wore dark rimmed glasses and frowned a lot.

She was lost for words. This was not the type of man she'd expect Michelle to be marrying. She'd thought it would be some long haired hippie type who supported the ban-the-bomb campaign and was heavily into arts and animal rights, but here stood a man, possibly old enough to be her father. He moved forward and offered her his hand.

"Pleased to meet you Jenny," .he said in a highly polished, very posh voice. "I've heard a lot about you. I understand you're to be Michelle's matron of honour." That made Jenny feel about ninety.

"Chief bridesmaid, I think" Jenny replied. "It's nice to meet you too."

"I'm afraid I haven't got long for lunch today, Poppet," he addressed Michelle. "Shall we go to the refectory?"

"Anywhere you want," Michelle answered in a totally submissive voice.

Donald didn't hold Michelle's hand or kiss her; he just walked next to her as he might walk next to any other student he was teaching. They sat at a table where Donald opened his briefcase to reveal a sandwich box and carton of fresh orange.

"Do you girls want anything?" he asked.

"No we're fine," Michelle stated, speaking for both of them. Jenny watched as Michelle sat gazing admiringly at Donald, hanging on to his every word as he spoke about the lecture he'd just given and the foolishness of the students who'd attended. As she listened, Jenny thought he sounded like her father rather than Michelle's boyfriend.

"Mum wants to know the final numbers for the wedding invites," Michelle said. Donald looked a little annoyed.

"I have asked you not to talk about it here in the university," he challenged. "Things like that we discuss at home." He sounded like a father chastising a small child. Donald finished his sentence, stood up and announced, "I must go now or I'll be late. Punctuality is so very important, as I'm always telling Michelle."

Without saying anything further, he walked out of the dining hall leaving Jenny a little stunned. He'd never even acknowledged that Michelle was his wife to be by kissing her or speaking nicely. He treated her just like a student.

"Well what do you think? Isn't he wonderful?" Michelle questioned, desperately seeking the approval of her close friend. Jenny wondered what to say.

"You seem to have found someone special there" was her tactful reply, which made Michelle smile.

"I knew you would like him," she said.

The following day they went shopping. Michelle told Jenny that the wedding was to be held in a little chapel near to the university, with just a few close friends and relatives being invited. There was to be a small reception in the evening at the golf club, where Donald was a member of course.

Michelle's dress was to be white broidery Anglaise in an empire line to disguise Michelle's growing bump. Jenny guessed she must be about three months pregnant. After much deliberation they chose a pale lemon full-length dress for Jenny. It fitted snugly and showed her figure off beautifully. The lemon colour accentuated her tan, and her dark hair looked lovely against the pale colour. Jenny chose a lemon headband and white shoes, all paid for by Donald.

"Well he does earn a fantastic salary," bragged her friend. Jenny knew that Michelle's parents were not well off, so this man would be seen as quite a catch to them but she wondered how they felt about the age difference.

As Jenny boarded the train home, Michelle waved her off at the end of the platform shouting instructions about not being late in a fortnight. She heaved a sigh of relief. Nice as it was to see her friend so happy, she'd found it difficult to be enthusiastic about the forthcoming marriage. She couldn't really say why, but she felt a sense of foreboding about their future together.

Her thoughts then went to Sue. She hoped she'd been alright and wondered if she should have gone on this trip, leaving her behind to fend for herself. She suddenly felt guilty. Not once did she think of her friend during her time with Michelle. She decided to go straight to Sue's house after she'd seen Mum.

It was about five in the evening when Jenny arrived at her own front door. It felt good to be home. She unlocked the door and went inside.

"Hi Mum, I'm back," she called.

"Hello Jenny," Mum returned. "Jenny, can you just come in here," Mum sounded serious.

"Is something wrong," Jenny asked. "Is everyone okay? I mean you and Dad, Mark or Lizzie?"

"No," Mum reassured. "It's not any of us, its Sue. I think we should sit down." Jenny sat and Mum sat next to her. "You know that Sue hasn't been herself since she came back from holiday, some fall out with a boy, her mum told me." Jenny nodded. The secret was still hers and Sue's. The only others that knew the truth were the offenders themselves.

"Well I'm afraid I have got some terrible news for you, Jenny love," Mum continued. "Sue died on Monday." Jenny looked at her mum blankly, totally disbelieving what she was hearing.

"Don't be ridiculous, Mum, I was with her on Sunday and she was fine. It was her that insisted I went to see Michelle."

"I now, love," Mum said, taking a hold of her hand.

What the hell happened?" Jenny pleaded, now in tears.

"I don't know all the details. It may be better speaking to Sue's mum," her mum admitted. "She's asked to see you as soon as you were back. I'll go with you if you like."

"Yes, but I need to know now, what did she die of?" Mum took a deep breath before she spoke, trying to find the right words to use.

"I'm sorry Jenny," Mum began, before dropping the bombshell. "She took her own life - suicide."

"Oh my lord," exclaimed Jenny "She can't have. It's my fault. I shouldn't have gone to Michelle's. If I'd been with her, she wouldn't have been able to do it." She sobbed hysterically, not believing her friend had gone.

"Come on, let's go see her mum. She needs to speak to you," Mum said gently. "Dry your eyes and get your coat on. We'll walk across together."

They walked to the house without speaking further. As they approached, Jenny could see that all the curtains were closed as a mark of respect to Sue. She knocked on the door as she had so many times before, but this time it felt different, because her friend wasn't there. Normally Sue would swan downstairs wearing some outrageous outfit and shouting orders to everyone, but not anymore. Today a relative of the family opened the door.

"Can I help you?" she asked.

"I'm Jenny, Sue's friend," Jenny said, biting her lip to stop herself from crying.

"Come in," the expressionless voice requested. Jenny could see Sue's mum sitting in the chair, with her dad standing in front of the fireplace. Their eyes were swollen from endless crying. Sue's mum looked up, saw Jenny and held out her hand.

"Oh Jenny what are we going to do?" It was a silly thing to say, but words didn't really matter. Jenny took hold of the hand extended to her and s squeezed it hard. Tears ran down her cheeks and the cheeks of everyone in the room. It was such a waste of a young life.

"What could have driven her to do this?" Sue's mum gasped. "Where did we go wrong? Why didn't she tell us what was bothering her? It's that damn boyfriend that has caused this! She got too involved and then when he dumped her she..." she didn't finish what she was saying and broke down and sobbed again. They'd been going over and over the same questions and searching for answers, but for them there weren't any.

Jenny wondered if there would be any point telling them about Sue's experience in Mallorca, but she'd made a promise that she intended to keep. Sue's dad coughed to gain his composure before speaking.

"She didn't leave any letter," he said. "We have searched and searched, but there's nothing."

Jenny wanted to ask how she'd taken her life, but couldn't. It would be unfair to put them through the ordeal of relating something that would hurt them so much. She would find out in due time. What she couldn't understand was the fact that Sue had not left a note. Did that mean she didn't really mean to go through with it? Was it just a cry for help?

"The police say they've carried out all of their investigations but found no suspicious circumstances, so it'll be recorded as suicide. We've been given permission to bury her, so the funeral will be on Wednesday next week," Sue's dad revealed.

"If there is anything I can do?" Jenny asked.

"No, Jenny," said Sue's mum. "You've done so much for her already, coming here every day and sitting with her. You were a true friend and no one could have done more." Although it was nice for Jenny to hear these words, it did not make her feel any less guilty. She still felt she could have done more for her friend.

Jenny and her mum left and walked home in silence. Upon arrival, she went straight to her room. She didn't tell Mum about the news of Michelle's wedding and her role as chief bridesmaid, about the beautiful dress she was to wear, or about Michelle's older husband to be. All this seemed unimportant and so trivial, when her best friend was dead!

Even though it was the height of summer, the air seemed decidedly chilly on the morning of the funeral. Because of her closeness to her late friend it was decided Jenny would travel in the second funeral car behind the hearse. She'd never been to a funeral before and was dreading it. She wore a pale grey suit covered with a black poncho, finished with a hat pulled low over her eyes. She walked to Sue's house on her own, almost in a trance like state. Sue's mum opened the door.

"Hello love," she said in quite a cheery voice. "Come in." Jenny followed hr inside, where there were several people in the room but she didn't know any of them. They nodded at her as she nodded back. She noticed they were speaking in whispers, making an eerie atmosphere in the room.

"She's here," someone suddenly announced. It sounded as if Sue herself had arrived, as if she'd just returned from holiday or a trip to the shops. What a silly thing to say!

The sombre looking men from the funeral parlour came in and asked Sue's mum if she was ready. She nodded in reply. Sue's mum, dad and grandma climbed into the car directly behind the hearse and Jenny went to the second car. She didn't know who else would be in the car and was very surprised when Pete climbed in next to her.

"Hi Jenny," he said in a soft voice. "Sue's mum asked me to come." Jenny acknowledged him, but continued to look out of the window. Another couple climbed in, nodded to them and closed the doors behind them.

The procession began with the hearse moving down the street at a snail's pace up, but speeded up a little when reaching the main road. When they reached the wrought iron gates, there were crowds of people waiting outside the small church.

Jenny got out of the car and stood by Pete. Her immediate family stood across the other side of the church entrance. When the pallbearers lifted the coffin from the hearse, Jenny felt a lump in her throat. She stared at the coffin as it passed her. On top of the coffin was a wreath of flowers in the shape of a cross, only the palest of lemon flowers had been used. It was beautiful. Sue's mum and dad walked slowly behind their daughter. At the front of the church the vicar stood waiting. Bouquets of flowers filled the aisles, filling the interior with the sweet scent of so many blooms.

Jenny's step faltered as she began to follow the procession inside. Pete took a hold of her hand and squeezed it tightly, which comforted her as they took their place on the second pew directly behind Sue's mum and dad.

The vicar began to recite the opening prayers and rituals but Jenny didn't hear his words, she could only look at the coffin and think, 'Why, why, why?' Pete offered her the hymn book, already open at the page of the hymn they were about to sing.

"Do not be afraid, for I have redeemed you," sang the choir. The congregation were finding it difficult to utter a single note, overcome by the situation. Jenny looked at Sue's mum and dad and thought they were doing really well, certainly better than she was. Having finished the first part of the service, the coffin was carried outside.

As they lowered the coffin into the grave, Jenny felt her legs begin to wobble and her head begin to swim. This was the moment she'd been dreading and thought she might faint. Pete took hold of her arm and she looked at him and saw that he too was overcome by emotion. The tears were running down his cheeks. She slipped her arm in his and hugged it.

She watched until the coffin had come to its final resting place. She saw Sue's mum and dad drop single yellow roses on the lid. She stepped forward to drop hers, kissing it gently before releasing it. After this, she turned away and buried her face in Pete's chest and cried uncontrollably.

When the service was completed, Sue's mum and dad left in the car to travel to the nearby hotel where the wake was to be held. Pete looked at Jenny.

"Fancy a walk" he asked. Jenny nodded. He put his arm around her and helped her walk away form the graveside. She turned for one last look to see men were already covering the coffin. 'Earth to earth, ashes to ashes,' kept going through her mind.

"I'll come and see you tomorrow" she whispered as she walked away from Sue.

They walked for a while without speaking, each lost in their own thoughts and memories of the girl they'd both loved in their own way. Pete broke the silence.

"I saw John last week," he said. "He asked how you were."

"Really?" she queried.

"He said you hadn't been together for a while."

"No, it's been quite a while now," said Jenny thinking, 'and so much has happened since then.'

"How is he?" she ventured to ask,

"He seemed okay. He's started a new job, though I don't know what." They walked on again in silence until reaching the hotel.

"Look Jenny, this really isn't my scene," Pete admitted. "I think I'll split if you don't mind."

"Fine, I understand," she replied. "I don't really want to go myself, but it's for Sue's parent's sake."

"Yes I know," he said, giving her a quick peck on the cheek. "I'll see you around. I'll tell John I've seen you and tell him how good you're looking too," he added.

"Okay," she blushed.

"Bye Jenny, take care," Pete offered.

"Take care yourself Pete," they parted and Jenny went inside.

Gone were the whispers now, people were chatting loudly, even laughing, even Sue's mum looked much better. She was busying herself offering sandwiches and stopping briefly to say a few words to each person before moving on. It was as if the funeral had been the end to one era and that life could begin again. Jenny knew that life would never be the same again, not without Sue. Her thoughts went back to the woman on the beach, and she wondered how her family had dealt with her untimely death.

She stayed at the wake for a little while, then said her goodbyes and left. She walked home alone deep in thought, trying to find a reason for life, for death, for love, for anything and everything, but could find no answers.

CHAPTER 6
DANGEROUS LIAISONS

It was the day before Michelle's wedding, just two weeks since the funeral. Jenny was rushing here and there preparing for Manchester, but still wanted to visit Sue's grave before leaving.

"Well you certainly got lots of flowers, Sue," Jenny said out loud. "I came to talk to you because, well because I didn't get the chance to say goodbye." A lump was forming in her throat as she continued. "We've been through a lot together you and me, some good times, some bad, but I didn't think things were this bad. Why Sue? Why did you do it? I need to know, Sue, I really need to know." Tears now ran unchecked down her cheeks.

She told Sue about the wedding the next day, about the dress she was going to wear, and how Donald was old enough to be Michelle's father. She began laughing as she spoke, but chastised herself. 'Fancy standing next to a grave and laughing!' she thought. 'Sue would have liked that.'

Suddenly it dawned on her that Sue would not want her to be sad. She'd expect her to carry on and not dwell on the past. This lifted her spirits.

A cold breeze blew across the graveyard and chilled her as she crouched next to the grave. She shivered. It was time to go.

"I promise I will come again soon," she promised her friend, and with this said, with tears still in her eyes she walked away.

The next day her friend, Michelle met her at the station in Manchester. She was very excited and told Jenny every last thing about the arrangements for the next day. It was great for Jenny to see somebody so happy, and it was infectious. Once at Michelle's, Jenny was shown to the spare room where her dress was hanging ready for the ceremony.

"Right then, I'll leave you here whilst I go to the hairdressers for my trial hairdo. Make yourself at home. I'll see you soon and then we can catch up on the gossip," Michelle said as she rushed out leaving Jenny alone.

Jenny emptied the overnight bag and then turned to Sue's vanity case, which her mum had given her to remember her daughter by. She took out the items she'd packed herself, but then revealed something Sue had left inside. She took each item out one at a time and examined it.

It was funny how each makeup item could be related to an event. The bright orange lipstick that Sue wore with the orange Kaftan coat when they went to the pop concert, the false eyelashes in their little box that had terrified Lizzie when she thought they were giant spiders, the fake tan that had made both of them go bright orange. Jenny smiled, hugging the items close to her chest.

Having removed everything she looked inside the empty case. The lining was stained with numerous different colours of lipstick and beginning to fray at the edges. She lifted the lining and the piece of cardboard that formed the base of the case, and a shiver went down her spine – She'd found Sue's secret hiding place. She had put her intimate diary here so her mum could not read it. She'd hidden condoms here when she first thought about sleeping with Pete. She'd even hidden her GCE results here and told her mum they'd been lost in the post!

Jenny took a deep breath and lifted the base completely. There were two envelopes. Jenny shivered again. There on one of the envelopes in Sue's handwriting was her name, JEN. She picked up the other envelope, but there was nothing written on it. She hesitated a moment, staring at the object in front of her, before tearing open the envelope addressed to her.

When she began to read the contents, the tears again rolled down her cheeks. She could not believe what was written inside.

Dear Jen, my oldest and only really true friend,

If you are reading this then you must have found it, as I hoped you would.

I knew that only you would look inside this vanity case, so I decided to leave this message here for you. I am so sorry to leave without saying goodbye, but I know you would have guessed something was wrong and you would have tried to stop me. Your invite to Michelle's was such a relief to me.

I had been thinking of ending it for some time, but neither you nor mum ever left me alone. I had to know that neither of you would be there to stop me.

I had made my mind up Jen; nothing was going to stop me. I couldn't cope with what happened to me in Mallorca. I have felt so dirty and so worthless since then, but last week I found out that Sean was married. How could he do that to me when he was already married! Not only was he married, but he also had two young children. I bet everybody else knew and were laughing at me. Did you know Jen?

("Oh my God" said Jenny out loud "I should have told here before she went away.")

I know I didn't have a very good name, but now everyone must have thought I really was a slut, going on holiday with a married man and with a bunch of blokes. I was asking for it and I got it! I guess it was my entire fault, Jen.

You were so good to me, taking control of the situation and rushing me off to the doctors. Well Jenny I have a confession to make. When we went to the doctors and he gave me those tablets I didn't take them. I decided to get my own back on Sean.

I lied to you when I said that I had my period, because I didn't. I was pregnant, just as you said I might be. So I went to see Sean and told him that I was having his baby. He laughed at me, saying that any one of the lads could be the father! He told me he was married and already had two kids so he didn't want any more, and he certainly didn't want to have anything to do with a slut like me! Jenny, I didn't know who the father might be. I couldn't cope with that. I had no choice but to end it this way. Please forgive me.

I have written a note to Mum and Dad and if you have kept your promise not to tell them about Sean then please pass it on to them. I want them to remember me as I was, not as I had become because of Sean.

I want you to remember me, Jen, and remember all the good times we had together. Please don't think badly of me. I have another confession to make to you. I want to ask for your forgiveness about John as well. I was so jealous of what you two had and I encouraged you to finish with him because I couldn't bear to see you two so happy. I am so sorry I split you up. Promise me Jen that you will get back with him. He is such a good guy. You were made for each other.

Remember how we talked about life after death. Well I will make sure I come back and haunt you if you don't get back with John. If there is a life after death, I'll make sure I let you know about it. I will find a way to communicate with you.

Jen please do not be unhappy for me, this is my doing and you are in no way to blame. You could not have stopped me. I'd made my mind up.

Goodbye Jenny. Thank you for being my friend. Take care of Mum for me please, and don't ever forget me.

All my love for the rest of eternity,

Sue.

Jenny noticed that the writing towards the end of the letter was more difficult to read. She began to realise that the tablets Sue must have taken had began to take effect. She was horrified to think that she could almost see the point at which her friend had passed. She dropped the letter on the bed and cried. She cried for Sue, for Sue's Mum, she even cried for John and for herself, for all that she'd lost.

By the time Michelle returned from the hairdressers, Jenny had returned the note to its secret place, along with the second envelope which she would deliver to Sue's mum as soon as she returned home. She'd washed her face and put on some fresh makeup. She didn't want Michelle to know anything, not wanting to spoil her euphoria at the prospect of the big day tomorrow. Later they sat on the end of Jenny's bed and chatted well into the night.

"Donald's brother is to be his best man," Michelle informed her. "I haven't met him yet. He's away at university in Bristol. The chief bridesmaid is supposed to get off with the best man. It could be your lucky day," she laughed. Jenny shivered inside at the thought of a forty year old man touching her in that way.

"Hey, don't you think you should get some beauty sleep, or else Donald will be running off with someone even younger!"

"Don't tease Jenny. I know Donald isn't exactly your ideal man, but I think he is wonderful."

"Well that's all that matters, isn't it? Now shut up and go to bed. I'll see you in the morning." Michele hugged Jenny and left.

Preparing herself for bed, Jenny suddenly felt very tired. The emotional strain of finding Sue's letter and the contents had completely drained her. She looked in the mirror to see dark circles under her eyes. She really needed a good night's sleep. Remarkably that night she slept considerably well, and when Michelle's mother woke her the next morning, she felt totally refreshed.

Jenny heard Michelle in the bathroom. Her morning sickness was getting the better of her. After a light breakfast, the hairdresser arrived. Jenny would have her hair done first, followed by

Michelle and then her mum. There was hustle and bustle and comings and goings all morning. The wedding flowers arrived mid-morning, with a bouquet of roses arriving personally for Michelle, sent 'with love from Donald,' with him reminding her not to be late.

At two, they were almost ready. Jenny helped Michelle into her dress and the hairdresser placed the tiny tiara on her head and applied the final touches. Jenny put her own dress on and the hairdresser secured the headband. They each looked in the mirror, turned and nodded approval to each other. They then fell into each other's arms, with no words needed.

Jenny knew Michelle well enough to know that she was totally in love with Donald at this moment in time and had no doubts that marrying him was the right thing to so. Hand in hand they walked downstairs, where Mum waited and dabbed her eyes with a tissue.

"You look lovely," she said. "No one would ever know that you are, well you know." It was hard for Michelle's mum to admit that her little girl (for that was how she still saw her) was three months pregnant.

At the little chapel near the university, a crowd had gathered and were waiting for a first glimpse of the wedding party. Jenny climbed out of the wedding car she'd shared with Michelle's mum, to be greeted with smiles of approval from the guests. Her choice of dress could not have been better. The sun was shining and the tan she'd gained in Cornwall was still obvious, and the lemon dress accentuated it.

Michelle's mum had chosen a conservative navy and white suit, with navy shoes and bag, and a large blue and white floppy hat. She fiddled a little nervously with her white gloves as she walked alone into the church, leaving Jenny to wait for Michelle and her dad. A few minutes later they arrived, and Jenny helped her out of the car and positioned her bouquet so that prying eyes would not notice the slight bump.

At the altar, Jenny took Michelle's bouquet and then her place directly behind the soon to be bride. She glanced slightly to the right to try and get a look at Donald's best man, but could only see the back of his head. He had quite a lot of long black hair for an older man, she thought.

The wedding service was over quickly and Jenny followed Michelle and Donald to the vestry for the signing of the register. Donald's best man followed behind her.

Michelle and Donald signed their names and Jenny witnessed the signatures. This was when she noticed Donald's brother, Ian, and was pleasantly surprised to see that he was much younger than Donald, she estimated him to be about twenty. He was quite good looking with his mop of black hair and piercing blue eyes, which seemed a strange combination. Spotting Jenny, he moved a little closer.

"Hello, I'm Ian," he said, announcing himself. "Donald told me you were a bit of a dragon, so I was frightened of meeting you," his eyes laughed as he said this.

"I thought you'd be as," she began to say, but then thought it better not to mention Donald's advanced years. Ian, knowing exactly what she was going to say, reassured her with a smile.

"I was an afterthought," he laughed.

"I'm glad," said Jenny, meaning it, but then thinking, 'did I really say that out loud?'

The official part of the ceremony over, the wedding march was played and the bride and groom led the procession down the aisle and out to the welcoming sunshine. Jenny followed with Ian, strangely feeling strange in the pit of her stomach. Perhaps today would turn out better than she'd first thought.

After the traditional photographs, taxis took all of the wedding party to the cricket club for the reception. Jenny took her place seated next to Ian. They chatted about their respective careers, hers in finance, his in biochemistry, their hobbies, his rugby, her art and design, their previous relationships and their aspirations for the future. By the end of the meal, they felt as though they'd known each other for ages.

When the time came for the speeches, Jenny listened with admiration, as Ian told stories of Donald's past and finished by toasting the 'lovely bridesmaid,' making Jenny blush. After the speeches the guests were asked to move into the bar area whist the tables were cleared in preparation for the impending dancing.

"Can I buy you a drink, Jenny?" Ian asked.

"Thanks. I'll have a white wine please," Jenny replied. They leant on the bar and continued to chat. Michelle caught up with them.

"Getting on okay are we?" she asked, winking at Jenny and making her friend feel a slight glow to her cheeks. "The dancing will be starting soon," Michelle continued. "I hope you two are going to join us?"

"Sure," said Ian, raising his glass to Michelle.

Donald and his new wife led the dancing, followed by the parents, best man Ian, and chief bridesmaid Jenny joining them. As they danced together for the first time, Ian certainly held Jenny firmly, as he controlled every move of the Waltz.

The evening passed quickly and they were soon announcing the last dance. Ian held out his hand, Jenny took it and he led them onto the floor, wrapped his arms around her and danced very close, a little too close, Jenny thought, but she could feel her heart beating faster and the butterflies in her stomach were now playing havoc!

His piercing blue eyes gazed down at her and she smiled at him, closing her eyes as they danced. It was obvious that Ian had learned to dance. He knew all the fancy footwork, but Jenny had noticed how he liked to show off his talent.

As the dance finished, Ian brushed his lips on her cheek and whispered, "Can I see you again?"

"I thought you were going back to university on Monday?" she queried.

"No, a week on Monday," he confirmed. "What would you say to a spot of bowling tomorrow?"

"Sounds good to me," said Jenny, hoping she didn't sound too eager.

"Right, I'll see you outside the alley at two." With that said he kissed her quickly on the cheek and went outside to join the crowd waving off the happy couple.

Jenny suddenly felt abandoned, but knew she'd be seeing him again tomorrow.

Leaving Michelle's house complete with her luggage at about one, she went directly to the station and placed her overnight bag and the vanity case (with its special contents) into a left luggage locker, and then made her way to the bowling alley to meet Ian. She arrived with ten minutes to spare and wondered if Ian was as keen as Donald on punctuality. She waited outside the main door, having to put up with whistles and comments from several males going in.

Ian arrived at two, wearing a black suede jacket, black jeans and a black T-shirt. All this made his blue eyes seem even more piercing. He pecked her on the cheek, took her hand and led her inside the alley, where he insisted on paying. After a few enjoyable games, narrowly won by Ian, they sat in the coffee bar and watched the other players.

"What now?" Ian asked.

"My train goes at seven," Jenny said.

"We could go for a pizza if you like," Ian suggested "There's a place just near the station. We could go there and then I can see you off."

"That sounds fine to me," Jenny replied, accepting the invitation.

They headed for the pizza parlour and managed to get a table in the corner, away from the children's party area. In no time at all it was time to catch her train. On the platform they exchanged phone numbers and he promised to call her. He kissed her quickly on the cheek and before she knew it, he was gone. It had been an unusual first date, with no show of affection from Ian. In fact, it was almost like being with a brother rather than a boyfriend.

As she boarded the train she wondered whether he would phone or not. She thought she'd visit Sue in the cemetery tomorrow and tell her about him, deciding that her friend would have liked him.

She also thought about writing to Jamie. He said that, this week, there might be a decision about the full-time lifeguard job he'd applied for and Jenny wanted to know the result.

Mum was waiting for her on the platform and they walked together to the car, where Dad was waiting.

"How are we then?" Dad asked.

"Fine," Jenny said, leaning forward and giving him a quick hug.

"Give over," he said smiling. It was nice to be hugged by such a beautiful daughter. He was so very proud of her.

The next morning the doorbell rang and Jenny found the delivery driver standing there.

"Parcel for Miss Mitchell," he stated.

"That's me," Jenny said, looking rather puzzled as she hadn't ordered anything.

The large box was fastened securely with scotch tape. She opened the box with kitchen scissors and was intrigued to find inside, two brown paper packages. Inside one was a book of love poems, inside the second box was a single red rose, but no note to say who it was from. She showed Mum.

"How lovely," she said, "a secret admirer."

"I would rather know," Jenny revealed, "then at least I could thank them." She put the rose in water and took the book up to her room.

She later went to visit Sue's grave and noticed fresh flowers had been placed there in a vase. She wondered if they were from Sue's mum. She knew she would have to visit Sue's mum and dad and give them the note. She decided not show them the note her friend had left for her to find, but would say she found it in the case and brought it to them as soon as she could. It would be up to them whether to tell the police or not.

As usual Sue's mum was pleased to see her, welcoming her in and putting the kettle on.

"Are you alone?" Jenny asked.

"Yes, Bill's playing darts down at the Miner's Arms, why do you ask?" Jenny pulled the note from her pocket, glad that Sue's dad wasn't here.

"I found this in Sue's case," Jenny told her. "It's addressed to you."

"A note?" she queried. "Please, let me see."

Jenny noticed that Sue's mum's hands were shaking as she tore the envelope open. She watched as tears formed and began to flow down her face as she read the letter she'd hoped for, the letter that would explain why Sue had committed suicide, the letter which would absolve them of blame.

Dear Mum and Dad

Please do not blame yourself for what has happened, you could not have been better parents to me and I love you both so much.

I have not been well since I returned from Spain and have been to see the doctor. He told me I had a growth inside me which there was no cure for.

I couldn't face being ill. You know I would hate it, so this is the best way out for all of us. I know I've hurt you, but I did this for all the right reasons. It would have hurt you far more to have seen me die in a great deal of pain, better for you to remember me as I am now. I have no regrets for what has happened in my life and thank you for being loving parents. Please remember me fondly and try to be happy.

Your loving daughter
Susan.

Sue's mum passed the letter to Jenny who read it several times, even though she knew what was in it.

"I don't think we should tell anyone else about this letter, Jenny," Sue's mum said, breaking the silence. "If Sue had wanted people to know, she would have told them. No, I think this should be between Bill, me and you." As she said this she nodded emphatically, as if convincing herself that this was the right thing to do.

Jenny stayed with her for a little while, all the time thinking, 'Another secret to keep!'

Days passed with no phone call from Ian, although Jenny was not too bothered by this. Had it been Jamie who'd not written or John in the past who'd not phoned, she'd have been upset. However, not being contacted by Ian didn't bother her in the slightest. Anyway, she was going back to college next week, so had no time for boys. Life was going to be hectic for her right up until Christmas.

She still made time to visit Sue's grave two or three times a week, updating her on the news and gossip and asking her for advice. It had become a part of her life.

The winter had been mild up until now, but with only a few days to go until Christmas it had taken a turn for the worse, with several flurries of snow.

College had finished and Jenny was busy doing her last minute shopping. She'd just rushed in with another load of brightly wrapped parcels when the phone began to ring.

"And how is my lovely bridesmaid doing?" she heard a chirpy voice say, a voice she didn't recognise. "Are you still good at bowling?"

"Ian!" she said in surprise.

"Well who else did you think it was?"

"Sorry, it was just a surprise. I didn't expect it to be you."

"I said I would ring, didn't I?"

"Well, yes. But that was three months ago!"

"Fancy coming out tonight?" Ian questioned. Jenny was still getting over the shock of the call and hesitated a little. "Well yes or no?" Ian asked, sounding a little annoyed.

"Yes, what time and where?"

"I'll pick you up at eight, okay?"

"Fine, but where are we going?"

"Does it matter?" he said, again sounding a little annoyed at her question.

"I'm asking so I'll know what to wear," Jenny said, feeling a little bullied by him.

"Sorry," he said, softly and sweetly. "I am taking you to the rugby club. We have a bit of a contest with a team from another uni, you know, games and that. It's just casual my darling," he explained. "Okay, see you at eight."

With that said, he put the phone down and was gone, leaving Jenny a little stunned by the whole thing. He doesn't ring for three months, but then acts as if it was yesterday when they last went out. He shouts and then charms the life out of me with his soft voice and calls me darling. She couldn't understand his attitude.

She looked at her watch, it was already five-thirty and she hadn't eaten anything since breakfast. Mum was out with Lizzie and Mark, so if she wanted tea it was up to her to make it. Deciding that she didn't have time to eat and have a bath, she decided a bath was more important for the date.

What to wear for a date at the rugby club? She finally decided on a fluffy lamb's wool short-sleeved jumper, with skin tight black pants. With these she could wear a flatter pair of shoes in case the games required her to participate athletically.

At five minutes to eight she heard the car horn tooting and glanced outside to see Ian sitting in a little convertible with the roof down, even in this icy cold weather! He waited a few moments and then sounded the horn again. Jenny was a little annoyed that and he wasn't even bothering to get out of the car to call for her, but grabbed her shoulder bag and rushed out of the front door, slamming it behind her.

"About time too," Ian said abruptly, flinging open the passenger door. She was just about to protest when he smiled lovingly at her. "You look lovely tonight, Jenny," he continued, now in his sugar sweet voice. "It will make me very proud to show you off in the club tonight." Jenny was taken aback by this.

He was wearing a blue silky shirt open at the neck, with a pair of navy corduroy pants. The blue shirt matched his eyes. He'd had the mop of black hair cut shorter, which really suited him. She observed that he was a very good-looking young man.

"New car?" she questioned.

"Present from Dad for passing the old exams," he revealed.

"Some present," Jenny said. "Good Dad!"

"Are you warm enough with the top down?" he asked with some degree of concern.

"I'm fine," she said, wrapping her wool jacket securely round her and wondering how her hair would look at the end of the drive.

"Sit back then and prepare to be thrilled," he announced.

Ian set off with the screeching of rubber on tarmac and careered at breakneck speed down the street towards Manchester. He sneaked the occasional glance at Jenny as they sped through the streets, but was more interested in the glances he received from other motorists when they paused at traffic lights or junctions.

He brought the car to an abrupt halt in the unlit car park at the rear of the rugby club, jumped out slammed the door shut behind him. As he began to walk away he suddenly remembered he'd 'left' something in the car.

"Are you coming?" he asked a little impatiently.

Jenny was about to say something when he smiled, offered his hand and helped her out of the car. He tucked her hand under his arm and walked inside the club. It was dimly lit and filled with cigarette smoke, but Jenny could see there were lots of men drinking beer and playing pool or darts, standing at the bar, or sitting with their arms round girlfriends and wives at the many little tables scattered around the room.

As they entered many of the occupants looked up, some waved whilst others shouted greetings to Ian, who raised his arm in acknowledgement, acting almost like royalty!

"Drink?" he said, more like an order than a question.

"Please could I have a Bianco and lemonade?"

"A little soft isn't it, Bianco and lemonade?" he remarked. Then realising he may have offended her, he smiled in her direction with charm oozing from every inch of his body. She really didn't know what to make of him tonight!

"Okay then, whiskey and dry," Jenny said, thinking 'I'll show him who's soft!'

"And who might this be?" a man asked Ian in a lurid voice, whilst placing his arm around him as he ordered the drinks.

"This is Jenny," Ian informed the man whilst playfully ruffling his hair. "And Jenny, this here is our scrum half, Dave."

"Hi Jenny, pleased to meet you," Dave said. "Just watch this one's up and under, won't you." Jenny smiled as Ian grabbed Dave's leg in a mock tackle, nearly sending him flying.

"Come on Jenny let's get away from this reprobate," Ian laughed. He picked up the glasses from the bar and set off in search of a table at the back of the room. Jenny found herself scurrying after him. Ian stood next to a table with three couples seated and as Jenny arrived he motioned her to sit down, making her feel like a dog being told to sit by its owner.

"Buzz, Chas, Ellie, Millie, Karen and Stewie," he announced conservatively, nodding in the general direction of the three men and three girls seated at the table. He then pointed at Jenny and simply said, "Jenny."

The drinks flowed and Jenny found herself somewhat abandoned by Ian, for each time he went to the bar or moved from the table he was stopped by someone wanting to talk over last weeks' match, or the team list for next week, or some other equally important topic. Jenny was included in the conversations of the other females at the table but the lads mostly ignored her, as they did the other girls.

Suddenly a whistle was blown and a voice over the microphone announced that the games would shortly begin. She wondered what the games might be and whether anyone was in a fit state to play anything.

"Could I have a couple to represent the blues and a couple to represent the reds?" asked the voice. Ian leapt up and grabbed Jenny by the hand.

"Come on, quickly," he shouted, dragging her across the floor toward the stage. There were jeers and cheers from the crowd, as Ian was obviously a popular member of the club.

The body belonging to the voice behind the microphone appeared. "You two there," the voice said pointing, "and you two there"

The game consisted of the female rushing into the crowd and collecting various items of clothing which the male had to put on, having first discarded most of his own clothes. Jenny found everyone was quite obliging when she ran to the audience and demanded items of clothing. They'd obviously played this game many times before. Some girls already had bras in their pockets, pre-prepared as they knew this item was regularly asked for. Unfortunately Jenny was not quite as quick as the other girl and they lost, making a real black look come over Ian's face. His eyes became icy and he furrowed his brow.

Jenny decided that Ian was a really bad loser. He walked back to his seat leaving her to find her own way back and ignored her for a while. Chas bought her another whiskey and she wished she'd had something to eat earlier, because she was now beginning to feel a little giddy.

A few games later, Ian again seized Jenny by the arm and pulled her to the centre of the room. This time it was a team event. The game was a wheelbarrow race, with the girls taking the part of the wheelbarrow. She was thankful that she'd opted for trousers and not the low cut short dress she'd first thought of wearing.

Jenny and Ian were last to go in their team, and when it came to their turn the team was slightly behind. She tried her utmost and her and Ian managed to win by a hairs breadth. This time she received a totally different reaction from Ian. He picked her up, twirled her round and a planted a passionate kiss on her lips, which made her gasp for breath.

"That's more like it," Ian cheered. "At least you tried this time". He took her in one hand and raised his other in acknowledgement of the cheers at their success. He led her back to the table where Chas congratulated Jenny. In fact, Chas was paying quite a lot of attention to Jenny. She was enjoying this, as Ian seemed to ignore her most of the time. Her head was spinning now and a vacant, permanent grin spread across her face.

"Come on. We're going," Ian suddenly announced, grabbing at her arm. Jenny struggled to her feet as he dragged her across the dance floor and out to the car park. He released his grip as they reached the car.

"Do you think you should be driving?" Jenny asked warily. Ian turned sharply to her.

"Do you think you should have been trying to get off with my mate?" he snapped angrily. She was about to protest her innocence when he pushed her against the car. "You are nothing more than a little tart," he said and slapped her harshly across the face. She struggled to remain upright such was the force of the blow. "Get in the car" he commanded.

Jenny focused on his face, which was now contorted with anger. He was no longer handsome, he was ugly. She began nursing her face which she could feel was puffing up!

Jenny didn't know how he managed to drive home, but he did. He stopped outside her house and saying nothing, waited for her to get out, and as soon as she did he sped off. She stood for a moment trying to collect her thoughts, trying to recall what had happened and what she'd possibly done that had so infuriated him.

She quietly opened the front door, crept upstairs and glanced in the mirror. All one side of her face was red and the area around her left eye was already beginning to darken. She would have a black eye in the morning! As she climbed into bed, tears fell gently down her swollen cheeks. She'd never been subjected to anything like this in her life before. Who did he think he was?

She wasn't sure what the time was when she heard her mother calling, but she knew her head hurt and her face felt sore. Taking another look in the mirror she noticed, sure enough, she had a black eye, as she'd thought she might the night before. Panic set in as she didn't know what to tell mum?

"You have a visitor," Mum shouted from downstairs.

Jenny slipped on a sweatshirt and tracksuit bottoms, combed her hair over her face as much as she could and went down stairs to see who the visitor might be. To her immense surprise, there in the hall stood Ian, almost totally concealed by an enormous bouquet of flowers. He smiled a radiant smile at her, his blue eyes sparkled and he looked nothing like the monster he had the night before. When he saw what he'd done, he visibly winced at the sight of her back eye. Jenny was unsure how to react to him.

"Come outside," he said, looking at her with such a pleading expression that she followed him. He gallantly opened the car door for her and then climbed into the driver seat.

"Look," he said. "I was completely out of order last night with the drink and all that and I'm really sorry. I was so frightened that you were going to dump me for Chas and I lost it." He really sounded like a little boy and she found herself feeling sorry for him, rather than angry at what he had done. "Say you'll forgive me." He looked at her with such a pleading expression that it was difficult to resist. Jenny nodded, and as soon as she did this, his expression changed.

"Right then, I have to get to the match," he announced casually. "I'll give you a ring okay?"

Jenny sensed that he was pushing her out of the car so that he could make his getaway. She climbed out but said nothing. Reaching the front door she turned to look at him, but he was already out of sight. She was stunned by his sudden change of character.

Mulling over the events of this morning and the night before, she forgot about her black eye. As she walked into the kitchen her mum let out such a shriek, it made Jenny jump.

"What on earth have you done?" Mum asked, brushing the hair from Jenny's face and examining the bruise on her cheek and the black eye.

"Oh I fell playing a game at the rugby club last night," Jenny lied. "It's getting better now." She hated lying to her mum, but knew what a commotion there would be if she discovered the truth.

After breakfast she returned to her room on the pretence of writing to Jamie. She wondered what he would think of this. Ian didn't ring that night, or the next. Jenny wondered if things were over between them but didn't really care either way. However, two days later he phoned.

"Hi - It's me," he said, sounding chirpy as ever. "Fancy a ride out?" Jenny hesitated, not knowing if she really wanted to see him again. Maybe that violent incident had been just a one off.

"Okay," she answered a little non-committal.

"Good," he replied. "Pick you up at eight." He then put the phone down. He certainly was an unusual guy!

Later, Jenny dressed in trousers and a jumper and threw a mohair cardigan around her shoulders. The evenings were getting cold now as it was only two days away from Christmas.

Ian arrived promptly at eight, looking stunning as usual in a brown leather bomber jacket, dark green sweatshirt and matching designer jeans. This time he came to the door and not sounded his horn as he'd done before. Jenny shouted 'goodbye' to Mum and Dad and left with Ian.

"Have you eaten?" he asked, once they'd begun their journey.

"Not really," she admitted.

"Good," he said, putting his foot down and racing out of town and onto the motorway. Breaking the speed limit most of the way, Ian drove to the Lake District. Swerving sharply into the car park of a stone walled inn, he brought the car to an abrupt stop.

"Right then, here we are," he announced.

Jenny looked at the clothes she was wearing and wondered if she was aptly dressed for what appeared to be a high-classed restaurant.

Ian took her hand and led her inside. With its low-beamed ceilings and sandstone walls adorned with Christmas decorations it looked like a Christmas card. Candles burned everywhere, their flickering lights reflected in the shiny brasses adorning the fireplace and window ledges. A fire roared in the open hearth of the huge stone fireplace, with the dark oak furniture adding to the character. A waiter showed them to a table.

"Shall I order?" Ian asked, taking command as usual. Jenny smiled in answer to him. "Fresh mussels to start, Duck Â l'orange with asparagus tips, broccoli and celery hearts, and for sweet, crème brûllée. We'll have a bottle of St Emillion." Without a please or thank you, he dismissed the waiter, turned to face Jenny and took hold of her hand.

"Well, what do you think?" he asked.

"It's beautiful," she said, finding herself smiling at him. He was just a different person from the last time they'd been out together. He chatted and listened attentively to her all through the delicious meal. He ordered coffees and liqueurs, which they drank seated in comfy chairs. It began to snow outside, which it had been threatening to do for the past few days.

"We'll have to set off soon," Ian said. "Unless that is, unless you'd like to stay the night," he looked across at her, his piercing blue eyes finding their way deep inside her.

"I have nothing with me," she protested, holding up her tiny handbag with not much inside. He shrugged his shoulders. Her heart beat faster. What was he suggesting? If she said yes, what was she agreeing to?

At this moment, the thought of spending the night with Ian filled her with excitement. The evening so far had been wonderful. The meal had been delicious, the atmosphere magical and he'd been the perfect gentleman.

Ian ordered two more drinks, "Whilst you make up your mind" he smiled, and she melted.

Ian went to arrange a room and when he returned he was carrying another two glasses. This time it was malt whiskey. Jenny declined hers so Ian drank them both. They chatted a little longer and then she could see from the look in his eyes, he was ready to go up to the room. This made her pulse race.

He unlocked the door to reveal a large room complete with canopied bed. There was a small bathroom which shone with cleanliness. Jenny suddenly felt a little awkward and crossed her arms over her body. Ian took her hand and sat on the bed, coaxing her to sit next to him. He ever so gently pulled her to him and kissed her. This kiss was sweet, so filled with feeling, so affectionate, so unlike any of his previous kisses.

Jenny felt her entire body relax. Her fears of him subsided and she was filled with a strange longing. There was a knock on the door, making her flinch.

"Steady," Ian said to comfort her, as he answered the door. It was the champagne that he'd ordered earlier. He sat back on the bed, placed the tiny silver tray beside them and opened the bottle, pouring the bubbling contents into two long stemmed glasses.

"To us," he toasted.

"To us," Jenny echoed.

Helped by the calm atmosphere of the room and the amount of alcohol consumed, Jenny began to fully relax. A warm glow of contentment washed over her body. Here she was with a tremendously good looking guy, in a top class hotel drinking champagne. What more could she ask for? It was the stuff of romantic novels.

"Tired?" he asked, not really meaning it.

"Sort of," she remarked, with a grin on her face.

Ian wrapped his arms round her and laid her back on the bed. He kissed her and ran his hand through her hair and brushed his fingers down her shoulders before lightly touching her breasts.

She felt a thrill run through her body. It had been such a long time since she'd felt that, when it had been Jamie sending shivers through her body when he'd held her in the sea.

She felt Ian tug at her jumper and didn't resist when he pulled it over her head. He gently cupped her breasts, secreted as they were in the pretty lilac lace bra. He kissed her longer and harder, caressing her breasts and letting his fingers stray inside the lace cups. She began to struggle for breath and came up for air, pushing Ian gently aside.

"Mind if I take a shower?" she asked.

"Go ahead," said Ian, whilst admiring her slim body and beautiful breasts as she stood before him in trousers and bra. As she searched the drawers for the guest soap, Ian helped himself to a couple of miniatures from the mini-bar.

Jenny went into the bathroom and locked the door behind her. After running the shower for a few moments she stepped inside and soaped herself, enjoying the steaming hot water caressing her nakedness. She was more pleased with her body now than she'd been as a teenager.

Satisfied that she was thoroughly clean, she got out of the shower and wrapped the warm fluffy white towel around her. She apprehensively opened the door of the bathroom, wondering if Ian would want to shower before….before….before what?

She could see an array of clothes scattered around the floor and raised her eyes to look at the bed. Ian was already in the bed and her heart began to beat rapidly again. She sat on the edge of the bed wrapped in her protective towel.

"Ian," she whispered, but received no response. "Ian," she said again, a little louder this time whilst placing her hand on his shoulder. His head flopped to one side as he was already sleeping soundly. Jenny saw the collection of empty miniatures on the floor, which he'd consumed whilst she showered.

Suddenly she felt stupid! She returned to the bathroom and took the robe from behind the door, wrapped herself in it, and then climbed into the far side of the bed. She slept fitfully, kept awake by his drunken snoring.

As light dawned the next morning, she went into the bathroom and stood in front of the mirror, looking directly into her own eyes.

'You nearly made the mistake of your life last night. You nearly slept with that man, didn't you?' she thought, mentally chastising herself.

She was lost in her thoughts as the bathroom door opened and a bleary eyed Ian pushed past her to use the toilet. He didn't even acknowledge she was there. He was completely naked and Jenny could see what an athletic body he had. After taking a leak, he wandered to the bed and climbed back in. Jenny put the supplied kettle on and began to make coffees for them. She gently nudged him and he opened his eyes, but then closed them again and let out a groan, rolled over and pulled the sheets round him.

Moments later, he opened his eyes again and looked at Jenny, who was now sitting on the edge of the bed, wrapped in a white bathrobe and looking lovely. He rubbed his tussled hair and reached out his hand to her.

"You okay?" he asked.

"Fine" she replied.

"I wasn't too rough with you was I?"

At first she didn't realise what he was asking, but then it dawned on her that he had no recollection of last night. The drink had wiped it from his memory. This made her smile, in fact, inside she was laughing to herself. Ian took this to be a smile of satisfaction and he pulled at her robe. She resisted and he didn't try again.

Ian got out of bed totally ignoring the fact that he was naked and walked across to Jenny, picked up a coffee and returned to his side of the bed. Having drunk the coffee, he collected his clothing from the floor and dressed. Jenny went into the bathroom, now feeling embarrassed about baring part of her body to him.

After a breakfast eaten in silence they began the journey home, but when reaching the outskirts of town, Ian stopped the car and looked at her.

"Do you mind if I drop you off here?" he said. "Only I have to go into town to get some presents."

"I don't think I have enough money for a taxi," Jenny explained, almost apologetically.

"That's rich after I have just spent a small fortune on you!" he shouted angry. He raised his hand and Jenny cowered instinctively.

"What the hell are you doing," he shouted.

"I thought you were…"

"You thought I was what?"

"I thought you were going to hit me"

"Hit you? You're not worth hitting," he snarled. "You're nothing but a slut! To be quite honest, you weren't much good at it last night." Jenny opened the car door to get out but Ian pulled her back, banging her head harshly on the doorframe as he did so.

"Not so quick you," he demanded, the darkness returning to his face. "You have made a fool of me once too often, chatting up my mates, pretending to be someone special. Let me tell you, you're nothing. A girl as easy as you to get into bed is just trash! Anyway I won my bet. I slept with you and now that's done. I find you quite boring really."

"Is that so?" said Jenny, mustering a degree of courage from somewhere deep inside. "Well let me tell you something. You couldn't even get it up. You're just a pathetic, drunken slob!"

She didn't see the punch coming, but certainly felt it as it struck her ribs and knocked the breath out of her. The second punch caught her on the side of her head, sending her spinning. As she banged her head on the car door, Ian grabbed hold of her hair and pulled her upright in the seat. He was just about to plant another punch when the driver of a passing car saw the commotion and stopped. Ian released his hold on Jenny's hair and she threw open the car door and escaped. Ian slammed the car into gear and screeched off leaving her stunned and alone.

She straightened her clothes and composed herself, but then felt a sharp pain in her ribs. She stood still for a moment until she could breathe more easily and then searched inside her handbag. Luckily she found a five-pound note in her purse, so was able to take a taxi home.

She arrived at the house to find nobody home, so went upstairs and undressed. Again she looked in the mirror, which seemed a regular occurrence following a date with that monster! A large bruise was forming on the left hand side of her chest, with the pain increasing as she breathed. She couldn't tell her mum she'd had another accident. Who would believe that?

She began to cry, crying out of relief to have escaped, and realising the mistake she'd almost made again.

A thought entered her head. It was Christmas Eve tomorrow and she would be alone. No Sue, John or Jamie. It would be just her.

CHAPTER 7
ARRIVALS

Christmas Eve and Jenny had no one special to spend it with, the first time in a long time that she was not going out with someone at Christmas. She wondered whether she should have gone with Mum and Dad to stay at the hotel in Blackpool. Lizzie and Mark had thought it really exciting to be away on Christmas Eve and then return to their presents on Christmas Day.

She wondered whether to phone the girls. Most of them were in long-term relationships or even married, so they'd probably already have plans. She'd expected to spend Christmas with Ian and wondered what he was doing.

Her thoughts went to Jamie in Cornwall. Last time she spoke to him he'd told her his family would be together at Christmas, but that she was welcome to join them. She'd declined the offer because of Ian, but now regretted that decision for obvious reasons. No, she was here on her own, surrounded by presents, wrapping paper and foil bows.

She decided to finish wrapping up the last of her presents and then settle in front of the television with a drink and some chocolates. There were usually some old films on Christmas Eve, perhaps they would keep her entertained

She piled all the presents under the tree and went upstairs to change into something more comfortable. As she did, the doorbell rang. She wasn't expecting anyone and opened the door to see a very heavily pregnant woman wrapped in a big coat with a large black scarf hiding her face.

"Jenny? It's me, Michelle. Can I come in?"

"Michelle!" Jenny said shocked. "What or earth are you doing here? Where's Donald, is he with you?"

"Oh Jenny," Michelle sighed, beginning to sob. "He's had to go away on business. I can't stand it on my own."

"Come in out of the cold," Jenny offered, opening the door wide to usher Michelle inside. "Give me your coat and sit down."

As Michelle removed her scarf, Jenny noticed a dark mark on her friend's face. Michelle saw her staring at her.

"I fell," she lied, covering the mark with her hand.

"Really," Jenny remarked sarcastically. "Right, I'll make us a cup of tea and then you can tell me all about it," she said reassuringly.

"It was just so lonely at home," Michelle began reluctantly. "I asked Donald if I could go with him and he got angry and told me to grow up. Now that I was a married woman, I should behave as such. I don't think I can live up to Donald's expectations. I seem to annoy him all the time."

As Michelle began to feel the warmth of the room, she removed her cardigan and Jenny noticed her arms were covered in bruises. Again Michelle gave an explanation.

"I have been moving furniture ready for the baby coming," she said, obviously lying.

"Moving furniture in your condition," Jenny challenged. "Why didn't you get Donald to do it?"

"He's far too busy with his lecture work, which he does to pay for everything." Jenny felt her friend was repeating a well rehearsed speech, but didn't question her about this as Michelle continued. "Would it be okay if I stay here tonight?"

"Of course," Jenny responded, always willing to help a friend in need, especially a very pregnant friend. They chatted for some time and were just about to go to bed when the phone rang.

"Hello Jenny, it's Donald," he said as she answered the phone. "Is Michelle there?"

"Yes do you want to speak to her?"

"No, tell her I'll be round to pick her up in half an hour. Tell her to be ready." It was an order and not a request! Jenny was about to speak but she heard the click of the receiver at the other end.

"It was Donald," she confirmed to Michelle. "He's coming for you now." Michelle looked surprised, then frightened, and then relieved. Jenny was unsure what to say.

They waited for the doorbell to ring, which it did about forty minutes later. Jenny opened the door. There was no one there, but down the path she could see someone scurrying back to a car parked in the road. Michelle rushed down the path after him.

"Thanks Jenny," she called. "I'll phone you soon. - Merry Christmas."

Jenny was stunned by the events of the evening but was also disturbed by dark thoughts of what might actually be happening in

Michelle's marriage. Feeling somewhat drained, she tidied up the remains of their suppers and went to bed.

It was several weeks later when she spoke to Michelle on the phone again. The call had sent her rushing to Manchester to collect her friend after a pitiful voice at the end of the line had pleaded with her to come.

Jenny raced through the traffic, parked up and ran through the streets to the coffee bar where Michelle had first told her about Donald and her intentions to marry him. In the far corner sat the forlorn figure of a young woman, now in the last weeks of pregnancy. Jenny noticed her friend had swelled to gigantic proportions. She also noticed that her eyes were red and swollen from continuous crying. She threw her arms around Michelle, but she winced with pain and Jenny pulled her arms away.

"I'll tell you later" Michelle said, as Jenny looked down at her before picking up the battered suitcase that lay on the floor beside her friend and helping her to her feet. They walked gingerly and Jenny noticed how difficult it was for Michelle to get into the car. She wondered whether it was because of the late stage of her pregnancy, or was it something more sinister.

Once at Jenny's house she ushered Michelle inside. Looking at her friend more closely now, she could still see tell tale bruises on her thin arms. With hands warming around the inevitable cup of tea, she began to question her friend.

"Oh Jenny," Michelle finally sobbed. "I've left him. I can't go on. I'm just not good enough for him. I always make him angry by my silly remarks and the mistakes I make. It's my fault it hasn't worked out. What am I going to do?" Jenny hugged her friend and noticed yet again how Michelle winced at her touch.

"Does your Mum know you've left Donald?" Jenny queried.

"No, I don't know what to say to her," Michelle replied. "Mum thinks he's a lovely man and I am very lucky to be with him." Jenny could well imagine this response from Michelle's mum. Obviously she did not know the real Donald!

They talked for a while with a mug of hot chocolate and then went to Jenny's bedroom. She pulled out the bed settee and covered it with a duvet.

"You take my bed and I'll sleep here, Jenny offered.

"No, I'll be fine on the settee," Michelle protested. "I'm used to sleeping on a chair when…" She didn't finish the sentence, but

Jenny already knew the end of it. She smiled at her friend and Michelle reluctantly sat on the bed.

As they both began to undress for bed, as she removed her clothes Jenny couldn't help but notice the bruises on Michelle's chest and legs. She decided she would have to say something and ask about Donald, but thought it best to wait until her friend had the courage to tell her herself.

"You know that I've been seeing Ian, don't you?" Jenny asked.

"Well you did seem to get on well at the wedding," Michelle laughed.

"It's over now," Jenny revealed. "He was very bad tempered and he even hit me!" She watched for Michelle's reaction and sure enough, there was one!

"At first I thought it was just a one off, but he had a dreadful temper. He accused me of doing all sorts of horrid things. It made me feel terrible, but when he actually hit me, I knew it was him and not me who had the problem."

Michelle began to sob as she said this. All this time she'd totally blamed herself for the beatings she'd received from Donald. But if Jenny had been hit by his brother, maybe domestic violence was a family trait.

Amidst a great deal of tears and sobbing, Michelle told Jenny of the constant verbal and physical abuse she'd been subjected to since they were first married. Jenny assured her that it was Donald in the wrong and not her.

"The most important thing now is you and that baby inside you. You are brave to leave Donald. I know it can't have been easy for you, but you have taken the first step and I'll be here to support you every inch of the way. You can depend on that," Jenny told her friend. Michelle smiled, with relief showing in her eyes. She'd found someone who understood what she'd been through. Jenny really was a very special friend to her.

After talking and hugging for some time they eventually went to sleep, but Jenny was awakened by a piercing scream. She saw Michelle was sitting bolt upright and clutching her stomach, obviously in extreme pain.

"Jenny, I think the baby's coming!" Michelle screamed, with eyes full of fear.

"Okay," Jenny said, trying to calm herself. "Do you have anything here with you for hospital?"

"No. The baby isn't due till next month and..." Michelle didn't finish her sentence as another excruciating pain overcame her. Jenny was about to run downstairs to phone for an ambulance when she heard Michelle shout to her.

"Don't leave me Jenny," her friend pleaded.

"I'll only be a moment," Jenny explained, trying to comfort her.

She phoned for an ambulance and very soon the two of them were on their way to the hospital maternity ward. Between contractions they talked.

"Do you want me to tell Donald?"

"Don't you dare?"

"Shall I ring your Mum"?

"No I don't want her to know."

"Almost there," said the extremely calm ambulance crewman, reassuring Michelle as she screamed again.

Upon arrival at the hospital a wheelchair was brought to meet them. Michelle was whisked away and transported directly to the delivery suite. The midwife examined her and then explained to Jenny that it could be quite some time yet before the baby made an appearance.

"They can't be hurried," the midwife smiled.

Michelle had been given some pain relief and was now sitting up in bed and looking much more relaxed. She held out her hand to Jenny.

"You will stay with me, won't you," she questioned. "I can't manage on my own."

"Of course," Jenny replied, a little unsure of how she was going to cope herself.

The midwife popped in and out of the room examining Michelle's progress, whilst Jenny sat beside the bed in a large comfy chair. The prospective mum dozed intermittently because of the effects of the drugs given to her. The midwife checked the foetal monitor, looked at Michelle and then at Jenny, and then rushed out of the room. Within seconds, a posse of doctors and midwives arrived in the room.

"The baby's heart is not very strong and we are a little concerned about it," the midwife explained. "We're going to deliver straight away." She went on to explain to the confused, expectant mother what the exact procedure would be.

They placed Michelle's legs in specially designed stirrups and brought in a ventouse machine to pull the baby out by suction. Jenny was given a gown to wear and Michelle clung tightly to her hand, digging her nails into it each time a contraction racked her body.

"Please let the baby be okay, please," Michelle pleaded.

Minutes later a tiny baby was lifted onto Michelle's chest and Jenny felt tears trickle down her cheeks. It was such a moving experience.

"Is it alright?" Michelle asked weakly, touching the baby.

"Yes. She seems to be fine."

"It's a girl?" Michelle asked for confirmation.

"Yes, you have a beautiful daughter," the midwife confirmed. "Do you have a name for this little one?"

"Jenny May," Michelle said confidently without hesitation. Jenny knew that May was Michelle's mum's name. She smiled in acknowledgement, proud for the girl to be given her name.

The little girl was washed and wrapped in clean blankets and handed back to the mother.

"Here Jenny, hold her," Michelle smiled.

Jenny carefully held the tiny bundle. As she did so, she wondered if she would ever have children of her own. She handed the baby back to the proud mother, who now looked exhausted. It had been an ordeal for her.

Jenny went home to allow Michelle to get some well deserved rest, promising to return later that day. She did so bearing presents of clothes for tiny Jenny May, with flowers and chocolates for the new mother. She'd hastily bought a nightdress, slippers and cosmetics for her friend, hoping that she'd managed to get the right size and make of everything. When she returned, Michelle looked refreshed and was sitting up in bed feeding her little daughter and looking as proud as punch.

"The midwife says I have to see a Social-worker because the baby might be at risk," Michelle said on seeing her friend enter the room. "What do they mean Jenny? They won't take her away from me will they?"

"I'll go and speak to them," Jenny told her and went to the Sister's office at the end of the corridor.

Although she already knew the reason why, Jenny asked about the Social Worker. She was told that, because it was very apparent Michelle had been abused, they were concerned for the baby's safety. Jenny assured them that Michelle would not be returning to her violent husband and explained that her friend would either be coming home with her, or returning to her own parents' home. She would take full responsibility for arranging that.

When she left that night, Michelle had agreed to phone her Mum and explain everything to her. Jenny was sure that her friend's mum would understand, especially when she saw little Jenny May.

CHAPTER 8
BRIEF ENCOUNTER

She stepped out of the taxi onto the wet street. She'd spent a long time doing her hair that evening and didn't want to get it wet, so she pulled her jacket up over her head and scurried blindly towards the entrance of the bar. The next thing she knew she was falling down, having caught the heel of her newly purchased shoes on the kerb edge. A strong arm caught her, stopping her fall just before impact with the ground. Her jacket fell to the floor and she reached down to retrieve it. She wondered how many people had witnessed her embarrassment.

She turned to thank her rescuer, but could never have imagined in her wildest dreams that her rescuer would be him. She checked again to make sure it was really him. He was taller now, and his body was much more muscular than before. His hair was cut shorter and he'd grown a moustache, but it was definitely him.

"John!" she exclaimed.

"Jen!" he replied, equally surprised at the meeting. It had been ages since anyone had called her, Jen. They both laughed.

"How are you?" John asked.

"I'm fine, and you?" Jenny replied.

"Great," John replied smiling. "Where are you off to?"

"Oscars," said Jenny.

"Me too," John divulged. They looked at each other, taking in all the changes. He noticed Jenny's hair had grown and she looked fantastic. Her legs seemed longer and shapelier, looking particularly good in the short skirt she was sporting. Lots of memories came flooding back.

"Are you meeting someone?" he asked.

"Just the girls from work," Jenny told him. "You?"

"I'm meeting the lads," he replied.

"Right then, well it's good to see you," Jenny added, not really wanting to leave it at that.

"Yea," said John, hesitating for a moment as if he was going to ask her something, but didn't, and the moment passed.

Jenny walked into the bar and turned to the right, through to the music room. John went left to the main bar area.

Jenny met the girls. They laughed, drank and danced for a while. A group of young men were attempting to chat them up, including Jenny, but she had other things on her mind.

"Excuse me, I need to get some air," she said, excusing herself to the guy sitting next to her.

"Want me to come?" said the guy, thinking it might be an invite. Without looking, Jenny shook her head, stood and headed towards the door.

In the main bar John had met his mates, listened to their conquests, and discussed last week's football results. They were now giving the girls in the club marks out of ten! He was bored with the somewhat juvenile banter and wondered what Jenny was up to. The last time he'd gone to the bar she was chatting to some bloke in a suit.

"I'm going outside for a smoke," he told the rest of the lads and headed for the door. It couldn't have been planned better, for they both reached the main door at the same time.

"Hi again," greeted Jenny.

"We can't go on meeting like this," John joked, "People will talk." Jenny remembered what a lovely smile he had, and how it lit up his lovely brown/green eyes.

"Let them, I say, how about you?" Jenny joked.

"Want to give them something to really talk about?" John suggested.

"I'm game," Jenny laughed. He grabbed her hand and - Wow! -The electric was still there.

"Bull's head?" he questioned.

"Sure," she accepted.

They ran hand in hand across the road. They'd escaped, just like they had from Sue and Pete that night at the fair, in what seemed like a lifetime ago. John spotted two chairs at a table in the corner and headed towards it. Jenny wondered what was going through his mind. They sat opposite each other across the small table and John signalled to the waiter.

"Is wine okay for you Jenny?"

"Lovely."

"Red or white?"

"Red please."

"Good. Red is also my choice." He turned to the waiter and requested, "A bottle of Chianti please and two glasses." Jenny thought how confident he'd become and how much he'd changed.

He looked across at her. She'd certainly become a beautiful young woman. He really missed her. No one ever meant as much to him as Jenny had, but he'd blown it last time by being such a boring waste of space. Was this the second chance he'd always wished for? He would have to play it carefully and not mess it up this time.

"Penny for your thoughts," Jenny said.

"Sorry, I was miles away."

"Am I so boring?" Jenny laughed. The waiter bought the wine and left it on the table without pouring it.

"You just can't get the service," John joked.

He poured the wine into two glasses, offered one to Jenny and raised the other. "A toast," he said, "to the two of us, past, present and future." As he said it he wondered if it might be the wrong thing to say, but it was too late now.

"To us," Jenny replied, raising her glass with the toast.

"So what have you been doing for the past three years?" Jenny enquired, genuinely interested in what had happened to John to make him the confident, well-groomed young man she saw before her.

"If you have two minutes to spare, I'll tell you everything," he joked with eyes sparkling.

"No really, John, I'd like to know," she stated. "Especially where you learnt your fashion sense, because you look terrific." Her saying this made his heart pound.

"Well then…" John began to relate the events of the three years since they'd been apart.

That last time they'd been together he'd walked down the path from Jenny's house, not believing what had just happened. He didn't dare turn round, knowing she'd be watching him. If he turned round he may run back and plead with her to take him back, and she would have seen the tears running down his cheeks and stinging his eyes. She would have seen the hurt and the anger on his face. He hated her but loved her, and missed her already.

Once out of sight from her, he didn't know why but he began to run, it just seemed to help. He still felt like his heart would burst! His world was falling apart!

He slowed down as he ran into the park and walked towards the rose garden where he'd taken Jenny on their first date. He went to the bench where they'd sat together, but this time he wept alone.

Arriving home he'd gone straight to his room and buried his troubles beneath the bedclothes, eventually sleeping fitfully. Tomorrow he would plan on how to get her back. He knew she was the only one for him and would never give up on her.

The next morning he dialled Jenny's number, but the line was engaged. He hoped she might be calling him. He quickly put the receiver down and waiting with bated breath. After a few minutes the telephone rang and he snatched up the receiver.

Without hesitating he said, "Jenny?"

There was a short pause before Pete's voice was heard to asked, "Have you lost the plot?"

"I thought it was Jenny calling," John admitted, "We've had a bit of a fall out."

"You mean she's dumped you," Pete mocked. "About time too, you boring old fart. I haven't seen you for weeks. How about making up a foursome tonight?"

"What do you mean – who with?" John quizzed.

"I met a couple of girls in the Ritzy last week," Pete divulged. "They're okay, a couple of good sorts. I'll meet you about eight at Bob's."

"No thanks. I don't feel like going out. Anyway Jenny might ring."

"You are thinking of staying in just in case Jenny might ring? You're crazy. Play hard to get. If she phones get you mum to say you're out with some other girl, it works every time. She'll come running back, you'll see."

"No Pete," John said, not wanting to take advice from this man.

"I will not take no for an answer. Bob's at eight," Pete demanded, not listening to his friend. "See you later."

John put down the receiver and stood by the phone for a while. It didn't ring again. Reluctantly John got ready to meet Pete. It was absolutely ages since he had been to a club. He and Jenny preferred to stay in together and watch television, or at least that was what he thought until yesterday. Now he wasn't sure. Perhaps if he'd taken Jenny out more, they might still be together. Pete was already there when John entered 'Bob's.'

"Good to see you, glad you came mate," Pete said. "Two girls are a bit of a handful, even for me!" John smiled, but wasn't really in the mood for this. They took a taxi to the club and went inside.

"I thought you were meeting the girls?" John queried.

"Yeah, but I'm not wasting money on the entrance fee for them. I told them I'd meet them in here."

'Typical,' thought John.

Pete looked towards the bar and two girls waved frantically back, having seen him come in. He put his arms around both of them, giving each a kiss in turn.

"Take your pick, John," offered Pete. John felt himself going red, whilst Pete pushed one of the girls towards him. "Here, meet Kate."

The girl in John's opinion was wearing far too much makeup. Her dress was very low-cut, revealing heaving breasts. Her perfume was strong and sickly, and John felt he might retch at the scent. Wasting no time, Kate pulled John towards her and planted a kiss on his lips.

"She seems to like you," Pete laughed, before turning to the other girl and saying, "Well Jane, how about me and you getting to know each other a little better?" Jane tittered as Pete patted her ample buttocks, which were almost covered by the minuscule skirt she was wearing. John thought the girls looked like prostitutes, but he could hardly say this in front of them.

Having bought drinks for just himself and John, Pete led Jane to the dance floor, leaving John and Kate alone at the bar.

"So what do you like to do?" Kate asked in a provocative, Marilyn Monroe style voice, whilst pouting her lips.

"Not much really," John said, feeling distinctly uncomfortable.

"Well if you like a lot, I'm your girl," Kate said, throwing her chest forward almost into his face. John pulled back.

"Shy, are we then?" she asked.

"Not really," John stammered.

Why on earth did he let Pete persuade him to come out tonight? This was not what he wanted. He compensated by drinking too much, too quickly. By the end of the evening he was legless!

Somehow he later found himself in a taxi with Kate. He was slumped against the window wondering where on earth she was taking him. The taxi came to a halt and Kate opened the door. She paid the fare and then taking hold of John's arm, she led him precariously down some steps to her basement bed-sit.

The flat was dimly lit. Kate sat John on her bed. He tried to focus while she went to make him coffee. She returned, sat next to him on the bed and then began undoing her top. (Perhaps she was a prostitute. Would he be expected to pay for this?) She took hold of his hand and placed it on her left breast.

"How does that make you feel?" Kate purred. He left his hand there for a few moments, and then without saying anything, dropped it to her lap.

She leaned forward and taking hold of John's head with both hands she kissed him, pushing her tongue inside his mouth. He was just not used to this. She began to unbutton his shirt. He wanted to resist but found he couldn't, as she removed his shirt and pushed him backwards onto the bed.

The room began to spin as he tried to focus on her. He could see that she'd removed her top and was now undoing her bra. He blinked again. Was this real or was he dreaming. When he looked again she was just wearing tiny panties and was climbing onto the bed to straddle him. Her breast was hanging right in front of his face and her hands found the zip on his trousers. This was the last thing he felt. He lapsed into unconsciousness with the effects of the enormous amount of alcohol he'd consumed.

A few hours later he was woken by bright sunlight coming through the window. He was confused – How did he get here? – Why was he in a state of undress – Why was there a totally naked girl in bed with him?

He tried to leave the bed and dress without disturbing the girl beneath the covers, but it was all in vain.

"Come back to bed," she urged as he woke her. "It's early yet." As she ran her fingers through her mop of hair, John began to remember the events of the previous night.

"Make us a coffee," she whined. John did as he was told and went to the kitchen. When he returned, she was sitting up in bed wearing nothing but a smile! She patted the bed next to her, gesturing for him to sit down. Instantly she put her arms around him and pushed her tongue into his ear. Again, he winced at this.

"Don't you like me?" she asked. John didn't know what to say. "You liked me well enough last night," she said pouting her lips like a hurt child. John nervously stood up, grabbed his jacket and made a beeline for the door. "Call me," she shouted after him.

Once out in the street, John tried to get his bearings. He realised he was about a mile from home and began to walk quickly, just in case she followed him.

He racked his brain for memories of the night before. Oh God what had he done. What would Jenny say, what would she think? He felt terrible, not just from the drink but also from the thought of what he might have done but couldn't remember doing.

As he entered through the front door, the phone was ringing. He answered and it was Pete.

"Well how did it go?" he asked.

"How did what go?" John remarked.

"Oh come on John, you're not telling me you didn't score with Kate last night," Pete laughed.

"To be honest, I'm not sure," John stammered.

"What do you mean - not sure," Pete remarked. "Don't go playing the innocent with me, John Peters. Are you worried Jenny might find out?

"Look mate, let me phone you later. I've only just got in."

"Just got in, in that case it must have been a good night!" Pate chuckled. "Did she take you back to her bed-sit?"

"Look Pete, I really don't want to talk about it right now. I'll speak to you later." John put down the phone. He felt disgusted with himself

When he spoke to Pete later, he arranged to meet him for a "lads only" drink in the local. Arriving at the bar of the busy 'Hindle Arms,' he was suddenly filled with dismay. Pete was there, but he was with Kate. John tried to hide, but was seen.

"Over here," Pete shouted, beckoning to John. Kate smiled at him when he finally joined them.

"Kate says you were quite a handful last night," Pete said laughing. John smiled but was embarrassed, wondering if she'd told him everything. Pete slipped away to the bar for a moment and Kate moved close to John.

"I won't tell if you don't," she teased. Confused, he thought back to the last thing he remembered before passing out, Kate undoing his trousers. "It will be our little secret," she said, winking at him.

"Look, tell me before Pete returns, what exactly appended?" John pleaded.

"Not a lot," Kate stated.

"And by that you mean we didn't..."

"No we didn't," she replied before he could finish the question. "You couldn't rise to the occasion. Without being too graphic you were one big flop. Still, we can't let Pete know, can we?" John was so happy upon hearing this he leaned forward and kissed her on the cheek. "Steady now," Kate said smiling. "You'll make Pete jealous. Yes we're going together now, since he asked me this afternoon."

'Bloody hell, this girl's a quick worker,' John thought. But at least it meant he was off the hook. When Pete returned, they both looked at him and laughed.

"Care to share the joke," he requested.

"Not really," John replied winking at Kate. With his nightmare finally over, he relaxed and enjoyed the evening.

Months later, John was playing football when he got injured. Standing on the touchline while nursing a badly bruised shin, he lit a cigarette and took a deep breathe.

"Shame," he heard a female voice say. "You were playing very well, except for continuously being caught by their offside trap." He looked at the female pundit and saw a young girl wrapped in heavy coat, scarf and hat.

"Know a lot about football do you?" John asked.

"Enough," she replied. "Enough to know you're quite a good player. But you'd be a lot better and fitter if you didn't smoke." Listening to her saying this reminded him of when Jenny always complained about his smoking.

"So who are you?" he asked.

"I'm Gillian, Dave's sister."

"I'm John."

"I know who you are. I've been watching you long enough."

"Really," John said, smiling a little at the attention she was paying him. He couldn't see what she looked like under all her winter woollies, but she sounded nice.

"Are you going to the clubhouse after?" he asked tentatively.

"Always do!" she replied. "I don't think I've seen you there before, have I?"

"Maybe not, but I have been there," he confirmed. "Okay, since you've been a loyal supporter for so long, I'll buy you a drink."

"Great - thanks. See you in here." With this said, she walked away. Later in the changing room, when Dave came in John collared him about his sibling.

"I didn't know you had a sister," he remarked.

"Our Gill," Dave said. "She comes here every week. She's been struck on you for ages but frightened to speak to you."

"I've just said I'll buy her a drink."

"Well, watch she doesn't faint at the prospect!" Dave laughed.

When John went into the clubhouse he wasn't sure if he'd recognise her without her outdoor gear. Luckily, Dave caught him up and tapped him on the shoulder.

"Our Gill's over there by the Juke box," Dave informed him.

As he approached her he could see she was quite petite, with front teeth that stuck out a little when she smiled. She looked very pleased to see him. She'd already got a drink so John didn't offer to buy her one this time. Dave arrived and sat next to them.

"Well Sis, what do you think of our leading scorer now you've finally met him?" Gill's face went red. She hated it when her brother teased her.

"You out tonight John?" Dave asked,

"Just to the club."

"I'll join you and bring our Gill if you like?"

John saw Gill's eyes light up. He hadn't planned on asking her out, just for a drink after the match. Now he was in a very awkward situation.

"Sure," he heard himself saying, without meaning it.

"Come on then Gill," Dave said to his sister. "You'd better get home and get your glad rags on. You can't be seen out with the star player looking anything but your best."

Gill smiled at John as she was led away by her brother. He finished his pint and went home to have tea and prepare for his night out, but couldn't help worrying about what tonight might bring.

....

Jenny had been totally engrossed with John's story and was surprised when the barman called last orders. She wondered if the girls were still waiting in the bar across the road.

"Well then," John said. "I've told you everything. That's my life story. I bet you think I am crazy."

"Not really," Jenny smiled. She thought he was lovely and all the old feelings she'd had for him were resurfacing. She wanted to grab hold of him and kiss him, long and hard.

The ringing of the last orders bell brought her back to reality. She really must go back and join the girls, but didn't really want to pay for a taxi home on her own.

"Want to share a taxi with me?" asked John, as if reading her mind.

"Okay, as long as we go halves," she smiled.

They went outside and soon hailed a passing cab. John opened the door and helped Jenny in. He wouldn't have done that in the past. He certainly had changed and seemed much more in control, much more confident and more attractive to Jenny. She wondered why she'd ever stopped seeing him.

During their conversation, John had asked Jenny if she was seeing anybody at the moment and she'd told him no. This had cheered him up, since it gave him the opportunity to ask her out again - Just as friends, of course. They chatted about events and people they both knew. As they neared Jenny's home she related a story about Dave, a boy who used to play football with him.

"Yes, "said John laughing. "I've been going out with his sister, Gillian." Jenny's heart sank. How foolish she'd been, thinking because John was meeting the boys that he must be free. He had a girlfriend and it was someone she knew.

Many emotions now racked her body, disappointment, anger, jealousy and frustration. How could he have held her hand that way as they talked when he was going out with someone else? She felt really foolish, assuming they would fall into each other's arms and start afresh.

The taxi came to a halt. "Here's my half of the fare" she said, quickly pushing a few coins into John's hand before slamming the taxi door and leaving John wondering what in the world he'd done wrong.

As the taxi pulled away, he watched Jenny run up the path to her house and hurry inside. He couldn't see the look of disappointment on her face. He was unaware how strong Jenny's feelings were for him at that moment, only knowing she was gone again.

Inside the house, Jenny called to Mum to say she was home and went straight up to her room. She threw herself on the bed and punched the pillow. Why hadn't he told her from the start that he had a girlfriend, and Gillian of all people? She'd always been a pushy girl and her front teeth were crooked, not the sort of girl

John usually went for! She suddenly realised how hurt and jealous she was.

'It should be me not her. I'll show her. I'll get him back somehow, and I'll never again let him go.'

CHAPTER 9
INVESTMENTS

It was the night of the Mayor's ball at the civic hall, always a grand affair. The men wore evening suits, while the ladies were dressed in beautiful evening gowns. It was always the event everyone hoped to be invited to, and Jenny had been invited as a guest of her director. Tonight her director would announce that she was to become a junior partner in the firm.

She'd worked hard and long for this. At twenty-one, she would be one of the youngest partners the firm had ever had and it was quite an accolade to be asked to join the board. Although excited, she wondered what the rest of the team at Franklins would have to say, but hoped they would accept her.

She'd decided to have her long hair cut short, feeling it would make her look more professional and mature. She hoped the new look would ensure the more senior partners and clients took her seriously.

The doorbell rang. It was the taxi to take her to the ball. Cinderella couldn't have felt as wonderful as she did now, wearing a dress made of silk in a beautiful sapphire blue. It fitted her perfectly, showing off her curves and flat stomach. To accompany the dress, she'd bought a diamante studded bag and a pair of high-heeled sandals, both in the same sapphire blue, and had chosen to wear simple drop diamante earrings. She looked and felt a million dollars as she climbed into the taxi.

"Where to?" asked the driver turning to face her.

"To the ball," Jenny said proudly. "To the Civic Hall please."

"Very well milady." he said, sounding like a posh chauffeur and touching an imaginary cap. "And may I say how wonderful you look tonight milady."

"Thank you, kind sir," Jenny replied, joining in the game. She then sat back in the seat and enjoyed the ride.

Mr Franklin stepped forward to open the door for her as she arrived.

"My, My," he sighed. "If only I was twenty years younger. You look really beautiful."

Jenny thanked him and walked to the line of waiting dignitaries to be formally introduced by her employer, and soon to be partner.

124

The main banqueting hall had been filled with circular tables, each seating twenty guests, with a long table at the head of the room where the Mayor and his entourage would be seated. The tables had deep blue velvet cloths with crisp white linen napkins, meticulously folded to resemble water lilies. Each table had a beautiful floral arrangement, with flowers in various hues of blue and white and chosen for their rich perfume.

With all the guests were beautifully dressed and wearing their most expensive jewellery, it was truly a beautiful sight, a scene to behold, and Jenny felt very excited to be there. She felt the evening was going to be very special indeed.

She took her place in between Mr Franklin senior and his son, Mr Franklin junior, who was himself over fifty. Other guests on the table included Mr James Dalton, the company accountant and his ever so pretty little wife, Louise, who he insisted on calling Lulu Belle; much to everyone's annoyance, even his wife's.

Before the first course was served, Mr Franklin Senior, seated next to Jenny as he was, like her alone, being a widower, asked for the waiter to serve champagne. He then rose to his feet and announced to the rest of the people on the table the secret that Jenny was to join the board of Franklins as a junior partner. Everyone looked pleased at the announcement, except Stuart Brown. Jenny was a bit of a threat to him and this step up meant he would be unable to stop her progression within the company.

All the guests at the table raised their glasses and toasted her, making her feel wonderful and very proud.

The food was delightful with each course carefully prepared to arouse the taste buds, served expertly by the many waiters who scurried here and there all evening, ensuring everybody's glasses remained full.

During the meal, Jenny chatted confidently to everyone. The evening went really well and it would certainly be a night to remember.

Later she went to the facilities to freshen up. Leaving the restroom, she suddenly felt that someone was staring at her, but was totally shocked to discover who it was. She looked up to see John standing there in a black dinner suit and sapphire blue bow tie. He looked terrific.

"Well, I did NOT expect to see you here," Jenny confessed.

"Likewise," he stuttered, regaining his composure as he took her hand to to shake it.

Jenny leaned forward and kissed John politely on the cheek. Her pulse was beginning to race. He really looked so distinguished and together. John also thought that she looked a million dollars in that designer dress.

"Who are you with?" he asked tentatively. God how he'd missed her.

"Franklins," she replied. "And you?"

"Alcocks," he smiled. "What's your table number?"

"Forty," Jenny replied.

"I'm on table twenty-six," he stated. "Do you mind if I come and ask you to dance?" Jenny's heart skipped as he continued. "That is if you are not with your boyfriend?"

"No - I mean yes," she muttered. "Yes for the dance, and no, I'm not with anyone, just the other partners. And you?"

"It's an all male group on our table," he told her. "No partners invited," he added quickly.

"When I said 'partners,' I meant partners in the firm" Jenny explained.

"Yeah I know," John reassured her.

"Have you left your partner at home? Last time we met you were going out with Gillian."

"No, I'm single again. Single, alone, unattached, and available. Interested?" he tried to make it sound like a joke, but in truth it was said in hope. Jenny laughed, he was so confident now.

"Maybe," she laughed. "Come and rescue me from the Franklins. See you shortly."

Not wishing to let her out of his sight, he rushed back to his table and explained to his colleagues that he was going in search of table forty. Jenny returned to her table feeling excited. She'd been trying to bump into John for months, ever since that night in the pub and here he was. She hoped he wouldn't wait too long before coming to ask her to dance. Her heart began to beat so fast when she saw him approaching and actually felt she might faint!

Ever the gentleman, John quite correctly introduced himself to Mr Franklin, both Junior and Senior, who in turn introduced him to the rest of the party. He shared a few words with them and then turned towards Jenny.

"Would you care to dance?" he asked, extending his hand to her.

"I would, thank you for asking," she said coyly.

Taking his hand, as they were crossing to the dance floor many people watching commented on what a handsome couple they made. The music began and John put his arms around her.

"I didn't know you could dance," Jenny said as they danced the waltz, somewhat stunned by the whole thing.

"There's a lot you don't know about me," he said as he span her round. "There's no end to my talents!" jenny was amazed by his dancing prowess.

"You look wonderful, Jenny, if you don't mind me saying."

"Thank you. You don't look too bad yourself."

They finished the dance and the master of ceremonies announced the next dance would be a quick step.

"Fancy it?" John enquired.

"Yes okay," Jenny replied, a little surprised that John was able to do more than just a slow waltz. He could, and she was amazed at his dancing talent.

A few dances later and the compare announced it was time for the raffle, so the pair took a rest and returned to the tables.

"Do you have to go back to your group?" John asked.

"I suppose I should," she replied. "But I think they've already moved through to the bar." Looking round the room she spotted Mr Franklin waving to her so waved back. He gestured to them both to come over. Hand in hand they went to his table.

"You two seem to be getting on rather well," Mr Franklin junior commented. "Have you met before?" Jenny looked at John and they both smiled.

"Yes, a long time ago," they both said in unison.

"Well you certainly look good together," Mr Franklin added. "There is certainly a spark between you."

After the raffle was completed, they returned to the dance floor and danced every dance, never noticing whether they were alone or if the floor was crowded, being so wrapped up in each other's company.

The last waltz played followed by the National Anthem, as was customary at all civic events, signalling that the ball was over. People left the dance floor and began to gather their belongings and made their way to the exits.

"Can I give you a lift home?" John asked, not wanting the evening to end, and certainly not wanting to let Jenny out of his sight.

"Do you think I'll be safe with you?" Jenny joked.

"I hope not," John laughed. "Can I ask if you're in a rush to get home?"

"I have no curfew," Jenny replied with curiosity.

"Good," said John. "Come with me. I want to show you something."

"That's the best offer I have had tonight," she laughed, as he took her hand and led her out of the dance hall, down the stairs and into the foyer, where they went to the cloakroom to retrieve their coats. John led the way to the car park.

"Where are we going?" Jenny asked.

"Wait and see" was his reply.

John took a set of keys from his pocket and stopped beside a blue Ford Corsair. He opened the passenger door and motioned to Jenny to get in.

"Is this yours?" she asked, looking impressed.

"Perk of the job," he replied. "Company car so yes, I guess so."

John drove carefully out of town and towards the moors. After a few miles, he pulled down a narrow lane. It was pitch black and Jenny would normally have felt very nervous about being alone with a man in such an isolated place, but with John it never even entered her mind, as she trusted him completely.

A little way along the lane John stopped the car, leant over and took a torch out of the glove compartment.

"Come on," he requested getting out of the car. "It isn't muddy, so you won't spoil your shoes." Jenny got out of the car and John took her by the arm. He pointed the flashlight towards a semi derelict building.

"This is my investment for the future," he announced proudly. Jenny could see that it was a detached, disused farmhouse, surrounded by trees. On either side of the main house were fields and outbuildings, but it was difficult to see exactly what they were.

"I have some fantastic plans for this place," John began. "It has a paddock and stables and several fields. It has fine views from very aspect. It's in a lovely location."

"It sounds perfect," Jenny said with genuine interest.

"That's what I thought," John replied. "Only there is one vital thing missing."

"What's that?" Jenny questioned, wondering what could spoil such a lovely scene.

"You!" John said emphatically. "It needs you!" Jenny stood in silence, her heart racing. "Come on, the best is yet to come," John urged.

Around the back of the house the hill fell steeply away and revealed the lights of Ashtown far below, looking like hundreds of diamonds glistening against the velvet black of the night.

"It's beautiful," she said breathlessly.

"Not as beautiful as you, Jenny," John told her. She felt his arm around her waist and turned towards him. "I have waited so long to do this Jenny," with this, he pulled her to him and kissed her. All the longing, the heartache and the loneliness, all the waiting and wanting went into that kiss. They were both quite breathless when the kiss ended.

"Oh Jenny, why has it taken so long?" he sighed. "I've really missed you. No day goes by when you are not in my thoughts. I thought we'd have gotten back together when we last met, but you just walked away." Hearing this, Jenny raised her hand in protest.

"Hang on; you were going out with Gillian, you told me so," she stated. "That's why I walked away. Until you told me that, I was thinking that things were going to work out for us."

"But I wasn't with Gillian that night," John protested. "That had long been over when we met that night. She was my friend's sister and I only saw her for a short while."

"Oh what fools we've been." Jenny said, as they both began to laugh.

"How much time have we wasted?" John agreed. They fell into each other's arms and their second kiss was no less passionate than the first.

Neither of them spoke for quite some time. Jenny kept pinching herself to check whether or not she was dreaming. She suddenly felt cold and began shivering and John pulled her closer. Turning up the collar of her coat around her face and neck, he kissed her gently on the nose.

"We'd better get back," she whispered eventually.

"I guess so," he reluctantly agreed.

They walked down the lane hand in hand and in silence, each with their own dreams and hopes about the future. Once in the car it seemed only minutes before they were outside Jenny's house. John turned off the engine and faced her. Jenny looked into his eyes and could see he looked serious.

"Jenny, do you remember that night in the Rose Garden?" he questioned. How could she ever forget? Their first kiss had been there. It was here he'd told her he would love her forever. "Well I still feel the same way as I did then," he continued. "I love you Jenny. I will always love you. I have always loved you from the first moment our eyes met at the fair. Please Jenny tell me you feel the same."

Jenny said nothing, but reached out her hands and placed them on either side of his face, leaned forward and kissed him. The kiss told John more than a thousand words. She loved him now and forever. She would never leave him again.

The next afternoon, John picked up Jenny and they returned to the derelict house on the moors. He wanted to show her the potential in the light if day. He showed her around, mostly in silence as she studied the structure and tried to imagine what it could look like.

"Are you ready now?" John asked, breaking the silence.

"Am I ready for what?" Jenny replied jokingly.

"To discuss our plans for the future," he instructed. Jenny looked at him quizzically. "Well there's no point me designing a kitchen that you won't cook in, or a bedroom that you won't...." he hesitated a moment before saying, "Sleep in."

"Are you asking me to live here?" Jenny queried.

"No," John exclaimed. "I'm asking you to marry me." Jenny said nothing, but looked as if she might cry and was waiting for the bubble to burst! "Well?" asked John.

"Well what?" replied Jenny.

"Will you marry me? I really mean it Jen; there has never been anyone else that I've felt this way about. I want us to grow old together. Please say you feel the same way." Jenny looked into his eyes and could see all his yearning for her, all the love he had for her.

"John, I love you too," she confessed. "I have always loved you and believe we were made for each other. Yes darling, of course I'll marry you."

For the first time ever, Jenny saw that John had started to cry. He had tears streaming down his face, but this time they were tears of joy. She really was the love of his life and today he was the happiest, luckiest man in the world.

CHAPTER 10
PREPARATIONS

The plans were really coming together now. The Church was booked, reception venue agreed and cars and flowers had been thoroughly discussed. The bridesmaids and ushers had been chosen. John asked Pete to be his best man, whilst Jenny had asked Michelle to be her chief bridesmaid. Of course it would have been Sue if things had been different.

They had written and re-written the guest lists and chosen and re-chosen items for wedding presents. All the while they were continuing to work on the house and were exhausted!

There had been the odd quarrel and disagreement here and there, brought on by the tension and tiredness, but any arguments were soon resolved. Jenny's mum had risen to the occasion, delighting in helping with the arrangements, whilst trying to include John's mum as much as possible.

The house was now really coming together. All the major building work had been finished, with the initial plastering and painting completed. The garden areas had been renovated and were now ready for Jenny to plan and seed once they moved in. They'd spent many hours searching for the correct furniture in character with the house, which all had to be stored whilst the renovations were taking place.

Jenny had to make a decision today, the decision of which wedding dress to buy. She'd been several times to all the wedding fitters in and out of town and narrowed it down to a choice of three dresses, luckily all at the same shop. Only her and mum had seen the dresses and they would both make the decision today, though obviously Jenny would he final say.

Once in the shop the assistant rushed about, bringing the dresses from beneath their dustsheets and handing them to Jenny. One by one she tried them on, each time walking to the waiting area to display them like a catwalk model to her mum and the assistant.

A strange thing happened when she put the third dress on. As she did so she swore she heard a familiar voice saying, "That's the one." Looking around she could see there was no one there. It sounded like her, but could it really have been Sue showing her appreciation?

The manageress of the store came and zipped up the dress. It fitted perfectly. The off the shoulder style really suited Jenny. It was made of ivory satin and trimmed with antique lace. The bodice fitted tightly at the waist and the full skirt fell onto a hoop, with a six foot train flowing behind.

"Well Mum?" Jenny asked her proud mum.

"That's the one Jenny, that's definitely the one," her mum replied with a beaming smile.

There would be another trip to the shop with the bridesmaids next weekend to decide the colour and style of their dresses, but no one but Mum would see her dress until the day of the wedding.

It was now only four weeks to the wedding. Mum's endless lists had been crossed, checked and re-checked. Church, choir, hymns, order of service leaflets, seating arrangements, hotel menu, wines, seating plan, table decorations, evening reception buffet, music, bar, and so it went on. Jenny left most of this side of the organisation to Mum. With John she'd chosen the hymns and designs on the invites, and alone she'd chosen the floral colours. Mum had done pretty much the rest, and loved every minute of it. Everything was going according to plan.

The future bride and groom had been particularly busy putting the final touches to the house, painting the walls in white, laying a deep blue carpet and furnishing with antique pine furniture. The place looked a picture and they were both very proud of it, feeling excited to move in. In fact they were so excited that, without telling their family or friends, they decided not to have a honeymoon but to move in immediately after the wedding. This was another reason why they'd worked so hard to get it ready.

A week before the actual day of the wedding, Jenny's friends arranged a hen party for her. Fifteen or so girls had agreed to accompany her on her last night of freedom! They were to meet in the local pub at seven-thirty and then a coach would take them to Manchester, where they'd go to a club.

After a long soak in the bath, Jenny was looking for an outfit in her wardrobe when the phone rang. It was John.

"I just thought I'd ring to say enjoy your night with the girls, but don't go finding any other bloke and leaving me stranded at the altar," he told her. "I'll be thinking of you." Although he'd learnt to accept that Jenny really did love him, he always had a lingering doubt underneath that one day he may lose her again.

"And what about you, going off to Bolton with a gang of lads," Jenny remarked. "There will be loads of girls just waiting to get their hands on you." She smiled when she said this, as she trusted John one hundred percent. "Anyway," she continued, "you enjoy yourself and come home safe to me."

"I will," he promised and then confirmed, "I love you Jen." With this said, he put the phone down. Jenny smiled to herself. She really did love him, and in just over a week she'd be beginning a new chapter in her life as a married woman. She couldn't wait.

Dressed in a low neck black lace top, with black leather pants accompanied with very high-heeled shoes, which made her look particularly tall, slim and sexy, she entered the local pub for her rendezvous with the girls.

All the ladies were already excited at the prospect of a good night out and were already attracting attention in the pub. Jenny looked at her mates and observed they were a good-looking bunch, some married, some engaged, some single and ready to mingle!

They had two or three drinks and then the coach arrived and they clambered aboard. The driver watched with interest as they climbed the steep steps. Many of them wore very short skirts and displayed a nice eyeful of thigh, much to the delight of the driver!

When the coach pulled up outside a club in Manchester, a shiver went though Jenny. She realised it was the same club that she'd visited all those years ago with Sean and Mike, although not only had it changed hands since then it also had a different name. She still prayed they wouldn't be in there.

They entered the club and found a large table where they all sat together. They decided the fairest way would be to have a kitty, so all put money into a pile.

Cheryl, a beautiful blonde girl, ordered the first round for the girls. When the waiter struggled back with the drinks on a tray, she asked, "Could you bring the same again please?" When the waiter looked confused she explained, "The first one will not touch the sides!" The waiter smiled thinking the girls looked like fun. He hoped to finish early and maybe join them later in the evening.

"Right girls," Cheryl announced, seemingly taking charge. "Raise your glasses to Jenny, who sadly will be getting married next week."

"To Jenny," echoed the crowd

Jenny looked round the club. The couches were the same, still there in the shadows. There were couples already sitting on them and entwined in each other's arms. This made her smile, although the memory of those couches was not a nice memory for her.

Later, the girls all danced around their handbags alone, but it wasn't long before various lads, most of them out on stag nights, approached them. Most girls welcomed the attention, although some felt a little uncomfortable.

Jenny was engrossed in her dancing when she felt a tap on her shoulder. She turned to see Mike and Sean. Her worst nightmare had come true, making her feel sick in the stomach. Sean looked her up and down as if undressing her – What a slime ball she thought. Mike recognised her immediately.

"Still sexy in black then aren't we, my little schoolgirl," he said. Jenny smiled. She remembered that at the end of that horrid night he'd been quite nice to her. Sean didn't seem to know who she was. Pushing Mike out of the way, he stood directly in front of her.

"Dance?" he grunted, rotating his hips and trusting them towards her.

"Dance with you? I wouldn't dance with you if you were the last man on earth!" she snarled. Sean wasn't used to being rejected, so took this as a joke and moved closer. Mike took hold of his shoulder.

"Come on mate," he remarked. "She doesn't want to know."

"Course she does," Sean said, shrugging off his friend's hand. "Look at her. She's gagging for it!"

These words hit through to the very heart of Jenny's soul, the same words Sue had written in her letter. She felt a surge of pure hatred and revulsion in the pit of her stomach. Instead of moving away she moved closer to Sean.

"Yea," she said in her sexiest voice. "Of course I'm gagging for it, but are you capable of giving it to me?"

The girls dancing beside her looked surprised to hear Jenny's words and wondered what she was playing at. Sean put his arm around her waist and pulled her towards him, thrusting his hips against her.

"Sure baby, anytime," he smiled.

"Come on then," Jenny said taking him by the hand and leading him off the dance floor to a vacant couch in the shadows.

Once he'd sat down she excused herself on the pretence of visiting the ladies, but she went to the bouncer at the door instead. A few seconds later two other bouncers came, grabbed hold of Sean and escorted him out through the side door. There were a few bangs and scuffling sounds, after which, they returned without Sean.

"I don't think he'll be bothering you again," the first bouncer said to Jenny. "A few boots to the nether regions has cooled his ardour!"

"Thanks," Jenny said, before returning to the girls.

"What was that all about?" asked one of them.

"Oh just settling an old score – Job done!" Jenny smiled.

Cheryl could see that the atmosphere was becoming a little flat, although unsure as to why. She though a round of shots could be the answer. They all went to the bar and each had a couple of Tequila slammers. It brought roses to their cheeks and renewed vigour to their dancing. It was with a great amount of reluctance that, at two thirty in the morning, they climbed onboard the coach for the journey home.

Some slept on the way while others chatted. Several tried to hold a conversation, but had difficulty stringing the words together. All in all it had been a good night.

At 'Journey's End' The driver poured the last of the girls off the bus before taking Jenny and Michelle to the door of Jenny's house. Michelle was staying there for the night. With arms around each other they climbed the stairs to the bedroom, where they collapsed in a heap on Jenny's bed.

"What a pity Sue wasn't here to join in the fun," Michelle said.

"I'm sure she was," Jenny replied. Michelle looked a little puzzled. "You probably think I'm crazy, but I believe she's with me a lot of the time. I don't mean physically, but spiritually."

"I've also thought that too," Michelle revealed. "Sometimes when I'm uncertain about things, it's as if she's there to help me make the right decision." Jenny nodded understanding exactly what Michelle was saying, then laughed when her friend said, "It's a pity I didn't listen to her about Donald!" They laughed together, chatted for a little longer, and then both fell into an alcohol-induced slumber.

It wasn't quite light when she rose and went downstairs. Mum wasn't even up, but Jenny knew it wouldn't be long before she was. She savoured these quiet moments alone. Today she would be getting married and leaving this home forever. It would be the happiest day of her life, yet she still felt a little pang of sadness that she'd be leaving her family behind.

She thought of John, and how he'd sounded nervous when he phoned last night to say goodnight. He'd made her promise not to keep him waiting at church. She smiled at how much she loved him. Mum came into the room wearing an apron over her dressing gown. Jenny couldn't help but laugh at her.

"Lizzie's still asleep. I'll leave her a while. Is Michelle okay?"

"Yes she's still asleep. Cup of tea, Mum?"

"Please," Mum said, beginning to busy herself, moving last night's supper pots into the sink. "Well today's the day, darling," she said looking at her daughter.

"Today's the day," echoed Jenny, beginning to feel nervous. Today was going to be a very special day, the day she'd become Mrs John Peters. She would become his in every sense of the word. This made her tremble with excitement and anticipation.

Mum insisted on a full breakfast for all of them and began to set the table. 'One less tomorrow,' she thought to herself. Lizzie and Michelle came down, followed shortly by Dad and Mark. They sat together and enjoyed the full English Mum had prepared.

There was a knock on the front door and Jenny went to answer. A delivery man from the flower shop was standing there with a small, but quite long box. He handed it to Jenny. Inside she smiled as she saw the single, pale yellow rose with a message attached. "Jen, I love you – John."

She began to cry with tears of joy, and very soon her mum joined her. After this, it was time to get busy. The hairdresser arrived to attend to Jenny and the bridesmaids, whilst Mum organised the rota for the bathroom. Michelle spent most of the morning upstairs with Jenny, helping to keep her nerves intact, while Mum began to lose her nerve as the morning progressed!

Soon the morning had almost gone before anyone noticed. It was Dad that happened to mention there was only an hour "before kick-off," which threw Mum into a right panic. She ensured the bridesmaids were dressed and their headdresses were firmly secured. She then handed each of them their flowers and hurried them into the lounge to wait for the taxis, not allowing them to sit down lest they creased their lovely dresses. Mum had chosen a pale grey Italian knitted suit with a heavily beaded jacket and a tightly pleated long skirt. Her shoes and bag were pale grey and her hat was grey and pink. She looked stunning. Jenny felt very proud of her.

It was now Jenny's turn to get ready. She slipped upstairs to her room, removed her dressing gown and stood before the mirror. She put on a brand new set off sexy underwear, a white lace bra with matching panties and suspender belt supporting white stockings with seams and pretty little silk bows at the back of the ankle. She smiled when she wondered how John would react when he saw her dressed like this later.

Michelle came in to deliver her 'something blue' present - a blue garter. Jenny slipped the dress off the hanger and carefully stepped into it. With trembling fingers, her mum zipped up the back and fastened the tiny pearl buttons. Jenny shook the dress so that it fell evenly over the hoop, while mum added the final touches of headdress, veil and long beaded gloves.

"You'll do," Mum smiled and then hugged her daughter. "Dad, come and look at your daughter," she shouted and they could hear him running up the stairs.

"Where have all the years gone," he asked out loud as he looked at the beautiful woman who'd once been his little baby. He held out his hand to her and taking it, Jenny could feel how much it was trembling.

"Well darling the cars are here," Mum announced.

"Are you sure you want to go ahead with this?" Dad questioned, already knowing the answer.

"Quite sure," his beautiful daughter replied.

"Then let's go," Dad shouted in jubilation. "Let's get this show on the road."

Mum left with the rest of the family, Michelle and bridesmaids in the cars which had been ordered, leaving Jenny alone with the proudest of fathers. He patted her hand as she linked his arm and they walked out of the front door. Many of the neighbours were outside waiting to catch a glimpse of the blushing bride. Jenny waved to them feeling like royalty, even more so when she saw the vintage Rolls Royce convertible draped in the palest yellow and white ribbon, which Dad had organised to transport her to the church.

"Thank God for sunny autumn days," she said when she saw the roof was down.

As they made their way to the church, she held on tightly to Dad's hand. She could feel that he too was trembling with fear and anticipation of what was to come. When they climbed out of the car after arriving at the Church, the bridesmaids were already having photographs taken under the church latch gate. Michelle hurried to arrange Jenny's dress. She looked like a fairytale princess as she walked up the church path in her father's arm.

The photos done, Dad nodded to the warden, who signalled to the organist to begin playing "Here Comes the Bride" and Jenny and Dad began their slow walk up the aisle.

Upon entering, she took a good look around at the magnitude and magnificence of the scene. The decor looked wonderful, and the church was filled with the perfume from the floral display.

John waited nervously, and was overcome with emotion at the sight of the beautiful woman who seemed to be floating towards him. She finally stood next to him, looked into his sparkling eyes and couldn't help but smile. This was the moment she'd waited for forever. From the moment she'd met him he'd been special to her. Over the years her love for him had grown and grown.

The vicars voice was heard greeting the congregation and welcoming them to "John and Jenny's special day" and all eyes were averted to him. He announced that the first hymn would be "Love Devine All Love Excelling," which the bride and groom had chosen together. The organ played the first few chords and was joined by the choir sounding wonderful, as they tried to coax the shy congregation to join them.

Hymn completed, the vicar invited everyone to be seated, and then began. "Dearly beloved, we are gathered here today to join this man and this woman in Holy Matrimony......."

Jenny's stomach was filled with butterflies and John's heart beat so hard and fast, he thought it would burst. Both hoped that they would not stumble over the words when it became their time to speak. They need not have worried. The service went beautifully and without a hitch, although Jenny did worry when the vicar asked if anyone knew of any lawful impediment why "these two should not be married," thinking it was the sort of thing Ian would do, turn up to spoil everything – But it didn't happen.

Wedding vows read and rings exchanged, the vicar pronounced them "Man and Wife," and John was given permission to "Kiss the bride. The party were then led into the vestry for the official part, the signing of the register and marriage certificate.

Michelle signed as witness, just as Jenny had done at her wedding, whilst Pete signed for John. He then came over to congratulate them both and kissed Jenny warmly on the cheek.

"You look gorgeous," he told her. "Shame you're a married woman now, I could have fancied you myself." Jenny slapped him playfully.

She couldn't be happier. She was officially Mrs Jennifer Peters and she wanted to shout it from the rooftops.

"Perhaps you could fix me up with the best man later," Michelle whispered in John's ear, as she kissed his cheek. "That's tradition isn't it?" He winked at her. It was impossible for him to describe how happy he felt.

Everything signed and the customary photos taken, the organist put his instrument through its paces and it reached crescendo as he belted out "The Wedding March" by Felix Mendelssohn. John led his new wife down the aisle and out into the beautiful autumn sunshine followed by Michelle and Pete, also arm in arm, Mark and Debbie, the younger bridesmaids and then the parents. Everyone in attendance seemed to have the same fixed smile etched upon their faces. They were all so happy for the wonderful couple.

Photos taken and the photographer happy that he'd finished except for, "Just one more." He instructed everyone to "Get ready – One two three GO!" The camera clicked continuously on motor drive as everyone bombarded the happy couple with confetti, much to the horror of the driver of the waiting Roller, although they were able to shake most of it off before getting into the car for the short journey to the Howard Crest Hotel for the reception. Once away from the crowds, John turned to his wife.

"I love you Mrs Peters," he informed her. Jenny smiled. Her happiness was now complete. He kissed her gently; scared he would wake up to find this was all just a wonderful dream.

The Howard Crest Hotel was set in its own grounds with a long, sweeping driveway and beautiful gardens; it resembled an ancient castle. They were met at the entrance by the Master of Ceremonies, who escorted them to the function room and handed them each a glass of champagne in celebration.

Both sets of parents stood beside the happy couple to welcome guests as they arrived. Jenny was introduced to members of John's family who she'd not met before, and John was introduced to family members of hers. The guests were all bearing gifts and cards, putting them on the table to the rear, which was filled to overflowing.

"Pleased to meet you at last, I have heard so much about you. So glad you could make the trip. I guess I owe you one," she heard John say and took a look to see who he was talking to. She was amazed to see that it was Jamie.

"Jamie," she shouted, unable to conceal her happiness at seeing him. She hadn't seen him since her trip to Cornwall, late last summer.

"It's so lovely to see you," she whispered in his ear while flinging her arms around his neck. He was her special friend, a friend whom she quite literally owed her life. For this, she loved him deeply and he would always have a special place in her heart.

"This is my girlfriend, Pat," Jamie announced, introducing the girl who'd travelled up with him. She was petite with red hair and freckles. Not at all like Jenny.

"We'll catch up later," Jenny promised, resuming her place in the line to meet and greet the rest of their guests.

When the guests were finally greeted and seated, the Master of Ceremony's called them to order and asked them all to stand to "Please receive the Bride and Groom, Mr and Mrs Peters." Jenny loved all this, but couldn't get used to that name.

As they entered to take their place at the top table, the guests clapped. Jenny was seated with John to the left and Dad on the right, the two most important men in her life. She felt blessed.

After a wonderful meal had been consumed, the MC called for the "Bride and Groom – John and Jenny Peters" to follow him to cut the cake. This they performed under a barrage of flashing cameras almost blinding them. Jenny felt like a pop star.

Returning to the table she could sense that Dad was getting a little nervous, shuffling some papers in his hands which she presumed was his speech. Order was called and he rose to his feet. He wasn't used to this sort of thing, being normally a very private person. Jenny was unsure just how he was going to cope. He picked up his notes, took a deep breath and began.

Dad needn't have worried. Once he got started, he began to enjoy being the centre of attention. The guests all laughed as he regaled stories of his daughter's younger days, how she was a "bit of a tomboy" and how she could be naughty but impossible to punish, as, "All she had to do was look at me with those sad eyes and pretend quivering lip, and my heart would just melt."

He welcomed John to the family with the mock warning, "Look after my daughter or you'll have me to deal with – And I know where you live!" This very nearly brought the house down.

He ended his speech by asking everyone to raise their glasses to welcome John's family into the fold, and finally proposing a "Toast – To the bride and groom – Mr and Mrs Peters." This said, he sat down to rapturous applause, raised his glass high in the air and coughed away the lump from his throat. He looked at Jenny and could see her face was filled with sheer pride for the father she loved so much.

John rose to his feet, hands shaking. Now it was his turn. After Jenny's dad's speech, this would be a tough act to follow, but follow it he did.

He began by thanking his new wife's parents for putting on such a marvellous day, with such a wonderful spread. He thanked the bridesmaids for being, "Well – Beautiful," and then went on to tell some funny stories about growing up with his best man, Pete, although Jenny was sure there were far more stories he could NOT tell the wedding guests.

He told the story of how he'd met Jenny at the fair all that time ago and had acted like, "A bit of an idiot!" although in those days it was how he thought it was, "How to impress girls!" Everyone laughed at this.

John's job done, he sat down and whispered in Jenny's ear, telling her he was happy that part was over and he could now relax.

"You were wonderful," she told him, gushing with pride.

The best man began his speech and John took in a sharp intake of breath, wondering what Pete was going to say about him and his colourful past. However, he had nothing to worry about. His friend did not give away too much detail about their murky past!

As he finished the speech, John shook hands with Pete. It hadn't been quite as bad as he thought it might. The Master of Ceremonies asked if everyone could, "Please retire to the bar area" so the tables could be cleared and the room arranged for the less formal part of the day. They could both relax now and thoroughly enjoy the rest of the evening.

"Would the Bride and Groom please come to the dance floor for the first dance," the DJ requested a little later over the microphone. Hand in hand they walked to the floor with the applause of the guests ringing in their ears. A Waltz was played, so they held each other close and moved slowly around the room. Others joined them and within no time the dance floor was full, and it remained full for the entire evening.

All too quickly it was time for the last song to be played, therefore the last dance of the evening. The DJ asked everyone to come on the floor and he played the song, "You'll Never Walk Alone." Not only did everyone smooch to the song, they also sang it at the tops of their voices. Quite drunkenly, it must be said.

The car was brought to the front entrance and guests gathered to wave off the happy couple. Jenny gave her mum and dad an extra long hug before throwing her bouquet over her shoulder, as is the custom. It was expertly caught by Michelle, whilst being lifted in the air by Pete.

"They seemed to have got on well tonight," Jenny suggested, to which John replied with a knowing smile.

They climbed inside the car and waved a last goodbye to family and friends. They then began their journey to where their married life would begin - The home on the moors.

Arriving at the front door, John put down the cases, unlocked the door and then picked up Jenny. "Well Mrs Peters, we should do this properly." With this said, he carried her over the threshold. "Now I've got you," he said crouching slightly and holding out his arms. Jenny pretending to be afraid and ran up the stairs to the bedroom. Upon entering the room she was amazed at the sight beholding her. John had filled the room with rose petals and the air smelt so sweet.

"Do you know I love you Mr Peters," Jenny said with a proud smile upon her face.

"And I love you too, Mrs Peters" he replied, taking her in his arms and kissing her.

Jenny's pulse began to race. This was the moment she'd been saving herself for, for all these years. John's heartbeat was also racing now. It had been difficult to hold back his feelings over the past few months, but they'd both made the decision to wait until their wedding night.

They began to slowly undress each other. She began to undo the buttons of his shirt, while he undid the buttons on her blouse. She exposed the dark brown hair on his chest and nuzzled her head against it. He removed her blouse revealing the pretty white lace bra. Her breathing increased as her excitement built to almost boiling point. With his arms around her he unzipped the back of her skirt and let it drop to the floor. Jenny unbuttoned the top of John's trousers. She stepped out of her skirt and stood before him in a pretty white lace bra with matching tiny briefs, suspender and stockings. John surveyed every inch of her and took a deep breath. She looked so beautiful, and she was his.

He stood before her wearing only white boxer shorts. He pulled her to him and pressed his body against hers. She could feel his excitement! They kissed each other frantically in their impatience to belong completely to each other. John lifted Jenny onto the bed and lay down beside her. They wrapped their limbs around each other and slowly removed the rest of their clothing, savouring very second of this magical moment.

She began to feel a pleasure she'd never felt before as John commenced to kiss every inch of her body. When he reached her 'special place,' she thought she would explode! It was like an electric shock running through every inch of her naked body. Finally she gave herself fully to him and felt him enter inside her. 'This must be how real love feels,' she thought.

As he began rhythmically gyrating on top of her, their passion increased. Suddenly they could contain themselves no more and both, at exactly the same moment, reached the height of orgasm. For Jenny an explosion of ultimate pleasure causing her body to convulse, whilst for John it was the release of all he'd held back for so long.

Breathless, they lay together without speaking, completely at one with each other. They had consummated their marriage and had shown their total love for each other.

Their passions sated, they slept in each other's arms until the early hours of the morning. When they woke, they made love again. Their happiness was complete.

CHAPTER 11
A SPECIAL GIFT

A couple of months after the wedding, Jenny was about to leave for work. She'd just waved off John and she'd gone back to the bedroom to pick up her briefcase when her head began to spin. She grabbed hold of the bedstead as she almost lost her balance and sat down on the bed. Her hands were shaking and she felt a cold sweat wash over her body. A few minutes later the dizziness had passed. She quickly grabbed her bag and rushed out to the car, not wanting to be late for a meeting with an important client.

Throughout the day she never gave the dizziness another thought, yet when she arrived home the symptoms returned. All she wanted to do was slump into a comfy chair and relax. The next thing she knew was the gentle touch of John's hand on her shoulder.

"Hi there sleepyhead," he said, kissing her on top of the head. "Sorry I'm a bit late." Jenny looked at her watch, it was eight o'clock. She'd been asleep for almost two hours!

A little later, John was eating his evening meal but noticed Jenny was just pushing the food around on her plate.

"Aren't you hungry?" John asked.

"Not really," she replied.

"Are you not feeling very well?" he asked concerned.

"A bit of a tummy upset. I think it may have been those prawns we had last night," she told him.

"I thought they were fine," said John. Jenny didn't answer.

After dinner, John sat down and had a cigarette. He kept looking at his wife, who really didn't look her normal self.

"If you don't mind, I think I'll have an early night," Jenny said, bending to kiss John on the cheek.

"Oh yeah," he said winking at her. Jenny smiled

"Sorry darling," she smiled. "But I really am tired" she said apologetically.

"Are you giving me the cold shoulder?" he asked jokingly. "Go on, get off to bed. I'll be up after the football finishes."

When John went to bed an hour later she was sleeping soundly. It was the first night since they'd been married that they hadn't gone to sleep in each other's arms. He climbed in beside her and wrapped his body around hers. She moaned a little at being disturbed, but did not wake.

John thought she smelt delicious, and could feel himself getting aroused just by holding her, but he knew how tired she was and thought she'd looked tired all this last week. Even though a little difficult to suppress his erotic thoughts, he soon drifted off into a deep sleep.

When he woke, Jenny was already up. John could hear her in the bathroom, so crept into the shower and surprised her. She threw her arms around him, kissed him and dragged him into the shower with her.

"You are going to make me late, Mrs Peters," he said as she began to lather the soap all over his body.

"Does it matter?" She asked playfully, knowing that it didn't.

"And to think last night I thought you were going off me," he said smiling.

Their lovemaking was fast and furious, but also incredibly enjoyable just the same. After, Jenny stood naked in the bedroom drying her hair.

"Are you putting on a bit of weight darling?" John asked seriously.

"Don't be cheeky - Of course not," she said, looking in the long mirror and patting her stomach.

She finished drying her hair, dressed, kissed John goodbye and rushed off to the office. She noticed that zipping up her skirt had been a little difficult this morning and decided she must check her weight tonight when she got home.

The following Sunday morning, as she prepared breakfast the smell of the bacon under the grill started to affect her, making her retch! She made a mental note to make an appointment to see the doctor. A few days later she was in her doctor's office, not believing what she was being told.

"Positive? Are you sure?" she asked.

"Yes I'm sure, the result is positive. Congratulations, you're pregnant," the doctor smiled.

Jenny slumped back in the chair, why on earth hadn't she thought that this could be the cause of her nausea. Her periods had always been a bit erratic so their absence hadn't triggered any alarms, yet here she was now, three months pregnant!

What was John going to say? They'd agreed to wait a couple of years before starting a family, wanting to get the house completely finished and then to travel abroad next summer, their first holiday abroad together.

Her thoughts went to her job. What would they say at work? She could imagine old Mr Franklin shaking his head in disbelief and saying, "Oh Jenny – Jenny – Jenny!"

She needed to get home and tell John, wondering what his reaction might be. Although shocked, she already felt a pang of excitement at the thought of being a mummy. Yes she must get home and tell her husband.

She thanked the doctor and made her first antenatal clinic appointment before leaving. The butterflies in her stomach were playing havoc and she felt sick with excitement. She hoped she could drive home safely and make it all the way without physically needing to vomit!

All sorts of thoughts were going through her head as she waited for John to arrive home from work. When she finally heard his key in the front door, she ran to him and threw herself into his arms. She burst out crying as she did so.

"Whatever's happened?" John asked, totally surprised by this greeting. He lifted her up off her feet and carried her into the lounge where he placed her on the couch.

"Oh john, something awful has happened," she said tearfully.

"Tell me darling, tell me."

"Well you know when you asked me if I was putting on weight, well I have."

"Silly, it doesn't matter. I'd still love you if you were twenty stone!" he said reassuringly, kissing the tears on her cheeks.

"Yes but I am going to get even fatter," she announced. John looked at her quizzically. "You gave me more than a wedding ring in October, you also made me pregnant!"

"Pregnant!" he shouted. A smile began to emerge on his face whilst his eyes began to sparkle.

"Yes!" she confirmed. "I'm three months pregnant. You're going to be a daddy!" She could see that he was genuinely thrilled and excited at the prospect of becoming a father and was able to heave a sigh of relief.

"Is it okay to hug you?" he asked, looking down at the non-existent bump in her stomach.

"It's okay to still do lots of things," she said, beginning to undo his tie and shirt buttons.

"Are you sure?" he asked.

"Quite sure," she confirmed, starting to remove his shirt. He responded by pulling at her jumper and lifting it easily over her head. She unzipped John's trousers and he removed her bra and began gently kissing her breasts. Within seconds, they were both completely naked. This time his love making was more gentle than normal, and she loved him for it.

Suddenly there was a knocking on the front door. John managed to dress himself first, so closing the lounge door behind him he went to investigate who the caller was. It was Pete and Michelle.

"We're not disturbing you are we?" Pete said, stepping forward to shake John by the hand. "Just thought we'd call to see how you're doing."

"No." John lied, keeping them at the door as long as possible to give Jenny more time to dress. Come on in."

As they entered, John looked down at his shirt to see that in his hurry to get dressed he'd buttoned it up wrongly. Perhaps they wouldn't notice.

"Would you like a drink, you two?" John asked opening the drinks cabinet.

"Thanks," Pete said, but then began to laugh.

"What's up?" John queried.

"You!" said Pete. "Have you seen yourself?" John looked in the mirror to see his hair was dishevelled, his face red, and his shirt buttoned incorrectly. "We did disturb you didn't we?" Pete continued, laughing. John coughed in embarrassment.

At this moment Jenny walked in. Although she'd managed to dress herself properly, the glow on her cheeks gave her away.

"Well it's nice to know that you two are still at it, even after all this time!" Pete commented whilst smiling at Jenny, who lowered her eyes in embarrassment.

"You'd better be careful though," added Michelle. "You might end up with child." John looked at Jenny and she looked at him. Immediately they both burst out laughing.

"Bit too late for that advice," John revealed, beaming all over his face. "Jenny is expecting already." Michelle leapt up and hugged Jenny. She was really thrilled for her friend.

"Congratulations mate," Pete said, happily shaking John firmly by the hand.

"Let's have those drinks now, shall we?" John said, pouring four glasses of sparkling wine.

"To the honeymoon baby and our very special friends, John and Jenny," Pete toasted. They all raised their glasses and took a mouthful. Michelle wanted to know all the details and offered advice, having had a daughter herself. Pete chatted to John about the outstanding work on the house and offered his help. They chatted on well into the early hours.

Too late to go home and too drunk to drive, Pete and Michelle agreed to stay the night, so Jenny hastily prepared the spare bedroom. She assumed that Pete and Michelle would occupy the same bed, although she didn't really know how serious their relationship was. She knew they'd been seeing each other since the wedding, and as Michelle had been married before, there was no reason for them not to be sharing a bed.

She laughed at the thoughts that went through her head next. She'd never told anyone that she'd been a virgin on her wedding night. Because she and John had known each other so long, people just assumed they'd slept together.

Finishing the night with Lumumba, (hot chocolate and brandy,) the slightly tipsy group made their way to bed. As they were undressing, John got hold of Jenny and pulled her to him, kissing her long and hard.

"I love you so much, Jenny," he whispered.

"And I love you too," she whispered in reply.

They climbed wearily into bed and, wrapped tightly in each other's arms, fell into a peaceful slumber.

Jenny had arranged to see Mr Franklin Junior at two that afternoon. She was feeling a little nervous, as she'd told the firm, when they had made her a junior partner that she'd planned not to have a family for a few years, yet here she was now telling them that in less than six months she'd be having a baby.

When she'd talked it over with John they'd decided it may be better for her to take a career break, rather than hire a nanny. He thought she would miss out on all the special milestones in her baby's life and regret it if she was working full time. Perhaps three years at home and then return part time. They hadn't made a final decision on this yet. Jenny thought it was only fair to tell Franklins immediately, so they could recruit and train someone before she left.

The company was closing tomorrow for the Christmas holiday and she he was glad, really feeling she needed the rest. However,

John had invited both sets of parents for Christmas lunch, so he could tell them the news - Some rest!

She fiddled nervously with the papers on her desk, it was almost time for her to go in and face the music. She wondered what his reaction would be, but very soon all her worries were forgotten.

Mr Franklin was very pleased by her news. He liked Jenny and John, they were a lovely couple and the world of finance could just about survive without her for a spell, as long as she promised to return. Also, with the agreement from John, she could work from home and email it to the office. She came out of the office smiling.

"Have you had a Christmas bonus?" asked one of the cashiers.

"Sort of," Jenny replied, laughing to herself.

Before she left the office the following afternoon, Mr Franklin took her to one side and placed an envelope in her hand.

"This is for you, Jenny," he told her. "There will be a lot of expenditure coming your way over the next few months. This should help a little."

Jenny didn't open the envelope until she'd arrived home. Inside she found a cheque for five hundred pounds, enough to put towards the nursery she thought, appreciating the gift.

John came home later dragging two large Christmas trees in through the back door. He returned to the car and brought in carrier bags filled with decorations. After carrying one tree into the front lounge, they decorated it with blue and white baubles to match the predominant blue and white colour of the room. The other tree, placed in the dining room, was decorated in burgundy and gold, complimenting the rich burgundy rug beneath the oak dining table. Satisfied with their handiwork, they returned to the back lounge to relax. Although this room was still a miss-match of furniture it was a really comfy room to hang out in, with lovely views across the garden and out to the valley. They loved to sit here with the curtains wide open even at night, watching the tiny lights of the town below twinkling against the black velvet of the sky. They slumped on the couch and put their feet up.

"Is that everything?" John asked, lighting a cigarette.

"Just the rest of the food tomorrow," said Jenny wearily.

"Fine, I'll take you downtown to collect everything then," John said, happy that the Christmas decorations were finally up on the trees and most of the downstairs rooms.

Christmas morning dawned crisp and cold. John reached across the bed to Jenny and pulled her to him.

"Merry Christmas darling," he whispered lovingly. Jenny snuggled into his chest.

"Merry Christmas," she replied. "The first of many as a married couple." They lay in silence for a few moments. Jenny knew that as soon as they left the bed they'd have to busy themselves preparing the Christmas meal in readiness for their parent's arrival at around midday. Jenny struggled to free herself from John's arms.

"What's the hurry?" he said, pulling her back towards him.

"Things to do, sweetheart," she reminded him.

"Stay a few minutes more," he said longingly. "This is our first Christmas together, and the last on our own." Jenny couldn't resist. John ran his hand down her spine and gently squeezed her bottom. She snuggled closer to him, knowing what was coming next. Both were so easily aroused by the closeness of their bodies and Jenny willingly surrendered herself to him. She loved making love in the early morning.

After showering, Jenny tidied away last evening's supper pots, made the bed and began taking out the fresh vegetables to prepare for the Christmas lunch. It was now eleven fifteen. She set the table in the dining room with all the best cutlery and dinner service, draped the table with a burgundy cloth, brass candlesticks, placemats and napkins, everything colour co-ordinated. She stepped back to take a look at her work and was pleased. The result was well worth the effort.

John lit the open fire and it was now fully ablaze, and with all the presents neatly stacked under the tree and all the food ready for serving, the working part of the day was now over. The rest of the day was to enjoy.

The sky was beginning to darken as the first knock came on the front door. It was John's parents bearing gifts for both of them. They kissed and hugged and John ushered them through into the lounge. He noticed how cold it had become. Jenny's parents arrived soon after, also heavily laden with brightly wrapped parcels. The atmosphere was ideal, everyone felt warm and full of Christmas cheer.

"Before we begin to eat, I would like to make a toast," John said, bursting to tell them their news and raising his own glass in the air. "I would like to propose a toast to a new member of the family who is coming to join us soon." He leant across and patted Jenny's stomach.

"No!" screamed John's mum in delight.

"Oh Yes!" confirmed John.

"When?"

"June."

"Wonderful."

"Fantastic."

"Congratulations."

Shrieks of delight could be heard all around the room and everyone hugged each other. They were all so happy and excited at this wonderful news. This Christmas Day would be remembered forever.

"I don't believe it," John's dad announced. "Look everyone, it's snowing – Magic!"

True enough, as they all looked through the window they could see the snow beginning to fall. This really was going to be a wonderful, special and magical Christmas.

CHAPTER 12
PRECIOUS MOMENTS

Jenny worked through her pregnancy for as long as she could. Now in the late stages, she'd finally agreed to finish work and spend the last weeks resting at home.

The early summer sun had started to become warmer and she spent many afternoons sitting out in the garden and enjoying the views, whilst knitting tiny garments for the baby. She still had nervous feelings at the thought of the imminent birth of their first child. She'd kept herself fit during her pregnancy, walking around their land and climbing up the moors carefully, chaperoned by John.

The swollen lump that held her unborn child had grown swiftly over the last few weeks, making her waddle a little as she walked. John called her his little duck. She began to tire easily; frequently dozing in the early evening wrapped protectively in John's arms.

The garden was in full bloom and the air was heavy with the scent of roses. She lay on the cushioned sun lounger enjoying the hot sunshine and reading yet another book on parenting. The two oldest dogs lay at her feet, as if protecting her in John's absence and Jenny shuffled herself to get comfortable. It was difficult now to find a comfortable position with the large lump in front of her.

She reached out to take hold of the iced tea she'd prepared when a searing pain racked her body. She gasped and caught her breath. Was this it? Was the baby about to arrive? She shivered nervously. Was it too soon to phone John? She knew he had a busy schedule today, but he'd made her promise to telephone the moment anything happened.

She waited a little while to see if any more pains arrived and sure enough, about twenty minutes later a similar pain racked her body. She rose gingerly from the lounger and made her way inside, realising just how isolated she was out here. As she reached for the phone, yet another pain hit her. This one was stronger than the others and there had been less time since the one previous. Reaching for the phone she dialled John's office number and his secretary answered.

"Could I speak to John please?" Jenny asked.

"I'm sorry but he's out of the office," the secretary answered. "Can I take a message?" Jenny froze. What should she do?

"When is he back?" she queried, beginning to panic.

"Is that you, Mrs Peters? I am sorry, it didn't sound like you. I'll just page him for you." Jenny heaved a sigh of relief when she heard his voice.

"Hello Jen, are you okay?" he asked a few seconds later.

"I am not sure," replied Jenny. "I think the bump might be about to make an appearance." Now it was John's turn to freeze as he heard this news. "Are you still there?" Jenny questioned, worried at the silence.

"Yes, sure, of course I am," he said as calmly as possible. "I'll leave now and be home in twenty minutes. Can you wait that long?"

"Of course I can. If the books are anything to go by, I could be hours yet" Although she said this, she still hoped he wouldn't be long as her body was dealing with yet another major contraction, only ten minutes after the previous one. In between contractions she put the final things in her suitcase, tidied round and washed the pots, changed into a sleeveless top and leggings, and then sat outside the front door waiting for John's arrival. As promised, he was about twenty minutes. He jumped out of the car and ran to pick up the case, kissing Jenny hurriedly on the head whilst doing so.

"Calm down John, you'll give yourself a heart attack," Jenny ordered. "I'm okay."

"Right then, are you ready?" a nervous but excited John asked.

"I think so" Jenny replied. She was just about to get up when an unexpected gush of water came from her body, completely soaking her freshly put on leggings. John looked at her in horror.

"It's okay," she said, feeling decidedly damp and soggy. "It's only my waters breaking. At least I know now it's the real thing and not a false alarm. I'll just go in and change. You ring the hospital and tell them we're on our way."

Arriving at the hospital, Jenny was ushered into a side ward and John was asked to wait outside whilst the doctor examined her. He felt alone and useless stood in the hospital corridor. After a few minutes, the doctor emerged from the room.

"You can go in now Mr Peters," the man in the white coat announced. "Your wife is quite established in labour. It shouldn't be too long now before she delivers"

John followed the doctor inside the room, where he saw Jenny sitting up in the bed surrounded by cushions.

"Well darling, it's for real," she said, smiling as he entered. "Before today is out, you will be a dad." It suddenly hit John that he was about to become a father. He took hold of Jenny's hand, squeezed it gently and looked directly into her eyes.

"Love you Jen," he said softly.

"Love you too you, dafty," she said, as the smile on her face changed to a wince as another contraction came.

It wasn't long before the doctor returned and began to prepare for the actual birth. John was positioned next to Jenny, holding her hand and offering her ice to wet her lips. The doctor and the midwife gave instructions to Jenny and minutes later, Miss Peters entered the world, showing what strong lung she possessed by issuing a long and very loud wail. John was overcome with emotion as they placed the tiny bundle in Jenny's arms. Instantly tears of joy trickled down both their cheeks.

"Have you got a name yet for this beautiful little girl?" the midwife asked, smiling at the happy parents.

"It has to be Suzie," Jenny blurted out without hesitation. "Suzie Elizabeth." Luckily, John nodded in agreement. The midwife wrote the name on the tag of the cot and secured another name band around Suzie's tiny pink ankle.

"Now we are a proper family," John grinned, kissing his new daughter first and then Jenny. Minutes later John phoned both sets of new grandparents and made the announcement. They were all delighted. Three days later, the proud parents took their little offspring home to their house on the moors. Their happiness was boundless.

Five months later, Jenny recognised the tell tale signs that again, she was expecting. Both she and John were delighted. Seven months later and with no less pleasure, James Alexander was born. Weighing in at eight and a half pounds, he was a whole pound heavier than his older sister's birth weight. Now their family really was complete. The children brought them immense joy.

When Suzie had celebrated her third birthday, she was seated proudly on a little Shetland pony John had bought her and joined the family tradition of riding across the open moorland. James did not have quite the same love of horses, choosing to run wild in the fresh air on the moor, rather than on a mount.

It was during James's third birthday celebrations that jenny first began to feel unwell. She felt a little giddy and was so very tired. She didn't think she might be pregnant again because she didn't have the same feelings as when pregnant before. However, a visit to the doctor's confirmed the third pregnancy, but this one brought problems from the start. She was confined to bed on several occasions because of bleeds, and she lost the sparkle that had previously accompanied her previous pregnancies.

She was now in her seventh month and was feeling particularly tired and out of sorts. She wandered out to the paddock to look at the new arrival, a welsh pony bought at auction for Suzie, who was becoming a very accomplished rider.

As she leant on the fence she felt a strange pain beginning low in her abdomen, which gained strength as it moved across her entire body. She doubled over with the pain. She knew it was far too early for it to be the onset of labour. Struggling to her feet and dragging herself across the courtyard, she returned to the house. Another excruciating pain overcame her almost making her lose consciousness, but she was able to pick up the phone.

"Please, please be in the office," she shouted out loud. Thankfully John arrived home twenty minutes later looking very concerned, for he too knew if this was labour it was far too early.

Taking no chances, an ambulance was called and Jenny was admitted into hospital, whilst John took the two children to his mothers. She was already ensconced in bed by the time he arrived at the hospital. He could see how worried she was by the look on her face, although she still tried to smile as he entered the room.

"This one is in a bit of a hurry to be born," she told him. He held her hand and she squeezed his gently.

The foetal monitor showed the baby was beginning to get distressed. It was imperative that the child be delivered quickly, if they were to avoid the need for a caesarean section. With the encouragement of the doctors and midwife, Jenny made full use of each contraction, bearing down and pushing for all she was worth.

One final elongated push and the tiny infant was delivered. This time there were none of the niceties experienced when Suzie and James had been born. The child was rushed away the moment it was delivered, without even telling the worried parents what sex it was. Jenny knew things were serious but tried to reassure John that this was standard procedure for a premature birth. They waited for what seemed forever for the doctor to return.

"We have taken the baby to the neo-natal intensive care unit because it's so small, so we'll need to help with its breathing," the doctor confirmed. "We'll take you there once we've set up all the equipment. We are a little concerned at the moment, but we will just have to wait and see."

Jenny turned to John with her eyes a brimful with tears, noticing the tears also trickling down his cheeks. They had been so lucky in the past, and with both their other children being born with no problems whatsoever, they never expected that it would be so different this time.

The midwife returned to see to Jenny but said nothing, they still didn't even know if it was a boy or girl! She felt a cold shiver run down her spine and bit her lip to stop her from screaming. An auxiliary brought a wheelchair and helped her into it. He wheeled her to the outside of the neo-natal unit, where a nurse came out to speak to them.

"I just want to prepare you before we go in," she said to the parents. "Your baby is connected up to quite a lot of equipment which can look quite frightening, but it's all there to help. You can come in now." John took hold of Jenny's hand and gave it a reassuring squeeze, even though his own legs were feeling like jelly. Nothing could have prepared them for the sight which greeted them. In an incubator lay a tiny baby, whose chest was being mechanically inflated by a machine. Drip lines were attached to the heels of each foot and the eyes were covered by a strip of plaster, whilst a tiny woollen bonnet was covering the head.

John felt his legs give way a little and he shook his head to pull himself to his senses. He needed to be strong for his wife's sake.

The wheelchair was pushed up close to the incubator and Jenny peered in. The tiny pink frame was nothing but skin and bone. No familiar roundness like the other two.

"Girls are usually better fighters," the nurse reassured.

"It's a girl?" Jenny questioned, sounding shocked.

"You didn't know?" the midwife questioned looking stunned.

"No, they just rushed the baby out the moment it was born. Nobody had time to tell us."

"Well it's a little girl and she weighs slightly over three pounds. She's very premature and..." she paused, "and the doctor will be able to tell you more when he comes back."

What more was there to tell? She'd been born premature, was very small and needed help to breathe. Surely that was enough for them to cope with. They were told that the next forty-eight hours were crucial. Their daughter was not breathing herself and the medical staff was concerned about any further complications which could manifest themselves.

Jenny agreed to stay at the hospital and arrangements were made for a room just down the corridor from the neo-natal ward. John reluctantly agreed to go home and care for the children, and would return later.

Jenny sat transfixed, watching the tiny chest rise and fall as the machine filled her tiny immature lungs with life giving oxygen. She watched the monitor above the incubator, as the tiny heartbeat continued to show that her baby daughter was still clinging to life.

John came back and sat with her for several hours before leaving, promising to return first thing in the morning.

Jenny was asked to move away from the incubator whilst they tended to the baby's needs, so stood at the window gazing up at the clear night sky. The stars were shining brightly and the almost full moon lit up the car park far below in the hospital grounds. When the nurse came to fetch her from her reverie, she dropped her eyes and did not meet Jenny's concerned look.

"We've just phoned for your husband and he's on his way," she told a confused Jenny.

"But why," Jenny questioned, although in her heart she knew the answer. Their little girl was not going to make it.

When John arrived he rushed to Jenny's side. The doctor came out to speak to them and what he said was the worst thing that any parents could be told. Their little girl was not responding to any of the treatment and was unable to survive without the machines breathing for her. They took the distressed couple into a small, dimly lit room, and seated them on low comfy chairs.

"The vicar is here and wants to know if you would like to have your baby christened," the doctor asked in muffled tones. Jenny nodded. "We will bring her to you."

The vicar conducted the christening ceremony in low sombre tones. "I baptize thee Emily Jane - in the name of the Father, the son and the Holy Ghost."

He left Jenny and John with their tiny daughter. She lay wrapped in a cotton blanket. Gone were the plasters and the drips, gone were the machines that had helped her to breathe. Here in her arms was a tiny human who'd struggled to live but moments later, she lost the battle. Jenny cradled her close to her chest and wept. John could not control his tears and stood gazing out of the window at the starlight sky. Jenny sat for some time, rocking the now lifeless infant.

"Shall I take her now?" asked the nurse with sympathy.

"Just a few more minutes," Jenny pleaded.

"Okay, I'll come back shortly." The nurse left as silently as she'd entered, closing the door behind her. Jenny stood up and carried the baby to the window where John was still standing gazing out into the night.

"You see these stars," she said softly. "Every time I look at these stars I will know you are there, and you will know that I am here thinking of you." At that moment, a bright shooting star crossed the dark sky. "That has just lit your way to heaven, little one," Jenny said kissing Emily on the cheek. "We will never forget you."

The nurse returned and took the tiny body away. John and Jenny fell into each other's arms and wept bitterly for the tiny daughter who'd come into their lives only briefly and stayed for such a short time before leaving them.

Dark days followed. John found sleeping impossible, haunted by dreadful nightmares where he relived the dreadful ordeal of carrying the tiny white coffin holding his dead daughter. He rose each morning feeling more drained than ever, and lost all his normal enthusiasm for life. Even worse was the fact that he no longer seemed to find enjoyment from being with his two surviving children. He moped around the house, sitting slumped in the armchair staring vacantly into space, losing his temper at the slightest thing. Even his work began to suffer, as it bored him! He spurned Jenny's advances and their sex life became non-existent. No one seemed to be able to get through to him, least of all his wife.

In desperation, at one stage Jenny even suggested he went for bereavement counselling. He laughed hurtfully at this suggestion. She felt that he blamed her for Emily's death, and this lead her into a deep depression, but not as deep as John's.

Sadly, she thought that this episode might have wiped out all the love they'd previously shared. One evening, it all came to a head.

They'd gone to bed early. As usual John could not sleep, so he got up and went downstairs. Jenny woke to find she was alone in bed, so also crept downstairs. The back door was open and she went out into the cold night air, where she found John leaning on the garden gate staring up at the stars. She put her hand on his shoulder and he winced, as if it were painful to receive her touch. He said nothing and just continued to look skywards.

"Come back to bed," she whispered softly.

"Why? I can't sleep, so what's the point?"

"It's so cold out here," Jenny pleaded.

"So?" John retorted coldly. "What is the point? What is the point in anything? I hate it here. I hate everything!"

"Even me?" Jenny questioned almost in tears. John did not reply, he just continued to stare into the darkness. Jenny thought this might be the end of them.

At that moment they heard a banging noise coming from the nearby stable. They hurried to find out what the noise could be. They had two horses in foal but neither was due to deliver. Putting the light on, John peered into the first stable. The occupant gave a soft whiney and raised her head to see who it was that had disturbed her at such a late hour. Seeing nothing was untoward he moved on to the next stable, closely followed by Jenny, who was wishing she'd put on her fleecy dressing gown rather than the cotton housecoat she was wearing.

John flung open the door of the stable and rushed in. The chestnut mare was breathing heavily and kicking at the straw on the floor of the stable. She was obviously in pain so John stroked her neck and talked to her softly. The tenderness in his voice brought a lump to Jenny's throat. She hadn't heard him speak like this for such a long time.

"You'd better phone the vet," he said sounding worried. Jenny went back to the house and called the number pinned on the board.

"I am sorry but Mr Henthorn is out at a farm at the moment and may be some time." Jenny was told by the voice at the other end. "I'll ask him to come up to you as soon as he gets back." John was not going to be pleased by this news and she hoped he wouldn't fly off the handle, as he had done so often of late.

Putting on her wax jacket and grabbing one for John, she returned to the stable where the mare now lay on the floor, with John gently stroking her neck and whispering reassuring words to her. Jenny explained what she'd been told, that the vet would not be coming immediately. John raised his eyebrows skywards.

"Well then, I suppose it's up to you and me to try and save this little one," John said gently.

Just after midnight, the skinny legged foal was delivered but it did not move, just lying in the damp straw. John reached for a towel and began to rub it vigorously, trying to encourage it to breathe. It did not respond. He tried shaking its head from side to side, but again, nothing. Panic set in and he tried rubbing it again. Jenny moved closer and could see the despair in his face.

"It's hopeless. We've lost her," he said with a sadness that almost broke Jenny's heart to hear.

"Let me try," she whispered. John shrugged his shoulders. It couldn't do any harm for her to try and he'd given up, so Jenny took hold of the towel and began to rub the foal rigorously. It still showed no signs of life.

"Please don't die, please don't die," Jenny chanted over and over again. It seemed an eternity since the foal had been delivered. It was obvious that it had been born too early, and like with little Emily it didn't have the strength to fight for life.

Jenny had just placed the foal's head gently on the straw when suddenly with a shudder the foal gasped, coughed and began to breathe. John who'd moved away and was staring out over the stable door, turned his head when he heard the spluttering. He couldn't believe it. He knelt down and gently lifted the foal to its feet. It wobbled and almost fell over, but then, helped by John it found its mother and began to suck hungrily. The mare shifted about a little and the tiny foal struggled to continue feeding. Its stubby tale swished rapidly as it enjoyed the warm milk.

"It looks like the little thing is a fighter," John said, smiling for the first time in months as they both looked on in awe. He turned to Jenny and she looked directly into his eyes. She could see all the hurt of the past few months welling up in them.

"Unlike our precious Emily, this one's going to make it." As he said these words he began to sob, sobbing uncontrollably and releasing all the emotions he'd bottled up since that dreadful day when he'd carried the tiny white coffin and placed it on the much too large podium in the cold church.

He put his arms around Jenny and wept letting his tears flow unchecked. She hugged him in return with all her strength. 'He's come back to me,' she thought happily to herself.

She was correct in her assumption. Over the next few days, weeks and months, John returned to his former self. Gone were the mood swings, the bad temper and the periods of inactivity. He wallowed in the responsibility of caring for the foal, which they'd named star, after the fact that she was born on such a starry night, but also in memory of Emily, who Jenny called her bright shining star that shone so brightly for such a brief amount of time. Happiness and contentment returned to their lives.

That summer, Suzie won her first red rosette at the local gymkhana, James received his first glowing report from primary school, and most importantly, John and Jenny fell in love all over again.

CHAPTER 13
YEARS HAVE FLOWN

How the years had flown. Next month they would have been married for twenty years. Suzie was now nineteen and had started university, James at eighteen was maturing into a handsome and confident young man, who'd just been accepted at Medical School following his excellent "A" level results. There had also been a new edition to the family, Laura, now thirteen, was discovering boys and enjoying life as a teenager. The family continued to live in their home on the moors and were still regarded by many as the perfect couple, a real tribute to the institution of marriage.

With their two older children fleeing the nest and their youngest child growing more independent by the day, they decided that the time was right for them to have their first holiday without them. They'd agonised over the decision to leave Laura behind, but had finally made up their mind when Pete and his wife had agreed to come and stay at their home and take care of everything whilst they took a well deserved break away from it all.

When the tickets arrived, Jenny felt real pangs of guilt. It felt very selfish to want to holiday without the family. They'd had such fun filled holiday s with them in the past, but now it was their time.

If she'd checked things once, she'd checked them a million times! Now that the taxi had finally arrived to take them to the airport, she did a final check again.

"Just get out of here," Pete said laughing. "And don't forget…"

"Don't forget what?" Jenny interrupted, wondering what on earth she could have forgotten.

"Don't forget to have fun," Pete finished, with Jenny hugging him.

"Please keep everyone safe until we get back," Jenny said, looking back at the house as the taxi pulled away. "Don't let anything happen to anyone, please."

"They'll be okay," John said, knowing full well what Jenny was thinking. She smiled back at him.

"Just think, I have you all to myself for a whole two weeks," he said with eyes sparkling.

"You might get bored with me," she protested.

"Not a chance," he confirmed, kissing her on the cheek.

They both sat back to enjoy the journey to the airport, where upon arrival, they checked in their luggage

"Drink," John said. Jenny nodded in agreement.

Hand in hand they walked to the bar area, but instead of sitting in the public bar, John led her to the executive lounge where he'd arranged champagne and strawberries as a special treat in celebration of their first holiday alone. Jenny looked at her husband lovingly.

"If you play your cards right, Mr Peters, you could be in for a good night tonight." They both laughed.

The flight was uneventful, and some four and a half hours later, the plane began its decent into Kos. With seat belts securely fastened as per instructions, the plane came down lower and lower. The sea below was inky black and the sparkling lights on the tiny islands below were all that was visible.

"We'll soon be there now," John offered, taking hold of Jenny's hand. Although not as scared as she used to be about flying, John knew only too well that the landing still filled her with dread. Suddenly the plane banked over steeply and began to climb.

"What's wrong?" Jenny asked.

"Nothing," John replied, shrugging his shoulders.

The plane levelled off and three massive bumps slowed it down as it landed. They'd arrived safely, much to Jenny's delight. Now the holiday could begin.

They passed through customs and went to the baggage reclaim. Unlike Manchester, there was only one conveyor belt and cases were placed onto it by hand by Greek airport workers who were in no rush at all, unlike the tired passengers anxious to get to their holiday destinations and check into their hotels.

Eventually Jenny recognised their overstuffed cases on the carousel and John strained to lift them off, amidst the throng of other passengers equally intent on rescuing their luggage before it disappeared through the hole in the wall at the end of the belt.

The holiday representatives holding up brightly coloured logo cards told them their bus was number four. Struggling with the heavy cases, John followed Jenny to the waiting transport. Once all the passengers were aboard the coach, the next leg of their journey began. The tour rep on board told them it would take about twenty minutes to arrive at resort and then went on to warn abut the ferocity of the sun, not drinking the water, and not putting toilet paper down the loo! The coach stopped at studios and apartments on route, allowing other fellow travellers to alight. Soon only the two of them were left.

"At the next stop is the Kappas Hotel," it was announced.

"Thank goodness for that. I thought they'd forgotten about us," John said with relief. But it was well worth the wait. Having seen the other hotels in the resort, it was more than apparent that this was probably the best of them all.

As they reached the double door entrance to the hotel, a small portly Greek man came out to greet them.

"Welcome, welcome," he repeated. "Come in. Can I have your passports and I will show you to your room."

By now it was three-thirty in the morning. All the lights were out in the bar area and they climbed up the stairs in the light of the emergency lighting. It was difficult to see anything, but everywhere smelt fresh and clean. Reaching the door, the hotel manager put the key in the lock and opened the door. John thanked him and they went inside.

The room was a reasonable size and contained two beds, a dressing table, a chair and a wardrobe. It was carpeted, which they both found unusual for a foreign hotel. Jenny opened the door to the bathroom. She was dreading looking at the facilities, as friends had told her how prehistoric the plumbing was in Greece. However, she was pleasantly surprised with what confronted her, as the entire room was tiled from floor to ceiling. In the corner was a shower, to one side a washbasin, and to the other side was the loo complete with a bin, for the toilet paper she reminded herself. It was all spotlessly clean.

Both were exhausted from their journey, so after hurriedly unpacking and putting their clothes in the wardrobe, they climbed into their separate twin beds and immediately fell fast asleep.

It was Jenny who woke first. The room was still dark because there were large shutters over the patio doors. Pulling these doors slowly open, trying to be as quiet as possible so as not to wake John, she stepped barefoot onto the balcony and into the bright sunshine. The fabulous view which greeted her took her breath away. The bay stretched out in a horseshoe shape. To one side of it stood a steep hill which fell sharply into the sea, to the other side was a small island with a minute white church perched on the steep cliff. The sea was a glorious blue and packed with windsurfers scooting across the bay, with tiny fishing boats dotted here and there. It was magnificent. It was Paradise.

She couldn't wait to wake John and show him this fantastic sight. He was beginning to stir, so she went back in the room with a smile as wide as a Cheshire cat's.

"Come and see," she pleaded. "It's just fabulous." John had to agree. He put his arms around Jenny and they stood drinking in the view for several minutes before either spoke, totally overcome by the beauty of the vista.

"Breakfast I think, and then we can explore," John said, sounding like an excited child. They dressed in shorts and t-shirts, and after slipping on flip flops they went downstairs to find the breakfast room.

They walked through the bar and reception area where they'd arrived last night and into the breakfast room. Clean white starched tablecloths were on the dozen or so tables, each with a vase of fresh flowers upon it. There was no one there to direct them, so they sat at a table near the large windows, where they could admire the view. The doors to the kitchen were swiftly kicked open and young Greek women came through carrying a tray of bread rolls and glasses of orange juice.

"Kalimera," she smiled. "Tea or coffee?"

"One tea, one coffee please," John requested. She vanished as quickly as she'd arrived, once she'd placed the two plates each bearing a fresh bread roll, two pats of butter and one sachet of Jam, along with the two glasses of freshly squeezed orange juice on the table. She quickly returned with the tea and coffee, smiling all the time. Being hungry, they soon devoured the bread rolls.

Others couples and families had now come into the breakfast room, some hesitating like they had, before choosing a table to sit at. Judging by their colour, some of them had obviously been here for several days already.

The owner of the hotel came into the room and bided 'good morning' to everybody as he passed them on his way to the kitchen. He came back carrying a cup of coffee and smiled at them. Jenny returned the smile. He then surprised them by coming to sit at their table.

"Is this your first time in Greece?" he asked.

"Yes, and our first holiday without the children," Jenny replied.

"It will be good for you here," the owner told them. "You will fall in love."

"With Greece?" Jenny questioned.

"Yes with Greece," he replied. "But also with each other." John and Jenny smiled at each other, remembering the wonderful feeling they'd experienced when they first saw the view from the balcony.

"I'm sure we will," Jenny said, finding the smile on the owners face quite contagious. Everyone seemed to smile here.

"You are going to the beach now?" he asked.

"Of course," Jenny answered, always the sun worshipper.

"Then enjoy your day," the very nice Greek man told them with sincerity.

Grabbing the bare necessities and an oversized beach towel each they meandered down the dusty lane to the beach, which was only a matter of twenty-five yards or so from the hotel. The sun was already scorching, so they were careful to ensure that both had plenty of high factor sun cream spread over their bodies.

There were a few sun beds with parasols dotted about the beach and they put their towels down on one near to the sea and walked to the water's edge. Brightly coloured fish darted here and there in the crystal clear water, the sun making every little ripple glisten like gold.

John dipped his foot in the water but it was icy cold, not at all what he was expecting. They would later learn that fresh water springs ran into the bay and this was what chilled the water. They were later told that bays further down the coast had much warmer water.

Returning to the sun beds, they both lay down and dozed for the rest of the morning. As the mid day sun caught them with its fierce rays, they decided to go to a local taverna for a refreshing drink. As they walked through the entrance they were met by a broad grin, with everyone smiling at them.

"Welcome, welcome, seet anyplace," the host said, motioning them to a chose a table.

It was not very busy in the bar at that moment, so Jenny and John picked a seat where they could look out at the bay. The man who'd greeted them fetched a menu.

"Please," he said, opening the menu at the first page. They were to learn that his English was not very good and he relied heavily on his young son, who was learning English at school.

"I'm a little peckish," John admitted, scanning through the pages of the menu. "How about you?" Jenny nodded. "How about a Greek salad?"

"Sound's good, and a fresh orange juice please."

And so they fell into the routine of enjoying themselves, doing what they wanted each day without having to consult the children. It was a really lovely holiday, and each day they discovered new things to see and do.

A few days later, when they woke it was a little overcast. After a light breakfast they decided to go for a drive in their rental car. John's confidence driving on the wrong side of the road had grown over the past few days and he was now happy to wander off the main roads and explore the side roads leading from them. One particular road seemed to go on forever, meandering continuously down the hill and towards the sea.

They passed isolated farm buildings, fields of goats, tiny churches and olive groves. The road changed to a sandy track but John carried on, thinking they couldn't be far from the sea now. They came to an abrupt end, where they left the car and looked at the sea a few yards in front of them. It was spectacular, with fantastic waves unlike the calm waters in Kamari Bay. Here the sea looked wild, with constant large waves breaking on the shoreline.

A narrow track led away from where they'd parked, so off they went to explore. It reminded Jenny of the paths over the cliffs in Cornwall. The path led to tiny coves, mostly rocky, some with a little sand. As they continued along the path, the gorse trees seemed to increase and began to make their walk more difficult. The pathway finally petered out and a large wall of gorse prevented them from going any further.

Jenny paused to admire the view. The sea still amazed her. John walked to the very edge of the cliff, where a gorse bush extended over the edge.

"Wow!" he exclaimed. "Take a look at this, Jen." A tiny pathway secreted by the outstretched gorse led down into a further tiny cove. "We could get down here if we're careful."

Jenny moved to John's side and gasped at the prettiness of the hidden cove. Large rocks and outcrops hid a tiny sandy inlet. They ventured down and stood on the soft sand in silence. It was awesome. From down here, all that could be seen was the rise of the cliffs behind and the foaming sea in front. It was totally isolated from the outside world.

"It's magic," John whispered, putting his arm round Jenny and feeling overcome by the beauty and the feeling of complete isolation. They stood for several minutes without moving or speaking.

"Fancy a swim?" John said breaking the silence.

"Why not," Jenny replied.

Without a thought they stripped naked and walked hand in hand into the frothing waves. They swam for a little while, held each other while the waves buffeted them, splashed each other and frolicked in the water like children.

John took Jenny's hand and led her out of the water. He gently picked her up and laid her on the sand. Although a little distracted by the fact that someone may be able to see them they made love on the warm sand, feeling totally at peace with the world and totally in love with each other. Satisfied, they lay for quite some time on the soft, warm sand.

"I love you John Peters," Jenny whispered.

"I love you too Jenny Peters," John replied, kissing her gently.

"This place is so magical," Jenny stated. "I defy anyone to come here and not fall in love with it."

They returned to the cove next day and the day after. In fact each day of the rest of their holiday they came back, rejoicing in the magic this cove seemed to hold.

"This cove is our special cove," Jenny said when they finally had to leave. "I will never forget this place."

And they never did - Over the following years they returned again and again to Kos, the island they'd fallen in love with just as the hotel owner said they would on that first visit. They spent time with the many Greek friends they made over the years, although as often as they could they came to visit their 'special cove.'

They'd visited other beaches on the island, but none had the special meaning in their hearts that this particular cove had for them. It was magical.

·

CHAPTER 14
PASTURES NEW

Jenny put away her book as they were coming in to land, returned the in-flight magazine to its place in the seat pocket in front and removed the earphones. Looking through the window she could see the blue Aegean Sea below. Straining her eyes she could just make out the tiny dots, which were boats and ferries. The sandy coastlines of the many islands were also clearly visible.

She felt the plane dropping in what felt like steep steps. She knew this flight so well. They would drop quite low above the sea, low enough to see the snow white buildings on the shore, low enough to see the coves and inlets and then to the surprise of first time visitors to Kos the plane would do a sharp incline, turning almost three hundred and sixty degrees over the sea before levelling off and flying low between the two mountainous outcrops and finally landing. This sequence, as they landed on Kos, always made her emotional, just as she would shed tears every time they left the island.

Over the years they'd come to love this place, and regarded it as their second home. This time lots of other emotions were at play, happiness, sorrow, anxiety, foreboding, excitement, anticipation, loneliness.

"We will shortly begin our descent into Kos, where the current temperature is twenty-eight degrees," the captain announced. "Estimated arrival time is eight-thirty. I hope you have enjoyed your flight with us today and we look forward to seeing you again in the future. Cabin crew, prepare for landing."

As the plane swept low above the sea, Jenny glanced behind her to see the nervous passenger looking straight ahead, unable to enjoy the fantastic views through the window. She wondered how she would deal with the steep banking over the sea just before landing. She returned to watching through the window. The plane did its customary sweep and then levelled for landing, flying low between the mountains over the lively resort of Kardamena, the new San Antonio for the youngsters who how visited the island.

Jenny and John had stayed there, but she'd never really liked it. Her love was for the quieter resort, where she now planned to stay.

"Welcome to Kos," a crew member announced. "Please remain seated until the aircraft has come to a halt and the captain has turned off the seatbelt signs." Almost there, Jenny told herself. She wondered if Demetrius would be there to meet her.

She stood at the baggage carousel amongst the crowd of holidaymakers, all anxious to retrieve their luggage and rush to the coaches outside, not wanting to lose a moment of sunshine.

"Have a lovely holiday," the nervous passenger called as she past, now looking completely recovered.

"Thanks, you too," Jenny called back.

She spotting her small case on the carousel and stepped forward to retrieve it. She remembered how in the early days of coming to the island, she and John would be travelling with four or more cases, all heavily laden with clothes, most of which were never worn! Compared to those days, today she was travelling light. She walked out of the terminal building, past the holiday reps trying to assemble the holidaymakers and point them to the right coach.

"Which resort?" one asked Jenny.

"It's okay, I'm travelling independently." She nearly said I'm travelling alone, but the thought brought a shiver.

Once outside she scanned along the rows of waiting cars and taxis, as the sun beat down mercilessly. She finally spotted Demetrius and he waved in recognition. She waved back and hurried towards him, relieved that he was here to meet her. He held out his hand to take her small case, which he placed in the boot. He embraced her warmly and kissed her on both cheeks.

"Dear Jenny, are you okay?" he asked, looking directly into her eyes as if searching the inner depths of her mind.

"Yes," she nodded. Instantly the tears began to well up in her eyes. She looked at Demetrius and could see that he too was close to tears.

"Come," he gestured warmly, "I take you home."

Home - She remembered how she'd always affectionately called this a second home, and how she'd said it was like coming home each time she visited. In fact at one time they'd planned that it would be John's and her home. Demetrius sensed how difficult it was for her, so he opened the car door in silence and motioned for her to get in.

Jenny knew the journey so well and knew it would take about twenty minutes to arrive at her destination. She knew every bend in the road, every road sign, every resort along the way. She'd travelled this route so many times before, but always with her lovely John.

She glanced out of the window to the see the dust flying from the car tyres as they sped along what was locally known as the M1, the only main road across the island.

She thought back to the first time they'd come here. It had been in the dead of night and they had no idea where they were going. No street lights illuminated the way and they had to rely on the coach driver to get them to their holiday destination. Today she was relying on Demetrius to take her home

CHAPTER 15
A ROOM WITH A VIEW

"This is the spot, just here. You have a fantastic view of the sea from here and if you look to the right, you can see the road leading to the forest," Demetrius instructed. "And your left view shows you the village. If you built balconies on all sides you cannot help but have tremendous views."

"This is just the perfect place to build our home," John said with real enthusiasm. "We must agree a price as soon as possible, and then I can get the architect up here."

The words rang out in Jenny's ears. She'd waited a long time for John to finally make his mind up, knowing that she could not force him into this decision, it had to be his.

She'd known that this was what she wanted since the first time they'd holidayed here, and now John was ready to commit to a life in the sun. She felt so happy and wanted to throw her arms around him and say thank you, but she knew she'd have to remain indifferent until everything had been finalised, just in case John changed his mind.

Her mind was working overtime, already designing room layouts and colour schemes for the finished home. There would be so much work to do once the purchase was finalised.

This was the ideal spot, just out of the village and perched high above the bay with sensational views. Jenny had always said that when she bought her dream house, she would ensure it had breath taking views, just like the guest house in Cornwall with its wondrous views of the sea.

John was speaking with the man from the real estate agency and there seemed to be lots of nodding of heads and shaking of hands. Jenny held her breath as he turned to her.

"We need to sort out the legal side of things with Antonio on Monday," John said, trying to remain calm. "It looks like we're in business."

Jenny wanted to shout "YES!" out loud, but resisted the temptation.

After months of to-ing and fro-ing between lawyers and councils, the purchase of the land was complete and planning permits given. The building work could finally begin. John commissioned a team from England who worked alongside the

Greek contractors, and slowly their dream home began to take shape.

Built on two floors with a basement, the basement housed a garage for two cars, a utility room with general storage space. John planned to build a games room complete with full size snooker table down there.

On the first floor there was a lounge with an enormous picture window with a view of the entire bay, a dining room with patio doors leading to a large Italian tiled balcony with another splendid view across the bay, and a dining room/kitchen with fitted units in bleached pine.

Leading off the corridor were three bedrooms. The main bedroom, John and Jenny's, had a walk in wardrobe with en-suite bathroom, tiled from floor to ceiling in decorative champagne coloured tiles and housing a deep burgundy bath and shower unit. The bedroom also had patio doors which led out to another balcony. The two other rooms would be be guest rooms, each with balconies and serviced by the main bathroom, which had been fashioned in grey and white.

The land surrounding the house had been landscaped and planted with colourful trees and shrubs, which would mature and blossom next summer. It was now down to Jenny to decorate and furnish the individual rooms, although for now the basement remained empty. They would have plenty time to work on this when they moved here next year.

During their last visit, they'd brought many bits and pieces, ornaments, linen and towels, and it was almost ready for them to move in.

They turned the lock on the ornate wrought iron gates in front of the door. Next time they came here it would be to live. Their dream home was complete, with their dream realised. This would become their new home when they left their beloved home on the moors. They would leave cold England behind and begin their new life in Kos.

Locking the house securely, they made their way to Marcos beach. Panos and Yiannis must have spotted them as they got out of the car, because immediately they ran towards them, warmly greeting and welcoming them back to Kos.

They chatted for a while about the weather, the lack of visitors, the problems with the exchange rate etc, and then they settled themselves on the sun beds close to the water's edge, ready for a relaxing day of serious sunbathing.

After all these years, it was clear they were still totally happy and madly in love with each other. However, being here in Kos seemed to make them fall in love all over again. This was another reason they wanted to make it their permanent home.

Although unfortunate for those whose livelihood relied on it, John and Jenny revelled in the fact there were only very few tourists on the beach today. It was quiet, with the only sound being the lapping of the sea and the occasional chattering of passers-by, whilst strolling at the edge of the water.

As usual Panos and Yiannis sat beneath the canopy of the beach hut drinking frappes and playing cards, interrupted occasionally by customers who wanted to go on the banana ride. Jenny could never understand why people wanted to be buffeted and bruised and then flung into the water at high speed. Even more confusing was the fact that they actual paid for it. She was content just to lie in the sun, napping or watching the odd tourist pass by, or just gazing at the calm blue sea. This was paradise for her, especially when she had the man she loved most lying next to her.

At one o'clock, when the sun was at its fiercest they sauntered up to the restaurant and took their time enjoying a Greek salad with fresh tuna, washed down by drinking long glasses of lemon. After this, they returned to the sun beds for the customary afternoon nap under the parasol. When they woke they ventured into the sea, after poking a toe in first. After lying in the hot, Greek sun, the water could appear to be very cold until becoming acclimatised.

As it was coming to the end of this holiday they decided that tonight they would eat at 'Stop In' and tomorrow it would be 'Captain Johns.' That way they'd be able to spend time with all their Greek friends.

Over the years they had made lots of really good Greek friends and had learned to love them all. They knew they would have their help and support when they finally moved out to live here, and that was a great reassurance to them.

At the end of the holiday they were sad to leave Kos, but knowing they'd be back very soon, made it much more bearable.

They made their way to the airport, cheered by the thought that their children would be at Manchester Airport, eagerly awaiting their return.

CHAPTER 16
PARADISE LOST

It was so unlike John to stay in bed when the weather was so fine. Even on bad mornings he would rise early to tend to the horses, but today he had said he was tired. Jenny brushed it off and carried on with the normal everyday chores about the house.

At eleven-thirty she took him a fresh cup of tea, but was surprised to see him still sleeping soundly, sprawled across the bed with the quilt discarded on the floor. Touching his shoulder, she found he was wet with a clammy sweat.

She roused him gently and he took a few seconds to open his eyes. Then as if confused, he muttered some words about work in progress before coming to his senses.

"Why are you looking so worried sweetheart?" he asked, smiling up at her. She leaned over and gently kissed him.

"It's not like you to be unwell," she replied.

"I'm not unwell," John said with annoyance in his voice, but then added apologetically. "I'm just tired."

"But you're wet through," Jenny observed.

"I know. I'm just a little warm," he replied, not very convincingly.

John sat and tried to get up from the bed, but his head started swimming and he suddenly felt very sick.

"I think I may have a bit of a chill," he said, looking at Jenny forlornly. "I might just stay put for today." Jenny was in total agreement with this, but was also slightly worried, as John was never ill.

"You rest now and I'll bring some lunch up later," she instructed. He positioned his head carefully on the pillow, and pulling himself into the foetal position, he closed his eyes. By the time she'd left the room, he was already sleeping soundly.

The next morning the alarm went off at its normal workday time of six-thirty, but John did not stir. Jenny leaned over him and switched it off.

"Time to get up sleepy head," she whispered softly. John stirred a little and half opened his bleary eyes.

"It can't be," he croaked. "I've only just gone to sleep."

"You've been asleep for hours and hours," Jenny told him. "In fact you slept all day yesterday!"

"Are you joking?" he queried, turning his head to look at the clock. Without further words he rose and went into the bathroom. He certainly felt extremely tired. Perhaps he'd slept too much.

Jenny went downstairs and prepared breakfast whilst he was showering. John came down dressed smartly as always in his navy blue suit with a crisp white shirt. Jenny noticed that his eyes didn't' sparkle quite a much as usual when he smiled at her. He picked up a glass of orange juice and promptly dropped it, spilling the contents all over the tablecloth.

"What is the matter with you?" Jenny laughed.

"I don't know, maybe too much sleep," John confessed. "I'll just have coffee and get on my way."

"Are you okay for driving or shall I take you?" Jenny questioned. John looked a little shocked at the suggestion that he would not be able to drive.

"Look Honey, I'm fine," he remarked. "Stop worrying. I'll have an early night tonight and then I'll be okay. You'll see," he said, kissing her on top of the head. He picked up his briefcase and left. Jenny cleared up the uneaten breakfast and got herself ready for work.

When John came home that evening, Jenny couldn't help but notice how drained he appeared. His skin looked pale and there were dark shadows under his eyes.

"Bit of a grueller today," he explained as he sat down heavily on the living room couch, looking exhausted. Jenny sat beside him and put her arm around him.

"Tired?" she asked.

"Worn out," John replied.

"I guess you won't want to go to the rotary club meeting tonight then?" she questioned.

"Oh God, I'd forgotten about that," he admitted. "Do you think they will miss me if I don't go?"

"No not really," she lied; being sure they would, as he was the main driving power behind anything and everything that went on there. She knew he must have been feeling really terrible, for he would never miss a meeting unless there was an absolute emergency.

"Perhaps you need a tonic or something," Jenny suggested. "Why not make an appointment at the doctors?"

"You know how I feel about doctors," John quickly replied.

"Yes but you've been working under a lot of pressure lately," she pleaded. "Perhaps you are a bit anaemic or something. It's worth checking."

John thought for a moment. He had felt a little ropey lately and things did seem to be getting on top of him. Perhaps he did need a bit of a pick-me-up.

"I'll call in tomorrow," he tried to assure Jenny, but it had the reverse effect. Now she was really worried. If john was agreeing to go to the doctors, then something must be wrong.

"Shall I come with you?" she asked.

"I'm a big boy now. I'm forty-seven! I can go on my own, thanks very much."

"But you'll always be my little soldier," she said, planting a kiss on the end of his nose.

Jenny watched as John struggled to eat his evening meal. She didn't comment on this, but hoped that he would go to the doctors and get sorted.

The next day John arrived home early. Jenny had only just got in herself and had not even taken off her coat.

"You're home early. My lover has only just left. Any earlier you would have caught us," she teased, making him smile.

"I'll catch you next time," he laughed. "I went to see the quack," he said, more serious now.

"And?" questioned Jenny.

"Nothing much, he wants to run a few tests. Like you said, I might be anaemic. He has taken some blood, a whole armful in fact," he laughed. "He says he'll get in touch when he gets the results."

"Did he say anything else?" Jenny queried.

"Stop panicking, Jen, I will tell you as soon as I know," he demanded. Jenny knew he was worried, she could tell from the way he joked about it. Perhaps it was best not to mention it and let him tell her when he knew something.

A few days later, they'd just sat down in the evening when the phone rang. Jenny answered to hear it was John's doctor wanting to speak to him. She handed him the phone and listened as best she could.

"Yes, I see, yes, right, okay yes, thanks bye." He put down the receiver and looked at Jenny. "It seems they want to run a few more tests, so he wants me to go to the private hospital in town on Saturday morning for the day."

"Well at least they are doing something." Jenny said, trying to hide the worry she felt inside.

"Fancy a walk and taking a look at the stars?" John said after a while, as the smile returned to his face.

They put on their wax jackets and went out through the kitchen door and into the garden. The heavy scent of herbs and flowers filled the air as they walked up the lane leading to the paddock. This was the spot where they'd stood all those years ago, when their little baby girl had passed away. This was their special place. John pulled Jenny to him and wrapped his arms protectively around her.

"Jenny my love, if anything was to happen to me, anything at all, promise me that you would still go to live in Greece. Promise me that you will look up at the stars and remember these moments, here on our hill. Remember I have always loved you and will never ever leave you."

"Hey don't be stupid," Jenny pleaded. "You stop that, John Peters, do you hear!" She fought back the tears as a cold shiver ran down her spine.

Jenny had to admit to herself that she had a sense of foreboding about John's illness. It had been worrying her since the morning he'd stayed in bed. She prayed it was nothing more than anaemia, but deep inside she knew differently.

They stood in silence for a while wrapped in each other's arms before returning home to bed. They made love that night with a gentleness that she was not accustomed to. After, he held her in his arms for a long time before finally drifting to sleep.

"I will never leave you, Jenny, Not ever," he whispered.

"Me neither," Jenny added.

"So what exactly are you saying?" John asked the doctor, who'd called him in a few days after the hospital visit.

"I'm afraid it's what I suspected," the GP said after sitting them both down in 'the quiet room.' "I'm sorry to say that you have a rare form of cancer attacking your entire system. I'm afraid the prognosis is very bad."

"Is there anything to be done?"Jenny questioned, as the first tear left the duct.

"We could try a new wonder drug. It's just been released, but we don't know if they offer any hope."

"How long, Doctor?" John asked, trying to be calm for Jenny's sake.

"If we're lucky it could be months, or even years," the doctor replied with a softly spoken voice. "But if not, it could be much sooner than any of us wish."

Although trying to be brave, John put his head in his hands and sat silent for a few moments. Jenny put her arms around his dropped shoulders. They fought back the tears until reaching home, where they instantly came in floods.

"Why me, Jenny," John gushed. "We are so happy. Why did this have to happen now?" He clung to her and wept.

Jenny refused to let herself cry. She knew she had to be the strong one. It was her who would explain everything to the children. She'd be the one who sat up with John long into the night when the pain became unbearable, the one who washed him and put clean clothes on his then frail body when he was unable to, and she'd be the one who would be there always. She would not let him down - He was her life.

Months passed and John's illness became a roller coaster ride. When he was feeling good, they ventured out on the horses, took long walks across the moors with the dogs and spent time with the children. When things were bad, they lay in each other's arms trying to find reasons for the illness and trying to comfort each other. In everything they did, their love for each other shone through and stood firm.

"The stars look particularly bright tonight," John said, as they sat in the garden late one evening. "They are the same stars in Kos you know, but they shine a little brighter there."

Jenny hugged him, knowing what he was hinting at. He'd said it so many times before and she'd finally given in, promising she would fulfil their plans and move to Greece the following spring, with or without him, although it was now more than obvious that John would not be with her. He was progressively having more and more bad days, with less good ones. They now spent every moment they could together or with the family, but they knew time was fast running out for them.

"I love you Jenny," John said, tuning to her and looking longingly into her eyes. "When you gaze at these stars in Greece, know that I will be there with you. I will always be with you. I will never leave you." As he smiled at his beautiful wife the twinkle came back to his eyes and they sparkled like they used to.

John was admitted to the hospital two days later. His was a familiar face there and a popular patient. Although saddened by his illness, the nurses laughed and joked with him as they'd always done. Jenny had taken extended leave to be with him, with the children coming as often as they could.

On John's final evening, all the family had been to visit and in a roundabout way, they'd all said their goodbyes. Now only Jenny remained in the room. The lights had been dimmed and the monitoring machine was the only real light in the room, apart from the moonlight which entered through the open window.

John was slipping in and out of consciousness. Each time he woke he turned to Jenny and smiled. He was finding it very difficult to speak because of the amount of drugs he'd been given. His once strong body was now frail and tired, and Jenny could see that he could no longer fight it. Much as she wanted him to stay with her, she prayed he would soon fall into a deep sleep, from which he wouldn't wake. Then, and only then, his suffering would be over.

He opened his eyes and smiled at her, reached out his hand and Jenny took it, touching her face with it and kissing it gently.

"Jenny, I am sorry. I'm so tired, I think I might have to take my leave of you," he said weakly. Jenny tried to hush him. She knew it was difficult for him to speak. "Listen," he said. "I want you to know that I am not frightened of dying, I'm only frightened of leaving you behind. Take care of yourself, and please Jenny, promise me you will be happy again."

"I promise," she reassured him.

"Whenever you feel sad or alone, look at the stars and I will be there," were the last words he ever spoke. John died in her arms, his grasp on her hand slackened.

"John?" she said, as a cold shiver ran down her spine as she realised he'd left her. Her prayers had been answered. He was finally at peace. The only man she'd ever loved had died.

"Would you like a few minutes on your own with him?" the nurse asked Jenny. Jenny looked round the room. The lights were bright again and it was cold and clinical now. No more beeping of the heart monitor or laboured breathing from John trying to hang on to life – nothing!

"I will go and tell the family," she said to the nurse, pulling herself up and taking a deep breath to compose herself.

She took one last look at the man she'd so dearly loved, as he lay lifeless on the bed. He looked so peaceful now and she wanted to run back and tug at him and try to wake him up, but knew she couldn't, and would never be able do so again.

She left the room and told everyone the sad, but inevitable news they were all dreading.

CHAPTER 17
FAREWELL BUT NOT GOODBYE

Nothing seemed real. She rose and showered in a trance. Dressing in front of the long mirror in the bedroom, she saw no reflection in it, putting on makeup without checking her face. Like a robot programmed to do certain things, she went to the back door, patted each dog on the head and let them out.

Suzie had promised to see to the horses and Jenny could see the water buckets had already gone. She must have been up early, but Jenny hadn't heard her. As she walked back in the kitchen her daughter, Suzie was there, looking so striking in a short black suit.

"You okay Mum?" she asked. Jenny nodded and sat at the pine table to drink a coffee. She couldn't remember whether it was her or Suzie who'd made it.

"People will be here in about an hour Mum," Suzie informed her, to which she nodded again.

They sat in silence at the kitchen table. There were no tears this morning, they'd shed so many over the past few days. Now Jenny was left with a dull ache in her chest. A deep longing that would never be satisfied, for she'd lost a most precious person.

This was different to when Emily died. She was too small, too fragile for this earth. She was only on loan for such a short period of time, but John had been with her forever; more than twenty-five years. They'd had such a wonderful life together, but now he was gone. Today they would commit his body to be cremated and would know he was really gone. This week she'd been in limbo, in a dreamlike state, but soon it would be over.

"Dad's here," whispered Suzie.

"Where?" Jenny gasped, thinking there had been a terrible mistake. The nightmare was over and John had come back!

Sadness returned as she realised what was really happening. They heard a knock on the front door and Suzie went to answer. Jenny looked up to see the two solemn faced men from the funeral company.

"Are you ready, Madam?" the older looking of the two asked. When Jenny told them she was, they escorted her to the waiting funeral car positioned behind the hearse, in which she could see John's coffin, almost covered entirely with flowers.

The younger of the two walked in front of the hearse as they slowly made their way to the main road where the young man climbed in and they picked up speed as they made their way to the crematorium. Travelling in the car with Jenny was Suzie and her husband, Daniel, both sitting opposite, while Laura was to stay with her grandparents in the car behind.

Arriving at the crematorium, James took hold of his mother's arm. She looked at him lovingly. He looked so much like John, with his dark brown hair and green/brown eyes. James' eyes were usually so full of laughter and fun, but today they were looking at her with concern, longing and sadness.

Jenny looked around to see who was here. She spotted Suzie's husband, Daniel, John's mum with his sister and her husband. Laura, who'd been staying with her grandparents, arrived with them in the car behind.

Everyone spoke in whispers as they had at Sue's funeral, as they do at everyone's funeral. Jenny was met with uncomfortable smiles as people struggled to find the right words to say. But Jenny could have told them, there are no right words. She'd already learned that.

The four pallbearers lifted the coffin from the hearse and began to carry it inside. As it passed Jenny, she noticed one single solitary yellow rose fell from the wreath and landed at her feet. She looked down at it and knew deep in her heart that this was a sign from John. Just as Sue had sent her a sign all those years ago, this was her wonderful husband's way of letting her know he was there watching over her. Instantly she felt an inner strength that she'd not known before.

Entering the crematorium's chapel, Jenny could feel her legs turning to jelly and a hot flush ran through her body. She took a deep breath to compose herself and looked straight ahead, as everyone else formed a queue to enter behind her. The coffin was carried past the onlookers and into the chapel, where it was placed on the podium at the front, behind the opened curtains.

Jenny walked down the aisle of the chapel with James at her side. The vicar greeted her and she was ushered to a seat on the front pew. James sat at one side and Suzie at the other. Laura sat next to James, with Jenny's mum and dad and John's parents at the far end.

Whilst sombre music was piped through the music system, James linked her arm as with his mother, while Suzie squeezed her other so hard it hurt. Jenny knew how difficult it was for them. She smiled at them both, but saw the sadness in their eyes. The vicar began the service with a hymn.

"Do not be afraid," Jenny tried to sing, but the words choked her. Many of the congregation were struggling, just as she was. She was thankful for the church choir, as their voices rang out above the other feeble efforts.

James stood to read the lesson, the same passage from 'John' that had been read at their wedding.

"What has a man if he has not love," James began, but stumbled a little, almost breaking down at one point but he carried on courageously. When finished, he took his seat back beside Jenny and gave her hand a quick squeeze as he did so. She was so proud of him.

Suzie was next and she read a poem that she'd personally written. It told of her love for her father and John's love for her. Much appreciated by the congregation, tears flowed as she read it, not only from her but from many others.

Next it was Jenny's turn. Although her legs were like jelly she walked proudly to the lectern, holding to it tightly for extra strength as she began the address. Normally this task would have been presented by the vicar, but Jenny felt that as she'd known John better than anyone, it was her who could tell everyone what a wonderful man and husband he'd been.

Now came the moment that Jenny had been dreading, the actual committal, when the curtains closed and she could no longer see the coffin. It had always upset her at other funerals and now it was going to be especially difficult for her not to break down.

She looked straight ahead as the curtains began to silently draw together. Laura called out, "Daddy," and burst into hysterical sobbing. Suzie and James wept silently, but Jenny stood tall and straight.

"Goodbye John," she whispered to herself. "Goodbye Darling."

The vicar came to Jenny and whispered in her ear, asking her to follow him. She felt numb as she walked out of the chapel and into the bright autumn sunshine. Now came the traditional shaking of hands and offering of condolences from all the people who'd come to show their respect for John. There were so many, the queue seemed endless.

Suddenly, standing before her was Jamie, the man who'd saved her life that time in Cornwall. He held out his arms and Jenny fell into them. They said nothing as he held her for several moments without lessening his hold on her. She knew he would understand how she was feeling.

She'd shared so much with Jamie, She owed her life to him and that had forged a bond between them that had held strong over many years. Releasing his hold, he looked into her eyes but said nothing – No words were necessary. They would talk later. But it still saddened him to see her grieving so.

Jenny continued to shake hands with what seemed an endless amount of people but then the crowd began to drift away, some going home, others returning to the hotel for the wake.

Hand shaking duties over, Jenny went to look at the floral tributes. There were so many. How could she ever thank all of these people? She read the cards. There were some wonderful messages from family and the many friends who loved John. The messages saddened her, but they also made her happy to see what a popular man she'd spent her life with.

Standing alone in solitude, she closed her eyes and thought about all the happy times they'd spent together.

"Goodnight Darling," she said out loud. "Thank you for everything. I will never ever stop loving you. My love for you has not ended today; it will last for the rest of my life."

CHAPTER 18
BANKING ON IT

She'd been putting this task off for as long as possible, but Jenny knew that she had to visit the bank to sign all the necessary documents and finalise matters regarding their joint finances. The problem for her was that, with John's name removed from everything, it all seemed so final. He was never coming back! She placed all the paperwork she thought might be required into a navy leather briefcase and went outside to the car.

It was a lovely morning. The dew lay heavy on the grass and an eerie white mist covered the valley below, shrouding the town and hiding it from view. The watery sunshine was peeping through the trees and the air was filled with the sweet smell of wet grass. Under normal circumstances, she would have been glad to be out on the moors enjoying this early morning stillness, but today was different. She had no one to share this beautiful morning with. She knew it was a morning John would have loved.

The drive into town was uneventful, with the early morning rush just beginning to fill the streets. She found a place to park and glanced at her watch. It was only eight-twenty and her appointment at the bank was not until nine-fifteen. She found a small coffee shop and took a seat at one of the small bistro style tables. Before she'd glanced at the menu, a waiter arrived wearing a broad grin.

"Good morning madam," he said "What can I get you?" Jenny noticed he had a foreign accent, not Italian or French, but possibly Greek.

"Do you do Frappe?" she questioned. The waiter looked a little surprised.

"It's not on the menu, but I can make it for you," he grinned. Shortly he returned bringing a tall glass with an extremely large amount of cream oozing down the sides. He placed it on the table in front of her. He was just about to walk away when he stopped and looked quizzically at her.

"May I ask where you learned about frappe?" the waiter questioned. Jenny smiled as her thoughts returned to the sunny days when she and John had drunk endless frappes.

"In Kos," she smiled. "Do you know it?"

"Madam, I know Kos well," he replied. "It was my home before I came to England."

Jenny took a better look at him. Of course he was Greek. The dark hair and olive complexion, he had to be Greek. She should have known the accent straight away, as she'd heard it so many times in the past.

"I'm moving to live there soon," she informed him.

"Everybody who goes there says that," he replied. "It's good to have a dream."

"No really, I'm going to live there next month. I have a house in Kefalos."

"Kefalos is very beautiful," he smiled. "What are you and your husband going to do there?" Jenny had not anticipated a question concerning her and John and was a little shaken.

"My husband is recently deceased," she told the young man, gathering her senses. "I'll be moving to Greece alone."

"You must be a very strong woman to carry on with this dream," the waiter observed with real emotion in his voice. "Your husband would be proud." He gently touched her shoulder as he left the table.

She finished her frappe and glanced at her watch. Nine o'clock. Five minutes to walk to the bank, time she was leaving. She gestured to the waiter for the bill.

"The frappe is from me," the young man said. "You have made me happy to think of my home and I have made you sad thinking about your husband."

"No you have made me strong, not sad," she confessed. "Efcharisto poli," she added.

"Ar you speak Greek," he commented.

"I try," Jenny said.

"Parakalo madam," he smiled, holding out his hand for a handshake, which Jenny happily accepted. "You will take your husband with you in your heart when you move to Kos. You will never be alone."

In such a small amount of time this young man had touched her deeply and given her comfort and strength to cope with what lay ahead. She left the café and walked tall into the now bustling street, and to the bank.

"Please take a seat, Mrs Peters," the girl on reception said. "I'll tell the manager you're here."

Jenny sat down clutching the briefcase close to her chest for comfort. Within a few minutes a nearby door opened and a dark suited man emerged. He crossed the banking hall and holding out his hand, greeted Jenny.

"Good morning, Mrs Peters. Would you like to come through?" Jenny rose and stretched out her hand to meet his. As she looked up to meet his gaze, she realised with horror just who the manager was. It was Sean, the man who'd robbed her of her best friend, Sue. He was the man who'd behaved in such an unspeakable way that time in Spain. It was obvious at this stage that he'd not recognised her.

He walked towards his office and gestured for her to follow. She did so reluctantly. Her palms became sweaty and her head was spinning. She did not want to speak to this monster, and certainly didn't want to discuss her affairs with him, yet she knew she must

She followed him into the office, which smelt strongly of aftershave. The blinds were partially drawn; keeping out the bright sunshine and making it seem dismal. Sean walked behind the large oak desk and sat down, gesturing for Jenny to the same.

"Now, Mrs Peters, what can we help you with today?" The voice sounded sincere, but it was a much-practised line. He didn't even look up from his desk as he opened the file that lay in front of him.

"I've come to sign the papers to transfer our joint accounts into my sole name," Jenny said.

"Oh, had a fall out with the old man have we?" he joked, or at least he thought he'd joked. "Making sure he doesn't get away with all the money."

"My husband died two months ago," she said softly. Inside she was seething. She loathed every inch of this man. Sean fiddled with his tie, experiencing just a moment of discomfort before returning to his thoughtless self.

"Well let's hope he's made you a merry widow and left you plenty of money to enjoy," he smirked.

Before Jenny could say anything, there was a knock on the door. A pretty young girl entered the room carrying a file close to her chest. As he took the file from the girl, Jenny noticed how his hand strayed and touched the breast of the young girl. The worker recoiled from the touch, obviously feeling violated by it.

"Sorry," Sean said smiling, but not meaning it. The girl scurried from the room. Sean cleared his throat and began to browse through the file. Jenny watched him, her revulsion of him growing by the second!

"Right, so John Peters, your husband, passed away and you, Jennifer need all he accounts transferred solely into your name," he said, but all of a sudden, a strange look came on his face. "Did you once call yourself, Jenny, many moons ago?"

"That's me," she admitted, feeling anxious that he seemed to remember her.

"Didn't you once go out with Mick?" he asked.

"I met him once," Jenny replied curtly.

"Yes, I remember now, you and that friend of yours – Sue I think was she called? She was a bit of alright, a bit of a goer if I remember rightly. Wonder what she's up to now. Married with a string of kids I guess!" Jenny couldn't believe what she was hearing. How could he speak of her friend like this?

"Sue died quite some time ago," she replied, struggling to contain her temper. "I thought you would have known that."

Oh yes, I remember now," he confessed. She topped herself, the silly mare!" Jenny was speechless. The rage inside was burning to her core!

"Shall we get these forms signed then?" he asked, totally oblivious to the way she was feeling and dismissing everything he'd just spoken of."

"Yes," she replied, flabbergasted!

Having signed all the forms, Sean summarised what would now happen. Jenny didn't want to speak to him anymore than was necessary, desperately wanting to get away from him and out of the office. He walked round to Jenny's side of the desk and placed his hand on her shoulder. She froze!

"Well now, that's all done," he smirked. "Now if there's anything else I can help you with, anything at all…" As he said this, he tightened the grip on her shoulder. "I mean we don't want you to go short of anything, do we?" The sexual tones of this question were more than obvious. She wasn't going to let him get away with this, but here and now was not the time or place.

"Goodbye," she muttered and walked out, head held high.

She needed a coffee to calm down and decided go back to the café she'd frequented before. She was disappointed when she arrived to find that the waiter was no longer there, but a young waitress came to take her order. She ordered a Latte and settled down in the chair, being in no hurry to return home, as there was no one there waiting for her.

The café door opened and Jenny noticed it was the girl from the bank. She sat at a table quite close to Jenny and the waitress, having recognised her too, greeted her warmly. Almost immediately, holding her head in her hands the girl broke down in tears and wept bitterly. The waitress, who was obviously a friend, put her arms around her shoulder.

What's that bastard done now?" she asked angrily, without considering whether Jenny could hear or not.

"It's what he's threatened to do," the bank worker replied weeping. "If I don't do what he wants, he says he'll sack me."

"You could easily get a job somewhere else," the waitress suggested. "It's just not worth putting yourself through this every day."

Jenny couldn't help but overhear the conversation. It was obvious that someone at work had caused the girl to be this upset. She continued to listen.

"It was the best thing I ever did, getting out of that place and away from him."

"Yes but if I leave, he'll only move on to someone else. I know it will be Maria, and she's my best mate and she couldn't cope with it."

"Neither can you," the waitress advised. "Just who does he think he is, touching everyone up like he does? It's about time somebody did something about it."

"I know, but who will believe me against him? He's the manager, after all!" lamented the bank girl. "I wouldn't know where to start." Jenny's ears pricked up when she realised they were talking about Sean.

"I guess I'll just have to do what he asks," the young girl sighed. "No one's going to back us against him, are they?"

"Oh yes they are," Jenny said, leaping to her feet. The girls turned to look at her as she continued. "Sorry to have listened in on your conversation, but are you talking about Sean, the manager at the bank across the road?"

The girls looked at Jenny a little puzzled. Who was this lady? Perhaps she was a friend of his. Neither said anything. They just looked at each other and then back at Jenny.

"I have known him for many years," she told the girls, trying to reassure them that she was on their side. "I know exactly the type of man he is and the trouble he causes women. I would like to see him dealt with. Maybe we could get together and try." The girls looked apprehensively at her as she gave them a smile. "Ladies, please, let me introduce myself. My name is Jenny Peters. I'm a customer of the bank and have just been to see Sean, I mean Mr – What is his name?"

"Cooper," the girls replied in unison.

"I have just been to see Mr Cooper and he behaved most inappropriately during our appointment," Jenny continued to say to a now attentive audience. "I was going to contact the Area Manager to discuss this with him, but you could file for sexual harassment as an employee and ex-employee. I hope I'm not jumping the gun here by assuming he's been abusing his position and bothering you in that way." The girls looked first at each other and then back at Jenny. They nodded hesitantly.

"Then we can get this sorted from two view points. We need to get together and discuss everything that has happened to you and any others we can find. Then we will put your case to a tribunal. I will of course also pursue my complaint."

The girls looked interested now at Jenny's proposal. Within minutes they'd agreed a time and place to meet, where they could put their cases together.

They met a few days later. It seemed that other girls had been bothered by Sean, but were reluctant to add their voices. Maria also found that there had been a problem of sorts at his last branch, where two female members of staff had left giving their reason for leaving as not being able to work under Mr Cooper's regime, which said a lot.

They chatted for ages, with Jenny recording as much as she could in her little notebook. She explained that she would arrange for them to see a Solicitor, who could formulize all this information and arrange for a tribunal to take place. She told them that she herself had written to the Regional Manager and had arranged to see him in a couple of days. The Regional Manager was called Mr Savage, which sounded quite frightening itself!

The appointment was at eleven and Jenny arrived in good time. She'd dressed in a dark blue suit to help her feel more businesslike but had left her hair loose, and it shone beautifully in the morning sun.

She had the girls' testimonies with her, but her prime objective was to talk about the incident in the office. Jenny was not familiar with this office, but soon found reception and confirmed her appointment. She was kept waiting only a few seconds when a tall, dark haired man emerged from a door linked to the reception.

"Mrs Peters," the man called. Jenny stood up and held out her hand to shake his. She looked at the man. He was distinguished looking, a little older than her and greying a little at the temples. He looked familiar.

Suddenly it dawned on her just who her appointment was with. It was Mick, Sean's friend, who Sue had matched her with all those years ago when her friend wanted her to come along and complete a foursome. Mick had been her blind date. Her heart sank. If he was Sean's friend, how or why would he help her?

Mick showed her into his office. The room was sparsely furnished, very minimalist. A dark mahogany desk was set at an angle in one corner, with an imposing executive chair behind it. Two chocolate coloured leather chairs were positioned either side of a square coffee table, with a vase of fresh lilies on it. Although minimalist, it was a very relaxed setting. Mick didn't go behind his desk; he gestured to Jenny to sit in one of the leather armchairs and he sat down on the other.

"I took the opportunity of browsing through your file before you arrived. I'm sorry to hear about your husband, I hope the bank have been able to sort everything out for you without too much upset." She nodded in acknowledgement of Mick's sympathies. "Now then," he continued, "how can I help you?" As he said this, he seemed to study her face, and as he did so he frowned quizzically. "You look familiar Mrs Peters, have we met before, perhaps at another branch?" Here was her opportunity. Should she tell him? He seemed friendly, not at all like Sean.

"Yes, we have met before. It was many years ago when my friend set us up. We went t a nightclub," Jenny could tell from his expression that he too remembered the night in question.

"Jenny, is that you?" he questioned with a look of recollection. "I'm afraid my behaviour last time we met was totally out of order," He looked embarrassed.

"It was a long time ago," Jenny said smiling.

"Yes, a lot of water under the bridge since then," he replied. "So how has life been treating you? Oh sorry, that was awful of me. You've just lost your husband. I really am sorry."

"It's okay," she reassured him, quite warming to his pleasant persona. "How about you?"

"Typical married man with two kids," he informed her.

"I have three" Jenny said. "They have been a great comfort to me since John passed away."

"They must be," Mick said softly. "So what are you planning on doing now?"

"Believe it or not, I'm going to live in Kos," she smiled.

"Good for you - How wonderful," he seemed genuinely happy for her. "Are your children going with you?"

"No I'm going alone. They will no doubt come to visit as often as they can, and will be very welcome," she replied. "I hope they will come to love Kos just as much as John and I did."

"It must be very difficult for you," Mick said with true feeling in his voice. "I don't know what I'd do if anything happened to my wife. I don't think that I could cope." Jenny felt comforted by this and was beginning to feel quite relaxed in his company.

"Well then, Mrs Peters," he paused, "or can I call you Jenny?"

"Jenny will be fine," she told him.

"What would you like to see me about?" Jenny hesitated for a moment, but then decided it was now or never.

"I've come to see you about Sean," she looked for a reaction from Mick and notice he raised his eyebrows. "His behaviour towards me was totally inappropriate when I went to see him at his office."

"Tell me everything," Mick said, looking straight at her. "And I mean everything," he said in a soft, but reassuring way.

Jenny told Mick everything that had happened in Sean's office and Mick listened without interruption. When Jenny finished, he sat back on his chair, took a deep breath and stared out the window for a few seconds. Her heart was racing. Did he believe her, or had she made a fool of herself by coming here and relating the facts to Sean's friend?

"He's a clever sort is old Sean. Wriggles his way out of situations, always got an explanation. Nothing's ever his fault," he offered. "I've got him out of quite a few sticky situations, but I've had enough of it. The trouble is he'll say you came on to him, you know grieving widow, needing a man. I really wish I could be there when he behaves like this. I believe every word you've told me, sorry Jenny. Please accept my apologies for the behaviour of a member of my staff." Jenny smiled at him. She could see it was difficult for him too. "Right then, let's nail the bastard!" he finally remarked.

Jenny was in the office for nearly two hours, during which time they'd become fellow conspirators in Sean's downfall. Reminiscing about their meeting years ago and the events that had peppered their lives from then till now, they became good friends. As she was about to leave the office, Mick took her hand to shake it, but then planted an affectionate kiss on her cheek. Jenny felt her face warm at the touch of his lips. She felt good inside, happy to have found someone to help fight the battle with her and could help her eliminate the feelings of guilt she still had over Sue's untimely death.

Jenny made an appointment at the bank. When the day arrived she dressed carefully, not wanting to look too obvious but not too unglamorous either. She chose a plain red dress, a little shorter than she would usually wear and opened it at the neck to reveal just a tantalising glimpse of cleavage. This was accompanied by her sexiest red high-heeled shoes.

"Mrs Peters to see Mr Cooper," she announced approaching reception.

"Just one moment," the girl said. "I will tell him you're here."

"Well hello Jenny," Sean Cooper said, breezing out from his office, "How very nice to see you again. Do come in,"

Holding her head up high and clutching at her bag to stop her hands from trembling, she followed him into his office. Once again he sat her in the comfy leather armchair, but this time he perched himself on the corner of the desk with his knees almost touching hers. Under normal circumstances she would have moved her legs, but this time she remained quite still.

"So you decided to take me up on my offer did you?" he smirked. Jenny's heart began to pound.

"And what offer was that?" she asked coyly.

"Whatever you would like, Jenny, I am sure it's within my power to help you with anything you need," he smiled.

"I just needed a bit of explanation about the papers we signed the last time." He looked disappointed hearing this.

"Is that all?" he asked with obvious suggestion in his voice that he'd expected more. "Well let's take a look shall we."

He pushed himself up from the desk and stood behind her. She could feel his eyes staring down the front of her dress. Inside she wanted to flinch, but outwardly gave no hint of her emotions. She took the papers from the folder and laid them on her knee. Sean leaned over to pick one of the papers, touching her knee as he did. He looked for a reaction, but she gave none.

"You didn't really come here for an explanation did you?" he said, his face very close to hers. He moved his hand, resting it on her shoulder. Jenny made no answer. "I know what you really want, you need a man. A beautiful, sexy woman like you, it must be difficult going without, if you know what I mean?"

Jenny knew exactly what he was implying, but was unsure what move she should make, if any. She didn't want to appear to be encouraging him, but wanted him to continue.

"Look, I can put a chair behind the door handle so no one can get in," he suggested, taking her lack of response as approval. Terror ran through Jenny. She didn't know what to say or do.

"See, very easy," Sean said picking up the chair and jamming the door closed. Jenny felt utter revulsion as he walked towards her. He loosened his tie and sat down beside her, their knees touching.

"So Jenny, how can I really help you?" he said with a slimy grin on his face. "Why don't you loosen up a bit, maybe undo a few buttons on that dress of yours so we can get down to business."

His hand reached towards Jenny's breast and he took hold of the top button, slowly undoing it. Jenny's heart was in her mouth. Should she resist or let him continue? She caught hold of his hand to stop him.

"Come on sweetheart," Sean protested. "Don't be shy. You know it's what you want, or why else did you come back to see me?"

At that the moment the chair holding the door was propelled across the room and Mick charged in. Sean shot to his feet, but his watch was caught on Jenny's undone button, leaving him with his hand touching her breast.

"Mick!" Sean shouted. "I was just trying to help Jen, er, Mrs Peters with some paperwork. It was awful. She just grabbed hold of my hand and put it on her chest. She's a widow you know, gagging for it! I couldn't keep her off me."

"Stop right there Sean, it's over," Mick demanded. "I've heard every word."

"No, you've got it all wrong," Sean claimed.

"No - you have it all wrong, Sean. Your bad behaviour has gone on too long!"

"Come on, Mick, we're old mates," Sean stammered. "We can sort this out."

"And can we also sort out the sexual harassment case that's pending with two members of your staff, Sean? Can we? Sean, you're finished!"

"You may be finished, but I'm not," Jenny interrupted "I won't be finished till you are punished for what you did to my friend, ruining her life and the lives of quite a few young girls here at the bank. You are the lowest of the low Sean." She could have said more but she didn't.

Mick escorted Sean out of the room, telling Jenny to remain there and he would return shortly. He smiled at her and nodded in appreciation of what she'd just been through.

"That was for you, Sue," she whispered to herself whilst alone.

Mick returned to explain that everything had been taped, and clever use of the office webcam had also caught the physical contact. Sean had been instantly dismissed for gross misconduct, and would have to appear at a sexual harassment tribunal in a few weeks.

"Are you going to prosecute Jenny?" he asked gently.

"I don't think so. The look on his face was enough for me," she stated. "Just make sure those girls win at the tribunal. That will do for me."

"Thanks for going through this, Jenny. I know getting justice for Sue has meant a lot to you." Mick looked down at his hands, looking embarrassed and not wanting to look directly at her. "Can I tell you something?" Jenny looked curious to hear what he wanted to say. "You may not believe it, Jenny, but I want to tell you anyway. That night on that holiday, I never forgave myself."

Jenny took a sharp intake of breathe. Was Mick now going to confess to raping Sue as well?

"I never forgave myself for not stopping them," he began. "I should have and could have, but I didn't, I just left the room and walked around for what seemed hours. When I returned, it was quiet. I went into the apartment and saw Sue lying there. She was naked and curled up like a small child. I took a blanket, wrapped her in it and then carried her to the bedroom. She thanked me. Thanked me for what? Letting it happen to her? I was a coward, Jenny. No day has gone by when I haven't felt the guilt."

Jenny could see shame and regret in his eyes. She stretched her hand out to him and touched his shoulder.

"If Sue is watching from up there, she would be proud of you today. She would forgive you, I'm sure of it," Jenny reassured him. They sat in silence for a few moments, each deep in their memories of Sue and of what ifs.

Eventually, Jenny said she had to leave. Mick thanked her again and shook her hand warmly.

CHAPTER 19
THE RESCUE

The sky was clear and blue with not a cloud in sight. The sun shone brightly and was already beginning to warm the early morning air.

Jenny woke early and walked out to the bedroom balcony and studied the view. She would never tire of this scenic beauty, especially at this hour before the streets began to fill with tourists, disturbing the silence.

She dressed casually and brushed her hair. By now her tan was developing into a rich golden brown, making her even more attractive, especially as she'd put back the weight she'd lost during the mourning process for the loss of John.

Later she went for a drive. Needing to buy a few things from the local shop, she set off to the village and the bakers. As she approached the top of the hill, instead of turning right towards the village she took a left turn, and without thinking, soon found herself on the narrow sandy track that led down the their secret beach. She hadn't visited this place since John's death. It was so very special there.

She felt a lump come into her throat and slowed the car down almost to a stop. What on earth was she doing come here? How stupid. She knew it would upset her and yet she didn't stop. She carried on past the little Church secreted in one of the bigger coves and past the rocky cliffs, where only the goats dare venture. Now as the prickly bushes reached out, touching the car as if to prevent it passing, she began to feel a funny sensation in the pit of her stomach. She was almost there at their special place.

She got out of the car and took a deep breath, inhaling all the atmosphere of the place. Instead of feeling sad, she felt very peaceful. All the happy memories flooded back and she couldn't help a little smile breaking out on her face.

"Oh John, how I wish you were here with me," she whispered to the sea, her words drowned out by the crashing waves.

She stood in silence for a moment, remembering the promises they'd made to each other. In that second, she knew John really would always be with her, because she held him in her heart.

The far end of the cove was bathed in shadow as the sun was still quite low in the sky. The sea at that part of the cove didn't appear like the inviting blue and white of the breakers, being almost black in appearance. Jenny felt her eyes drawn to this darkness. She remembered the darkness of the sea that day when she'd almost drowned, and felt a shiver run down her spine.

Jenny studied the darkness for some time. She then began to make out a shape floating on the surface, moving slowly backwards and forwards with the swell. Unsure of what it was, she stood up to get a better look, but still couldn't make it out. It was certainly quite a large object. Curiosity got the better of her and she began to walk slowly across the sand. As she neared the middle of the cove, she stopped in her tracks - It was a body!

She threw off her flip-flop as she ran towards it and waded into the water until it was up to her waist. The chill of the sea took her breath away! She moved towards the body and could see it was dressed in jeans and a white T-shirt. From the hair on the bare arms, she could see it was a male.

Taking the body by both arms, she pulled the body ashore and dragged it onto the sand. As she turned it over she could see the face was swollen and blue. She put her head on the chest and listened intently. Miraculously she could make out a faint heartbeat. He was alive.

Summoning up all she could remember about mouth-to-mouth resuscitation she took a long deep breath, pushed her lips to his and blew with all the puff in her body. She repeated this for several minutes but without any obvious response. She took a deep breath and bent down to place her lips over his again. Just as she did so there was a flickering of his eyelids, followed by a convulsive coughing and spluttering. Turning his head to the side, the man spewed out the watery contents of his lungs. Jenny watched in disbelief as he turned his head back and opened his eyes slowly.

Jenny looked at him and noticed he had green/brown eyes like John, and they were gazing up at her. For a split second she felt a shiver course threw her body.

After rolling him into the recovery position she ran back over the beach, scrambled up the cliff side and ran to her car to get her mobile phone. She was so glad she'd persevered with those Greek lessons, as it meant she was able to make herself understood when she phoned the emergency services, giving them explicit directions to her cove. She took a beach towel from the car to act as a makeshift blanket and hurried back to the body lying motionless on the beach. After covering his body, she sat beside it and waited for the experts, checking occasionally that he was still breathing and the heartbeat was still there.

The emergency crew were there quickly. They took over the situation, whisked the man quickly onto a stretcher and carried him up the cliff to the waiting ambulance, with Jenny following.

"Hee veery lucky you come heeere," said one of the crew in broken English. "Theese ees veery lonely place." Very lovely place indeed, thought Jenny.

"You come too?" the driver asked, before closing the back door of the ambulance. Without even thinking, Jenny nodded and said she would follow them to the medical centre.

The ambulance raced along the sandy track ignoring the deep ruts in it. Jenny was bounced up and down in her little car as she kept pace with it. Once on the main road, the siren was put on and Jenny followed in its path all the way through the village and on to the medical centre. When they arrived the crew leapt out of the vehicle, threw open the rear doors and carried the stretcher inside to the waiting staff. The doors of the emergency room swung open and they entered, leaving Jenny alone. She shivered, standing in her wet clothes. What should she do now? Should she go home? She didn't know why she'd said she would follow the ambulance.

At that moment the doors swung open and a nurse came out saying something in Greek. Speaking too quickly for Jenny to understand, she shook her head

"I'm English," she said apologetically.

"Your husband ees very poorly," the nurse said in broken English. "You come to see him." Jenny was about to protest that this was not her husband, but the nurse had already returned through the swing doors and had motioned for her to follow.

On a bed in the centre of the room she could see the outline of the man from the beach covered in a blanket and surrounded by various members of medical staff all talking at the same time, as the Greeks always did. As she crossed the room, they all fell silent and moved away, leaving Jenny alone with this complete stranger, whom they all thought was her Greek husband! She couldn't help but smile. This could be a REAL Greek tragedy!

There was an eerie silence in the room. She wondered if this man really was alive and moved closer to listen. His breathing now seemed normal and he looked as if he was just sleeping. She walked round to the head of the bed and stood looking down at his face. His eyelids flickered and he slowly opened his eyes and tried to focus. His eyes eventually opened fully and looked at Jenny, who met his gaze. She was instantly taken aback. He looked so much like John. Strangely, she was full of mixed emotions. She didn't know why, but she felt that she'd known this man for ages.

"It's the pretty Angel who saved my life," he said in perfect English, lifting his hand to shake hers in thanks. As their hands touched, she felt electric run through her. He also looked visibly shaken.

"Do I know you?" he asked. "I'm sure I do." He saw Jenny shivering. "Oh my word, you are cold and wet. You must get dry and put on fresh clothes." She was moved at his concern for her, since it was him who'd just escaped death and not her.

"I'm okay," she replied. "I just wanted to make sure you were feeling good before I left," she explained.

"You are leaving me already. Please don't leave," he pleaded. These words pulled at her heartstrings. Why was he asking her this?

"I must go and get changed," she told him.

"But come back please," he said sorrowfully.

"What about me letting your family know you where you are," she suggested. He shook his head, and she didn't push the matter any further.

"I live close so I won't be long," she confided.

"Promise you will return," he begged.

"I promise," Jenny found herself saying to this man she'd only just met. He smiled; relieved she'd accepted his request.

Arriving home, she quickly removed the wet clothes and jumped into the shower. It was lovely to feel the hot water warming her. She dried herself, dressed and applied fresh makeup before making her way back to the medical centre.

Driving back towards the centre, she began to mull over the morning. She wondered why she was rushing back to see this complete stranger. Who was he, and why did her heart skip a beat when with him?

She felt a sudden rush of warmth in her cheeks, feeling like a teenager rushing to see a new boyfriend, certainly not like a woman recently widowed! Perhaps she shouldn't go back. His family may be there by now and it would be very embarrassing. No, she'd given the stranger her promise to return and she knew how important promises were.

201

As she opened the door of the medical centre, a young receptionist was now manning the desk. She called out a greeting to Jenny as she entered.

"Yassas Te thelete," she said.

"Yas," Jenny replied. I've come to see the man who was brought in this morning."

"Ar yes," she replied. "He's been moved into a side ward. Go through to number three."

Jenny stood outside the door of room three, but panicked. What if he wasn't alone? Had family with him? Had a WIFE with him? She knocked gently and pushed the door open. The room was small but cheery, with a large window that gave wonderful views right down to the sea below.

She looked across towards the bed and was met by the most beautiful eyes, and a smile that lit up the entire room.

"You came back," he said, again in perfect English.

"I said I would," Jenny said returning his smile. She felt so comfortable speaking to him. It was as if she was speaking to someone she'd known forever.

"Come, please sit down," he said, motioning towards the chair next to the bed.

"I just ran home to change," she said, not knowing why she'd said the obvious. "Everything was wet." He nodded and continued to look at her, as if carrying out an inspection and wanting to make a mental note of every last detail.

"I'm sorry," he said, noticing Jenny's uneasiness at his attention. "You look so beautiful I cannot take my eyes off you." Jenny's felt flushed as he continued. "I'm trying to think where I know you from, but just cannot think."

"I was thinking the same," Jenny confessed. She was also sure they must have met before, but really could not think where or when. She felt strangely attracted to this man about whom she knew nothing.

"I want to thank you for saving my life," he smiled. "If you had not gone to my cove, I would not be here now."

'His Cove,' it was hers and Johns, not his. However, Jenny nodded in receipt of his thanks.

"They say I can go home" he mentioned, "I'm being collected later." Again, Jenny wondered if he was married and his wife would be collecting him.

"Well as long as you're okay," she replied. He smiled again. Jenny thought again what lovely eyes he had. They really were just like John's.

You remind me of my wife," he announced, almost confirming to Jenny that he was indeed married. Maybe it's time to make a sharp exit before the wife arrives to collect him, she thought.

"Well I must go. I'm happy to see you're making a good recovery," she said, edging towards the door.

"Bye," he said looking disappointed. He held up his hand in protest at her leaving, but before he could say anything, she was through the door and rushing along the corridor and out to her car.

When she arrived home, again, she felt a pang of disappointment at the thought of him belonging to someone else. This Greek man had stirred feelings in her that had lain dormant for a long time. He'd reminded her so much of John for some reason, and yet he was so different. Jenny felt silly and a little ashamed at some of the thoughts she'd had about this stranger.

Although making a cup of tea, she reached instead for the bottle of Ouzo. She half filled a glass, added some lemonade and took it out to the balcony. She sighed deeply, sat on the wicker sun lounger and sipped at her beverage.

She suddenly realised that she didn't even know his name, and probably, she never would!

CHAPTER 20
NICE TO SEE YOU

It was wonderful to see her son, James, when he came for a two week visit. How tall he'd grown and how much like his father he now looked. She spotted him as he came through passport control, clutching his passport in one hand and an oversized flight bag over his shoulder.

At first, she didn't notice the beautiful, long-legged blonde behind him. She stood behind James, not quite in full view as they waited for the luggage to appear on the conveyor belt. James was tall enough to see above the heads of the bustling holidaymakers, as they also tried to find their own luggage on the overcrowded carousel. He'd still not seen Jenny, but hoped she was there to meet him as he was not sure where they were going. At last his luggage and that of his leggy companion finally appeared on the carousel. His case was relatively small, but hers was large and heavy.

They began pushing their way through the crowds towards the exit, all the time scouring the area more intensely. A bronzed slim lady waved furiously at him and pushed forward. It couldn't possibly be his mother, could it? She looked so young and full of life, not at all like the woman he'd left at Manchester airport a few months ago.

Jenny ran forward and embraced him, kissing him on both cheeks in the customary Greek way. The tears in her eyes this time were tears of joy at seeing her son in the flesh and being able to hold him. They'd spoken on the phone many times since she'd been here and written often to each other, but now he was standing in front of her, every inch the man and so like John. She hugged him again and then relaxing him from her grip, he took a step back.

"Sun gets in your eyes, doesn't it?" he said, wiping a tear from his face. Jenny understood his tears. "Mum can I introduce you to Caitlin?" The long legged blonde who'd remained in the background, not wanting to intrude on the mother-son reunion now stepped confidently forward. Jenny smiled, took her hand and then kissed her on both cheeks.

"Welcome to Kos," she said.

Jenny needed no explanation from James as to whom this person was. She could tell from the look in his eyes that this was the love of his life. She knew the look only too well. It was the look of love that John had bestowed on her when they first met, and throughout all their life together.

"The car's outside. Can you manage the luggage?" Jenny asked James. It was a silly question really. He was clearly a strong, fit young man, a little pale, but that would soon change over the next few days in the sunny climate in Kos.

Not wanting to scrutinise James companion too obviously, she glanced at her from time to time as they made their way to the car. She looked about the same age as James and was almost as tall, with her long slim legs and trim figure. She had beautiful sapphire blue eyes that made Jenny think her blonde locks were not from a bottle.

James heaved the large suitcase into the boot of the car and placed his own smaller one next to it. Caitlin still clung to the vanity case, as if it contained something of great value. James opened the rear door of the car for Caitlin to get in and then opened the front door for himself.

"Are you going to drive then?" Jenny asked smiling.

"Oh yeah, I forgot," he laughed, and walked around to the passenger side.

"Ten minutes and we'll be home," Jenny said, turning the ignition key and firing the car into action. "Do you want the tour rep spiel on the way?"

"Of course," James replied. "We are first time visitors and need to know everything."

As she drove, Jenny pointed out places of interest, and places they may like to visit during their stay. James and Caitlin had remained silent during the talk, unlike many holidaymakers on transfer buses. They had listened to every detail and been overwhelmed at the fantastic views. They could hear how proud Jenny was of Kefalos, and how much she obviously loved it. From what they'd seen on their journey from the airport, they were already beginning to understand why she and John had been so keen to move here.

As they climbed up the hill, Jenny indicated to turn right and drove up the steep driveway to her home. James gasped at the beauty of the setting. The house stood out from the rocky side of the hill, with its large verandas offering magnificent views over the entire bay.

The garden was beautiful, filled with flowers and shrubs of every colour and fragrance. Gardening had been Jenny's salvation when she first arrived and she'd put a great amount of time and energy into creating these grounds. An impressive curved, wrought iron staircase led to the veranda at the front of the house, where there was a set of table and chairs and numerous earthenware pots containing more plants upon it.

James and Caitlin got out of the car and retrieved their luggage from the boot and following Jenny, they climbed up the steep staircase. Sweat poured from James's forehead as he struggled up the steep stairs carrying the cases. He was more than relieved to reach the top and place them on the tiled veranda floor. Both he and Caitlin walked to the rail and took in the breathtaking views, before surveying the house itself.

It was painted traditionally blue and white, but was nothing like he'd imagined from the photographs he'd previously seen. He was quite overcome, not only by the wonderful setting but the beauty of the house itself, with its hanging baskets overflowing with bright red geraniums and its numerous balconies.

The pair followed Jenny in silence as she gave them the guided tour. They were both in total awe of the basic beauty of the house. Each room had its own character; filled with fresh flowers and with the minimum of accessories, making it look designer through and through.

It suddenly dawned on Jenny that she'd only been expecting James to stay. She supposed they would want to share a room. After all, it was not like thirty years ago, when that would not even have been a consideration. She remembered deliberating about Pete and Michelle sharing a room on that first Christmas, all those years ago.

"Will you be okay in here?" she asked, gesturing towards the black and white bedroom.

"Mum it's just too lovely for words," James finally managed to say. The sparkle clearly visible in Caitlin's eyes showed that she too was more than pleased with the room. "I'll give you a few moments to unpack and then if you like we can have a frappe on the front balcony.

"A what?" James quizzed.

"Iced coffee," Jenny informed her son. "It's what the Greeks dink."

"Fine," James said.

"I'll try anything," Caitlin joined in.

Whilst James and his girlfriend busied themselves unpacking, Jenny prepared the drinks. She placed a hand embroidered tablecloth on the balcony table and brought freshly baked cakes and a tray of fresh fruit, with freshly baked rolls and feta cheese. She knew they'd be peckish after the journey. Airplane meals were no substitute for real food.

It felt good to have people in the house and to be able to prepare food for them. She hoped that James and Caitlin would enjoy their stay and would come to love Kefalos as she and John did.

Jenny still did not visit Kos Town unless she really had to. It was always a case of travelling there, doing what had to be done, and returning to Kefalos as soon as possible. Although the shopping there was excellent, it always felt sticky and airless. She was always glad to return to the breeze, which was always present in Kefalos. However, James wanted to visit, so she agreed to take them. They also wanted a flying visit to the lively resort of Kardamena.

When John and Jenny had first come to Kos, Kardamena had been a reasonably quiet place, with only two parallel streets of shops and bars. Over the years it had changed dramatically and was now the youngster's holiday resort, with its endless blocks of apartments and bars spewing out incessant music and offering videos of UK comedy shows constantly! It certainly wasn't Jenny's cup of tea and having visited today, James and Caitlin both agreed they much preferred the quiet, relaxed lifestyle of Kefalos.

Leaving Kardamena they took the road towards Kos Town. As they drove, Jenny explained that the island visible to their left was Kalymnos, known as the sponge island, where for years divers collected sponges and coral from the seabed, selling it to holidaymakers. Although paying attention to what they were being told by Jenny, they seemed more interested when she pointed to the sign to Tigaki Beach, the local nudist hotspot!

They soon noticed an increase of large furniture shops, electrical stores and supermarkets. This was the outskirts of Kos Town. After finding somewhere to park, Jenny gave some simple instruction to James and Caitlin regarding places of interest, the best shops, where to eat and the overpriced restaurants on the harbour to avoid. They made arrangements where and at what time to meet later and then Jenny said goodbye, leaving them to explore the town alone.

She crossed the square near the market and made her way to the bank, carefully rehearsing the Greek phrases she would need to use to conduct her business there. Ten minutes later everything was completed and the time was now hers, until the agreed meeting time.

She wandered round the shops for a while buying a few things for herself, then decided to go for a coffee. She found a small kafeneio and sat down outside at a table, shaded a little from the now fierce glare of the sun. She ordered a coffee and decided to spoil herself with a cream cake, sat back and relaxed.

As she sat there, a strange sensation came over her, as if someone was about to speak to her but nobody did. Having savoured the last drops of her flavoursome liquid, she glanced up and caught sight of a Greek couple crossing the square in front of her. They were heavily laden with shopping bags and were laughing loudly.

She continued to watch and suddenly her heart fluttered, as she realised it was the man from the beach and this was obviously his wife with him. She remembered how the man had said that she looked like his wife, but looking at this woman now she could see no similarity.

She watched as they passed by and then began to feel a little disappointed that he'd not noticed her and come to say hello. Giving up on any connection with the man, she strolled to the arranged meeting place and soon met James and Caitlin, who were each carrying a selection of carrier bags and waiting beside the car.

"You look a little flushed, Mum. Are you okay?" James asked as she approached them. Jenny dismissed his concerns with a wave of her hand.

Kos Town is a bit too much for me," she admitted. Surely seeing that man hadn't made her blood pressure rise, making her cheeks blush so obviously.

All too soon, their stay in Kos had come to an end. Jenny reluctantly drove them to the airport and said a tearful goodbye. They told her how they'd fallen in love with the place, especially Kefalos, and could truly understand why she'd chosen to live there. They confirmed they would definitely be coming back. It seemed that Kos had performed its special magic on them, as it does for so many.

Driving back, she felt suddenly very alone again. It had been wonderful having James there, Caitlin too. Her son had become so like his father, both in his looks and his ways, even in the way he showed love to his girlfriend, just like John had shown his love for her. She smiled at such happy memories. No one could take those away from her.

As she entered the house she found herself humming a tune, an old sixties song that she and John used to dance to. She laughed to herself.

"I'm sure you are haunting me, John Peters," she said out loud. It felt comforting to think that he might be.

CHAPTER 21
STRANGER ON THE SHORE

It was now late August. Although the sun already held a sting, there was none of the customary breeze that refreshed the air. A haze covered the sea, blanketing the island of Nisyros. Early sun worshippers had already secured their spots on the beach.

Jenny's thoughts that morning were the same as every morning, they were of John and how he so loved the sun. They had always gone to the beach early in an attempt to catch every second of sunshine, making sure they returned to England with a deep, long lasting tan.

She showered and put on a short shift dress over her bikini. Nothing was planned for today. No one would be visiting, no errands to run or cleaning to do. The day was hers and hers alone.

'Alone' - What a sad word that was.

Packing a small bag with the bare essentials, she drove to 'their beach.' The sea was high up the cove and the waves were furiously breaking against the rocks, filling the air with spray. She placed her bag on a large rock in the centre of the cove and removed her dress. Her body had become bronzed with many long weeks in the sun, with her figure slimmed and toned with swimming as often as she had. Physically she looked and felt great, yet psychologically she still needed to heal the deep wound which left her feeling empty inside. Only time would help, and time was something she had plenty of.

After securing her towel on the sand with a large pebble, she waded into the waves. The chill of the water caught her breath, making her pause momentarily between each breaker, ready for the onslaught of the foaming mass of cold water that accompanied the next wave.

She swam for some time, totally relaxed and at one with herself and the world for it was in this, their special cove that she felt closest to John.

Lost in the memory of her deceased husband, she swam back and forth across the cove. Then refreshed she returned ashore, lay in the hot sun she dozed for quite some time. On waking fully she decided to take another dip before returning home. She didn't linger as long this time, just taking enough to refresh herself. As she paddled back to shore she'd the strong sensation of being watched. She glanced around the cove but saw no one. Perhaps it was her over active imagination playing tricks on her. She wrapped the soft fluffy towel around her body, glad of its protection.

She gazed towards the rocks in the corner of the cove and spotted someone sitting there. The strong sun prevented her from seeing any features, but the outline of the body told her it was a man.

She rarely felt threatened here in their cove. Few people ever ventured here, unaware that it existed, hidden away as it was behind the outreaching gorse bushes. Today however, for some reason she felt a little uneasy at the presence of this man, for the cove was quite far from the road and civilisation. Yet after drying herself, when she looked again the man was gone. She put on her shift dress, fastened back her long dark hair and gathered her few belongings. Now ready she returned to her car and noticed, parked close to it was a black Mercedes sports car. Perhaps it belonged to the 'trespasser,' for that was how she regarded anyone who happened on their special cove. She put the keys into the lock of her car and was about to open the door when just at that moment, she felt a hand on her shoulder and was startled to hear a man's voice.

"Do you not know how dangerous it is to bathe alone?" the voice was heard to say. Jenny turned fully to be met by the most beautiful pair of green/brown eyes. "My little lifesaver, if you are not careful, I may have to return the favour."

He smiled as he said these words, making Jenny feel a little uncomfortable. Standing so close, she found herself smiling back in response to his wide grin, which displayed perfectly formed white teeth. A little like John's, she thought to herself.

"May I buy you a coffee?" he asked. "You ran away so quickly last time we met, I never had the chance to thank you." Jenny could not find an excuse not to go so she agreed to follow him in her car. His car was the black Mercedes.

They drove in convoy up the winding lane from the cove. At the top of the hill he indicated to turn left. Jenny had not been down this road before. It was unmade and very rutted, as many of the roads had been in Kos before the council finally consented to tarmac them. This road must not have been on their list.

Jenny followed slowly but eagerly, eager to find out where it led. About a mile down the road, the road veered sharply to the left and downward. At the end of the track lay another smallish cove, and nestled behind some large trees was a small taverna, painted in the traditional blue and white and offering spectacular views out to the sea. He got out of his car and came to open the door of Jenny's, offering a hand to help her out. A sleepy taverna owner came out to greet them.

"Yasou Manolis," her escort said in greeting.

"Yasou Yannis," the owner replied, shaking hands and hugging each other. A shiver ran down her spine at discovering his name. His name, Yannis was Greek for John.

"Come sit down, I bring you drinks," Manolis said, waving his arms toward the blue table nearest to the front of the taverna, having the best views of the beach. Yannis pulled out a chair to seat Jenny.

He spoke quickly in Greek to Manolis, too quick for Jenny to understand, even though her Greek was much improved since she moved here to live

"Well now," Yannis said, giving Jenny his full attention. "Why have I not seen you for such a long time? You do not visit my cove." 'His cove!' Jenny thought again.

"I didn't think you would go there again after your accident," Jenny proclaimed. "I thought you'd no longer like it there."

"Not like it!" he replied. "It saved my life. YOU saved my life! It's a very special cove and I can see when I watch you there, it's special to you too - Yes?" Jenny nodded. "I think it has happy memories for you also?"

"Very happy memories," Jenny sighed. "I went there often with my husband."

"Ar," said Yannis knowingly and with disappointment clearly showing in his voice. He'd only met her briefly and in extremely unusual circumstances, yet since that meeting he'd been unable to get her image out of his mind. He'd tried several times to find out who she was and where she lived but with no success until today, when he'd happened upon her quite by accident.

"Your husband, he does not come with you now?" he questioned Jenny.

"No, sadly he cannot," she revealed sadly. Before she knew it she was telling him all about her life with John and how much love they had for each other. She told Yannis how she'd promised to fulfil his dream of living in Kos and how much she ached with emptiness because he was not here with her.

212

Yannis was visibly moved by her story. Suddenly Jenny realised he was clasping her hands in his, across the table.

"He sounds like a wonderful man," he said.

"He was," Jenny sighed in agreement. "Do you go the cove often?" she questioned.

"Not as much as before....." he paused. "My wife lost her battle to live and left me alone with only memories."

Yannis gazed out to sea and Jenny could see the hurt and sorrow building inside him. She found herself reaching across to take his hands and offer him solace, as he'd done for her. They sat in silence, holding hands and each lost in their own thought and memories. Anyone seeing the two of them sitting there would have thought they were lovers, so strong was their hold on each other. In this instance, it was healing and a deep respect which was passing between them, a respect for what each must have suffered, losing someone they'd clearly loved so deeply.

They were interrupted by Manolis, bringing fresh coffee and hot bread rolls. He smiled and knowingly nodded his head towards their joined hands. Yannis and Jenny both looked at their hands and released their grip on each other, embarrassed at what Manolis was obviously thinking

Yannis looked sadly across the table and began to tell Jenny his brief life story. How he'd grown up in Kefalos, met and fell in love with his wife, Eleni and now sadly had lost her. He told Jenny about how happy their lives had been before his wife passed away of cancer.

He'd met Eleni when they were very young and at school together. They'd become inseparable friends. They sat together all day at school, played together by the sea in the evenings and spent the long summer holidays together. Even in those days everyone said they were made for each other and destined to be together forever.

He went on to tell Jenny about how they were both devastated when at the age of twelve, Yannis' parents decided to move to America, as many other villagers had done.

On the day they were leaving they clung to each other for hours. Yannis was finally dragged away so the family would not miss the ferry taking him and his family far away, to a new life on the other side of the world.

He promised Eleni he would never forget her and would write daily. This he did for several months, but then slowly and surely, as with many long distance relationships the letter writing dried up, soon becoming the annual birthday and Christmas wishes.

It was six years before Yannis returned to Kefalos. Gone were the childish good looks, replaced with a handsome face and the strong body of a man.

When returning, his first thought was of Eleni. She too had changed dramatically. Her girlish body had transformed into that of a shapely young woman. She was stunning and had attracted many suitors over the years, but she wanted none of them. Her heart had always belonged to Yannis.

Upon seeing her, it was only seconds before Yannis had fallen madly in love with her all over again. They spent every moment they could together, closely watched by both sets of parents. They were the talk of the village, known as the ideal couple. Everyone smiled when seeing them together. They were so clearly meant for each other.

Eleni thought her heart would break when Yannis had to do his obligatory national service in the army. She wrote to him daily, gazing out to sea each night waiting for his safe return.

It was at the end of this spell of duty when he decided to ask her to marry him, after first asking permission from her father. It came as no surprise to her father or indeed to the rest of the village, as they'd seen the romance blossoming over the years.

Early in their married life, Yannis worked hard as a waiter in one of the many hotels that had begun to spring up in the beach area of Kamari Bay, as the island of Kos became a popular tourist spot. His amazing good looks and lively personality made him popular with the female guests, much to Eleni's sorrow, but he only had eyes for her and their love only grew stronger.

Yannis worked hard and progressed well within the hotel business, gaining promotion to manager of a small hotel and eventually becoming a partner in it He was eventually able to own a small hotel of his own, which he and Eleni ran together. They prospered and were able to add further hotels around the island. They themselves remained at their first hotel in Kamari Bay, preferring to stay near the village of Kefalos, where they were both born and raised.

Sensing that the atmosphere was beginning to get a little too sad, Yannis changed the subject and told Jenny a most fascinating story about his father, amd how he'd been involved in the liberation of Kos from the German occupation during the Second World War.

"The village of Kefalos still celebrates Liberation Day annually," Yannis told Jenny proudly. "My father was a war hero." Jenny looked impressed. "Maybe we can see the celebrations together next year?" Yannis said, more in hope than as a question, but then the conversation turned back to family life.

"My one true regret is not having children, because Eleni would have given me beautiful children," he said pausing for a moment. "Do you have children?" he questioned clearing his throat, overcome with emotion.

"Three, all grown up now," she revealed.

"How can that be, you are so young?" he told her. Jenny blushed. It was such a long time since anyone had paid her a compliment.

"Well I am quite old enough to have three grown up children, and I'm very proud of them," she informed him. "We also lost a daughter after only a short time. Her name was Emily, and the sadness of losing her never went away."

"So much sadness in your short life," Yannis observed with sincere feeling.

"And so much happiness too," Jenny stated. "I had a wonderful husband who I loved dearly and he also adored me. No one can take that away."

"I understand, I have my memories of Eleni and they are happy too," Yannis said looking at his watch. "I must go now. I have business in Kos Town. Please have coffee with me again next week." Jenny felt a surge of excitement. She'd really enjoyed being with Yannis and welcomed the idea of seeing him again. "We meet at the cove at nine- thirty - Yes?" His eyes sparkled as he asked her this. He hoped she would accept the invitation.

"Okay," she replied. He smiled in relief.

"I will walk you to your car," he said, rising to go.

He walked close to her, their hands not quite touching. Jenny put the key in the lock and Yannis opened the door. She climbed inside, shut the door and wound down the window.

"Thanks for the coffee," she said.

"Thanks for being with me," he smiled. "See you Saturday."

Jenny returned to her house and sat on the balcony. The feelings that ran through her disturbed her a little. Here was a man so like John, and yet so different. He rekindled emotions she'd suppressed for a long time. She felt euphoria when she thought of him.

In her excitement she'd almost forgotten that Michelle was arriving from England the next day. It was her first trip to Kos since Jenny had moved there. Although they'd written often, Jenny was anxious for news from England. She no longer referred to England as home. Kos was her home now, and she'd adapted reasonably well to the slower pace of life.

Michelle's daughter Jenny May was to have come with her, but had just found out that she was expecting her first baby. Michelle would be a Grandma at forty-five. The last time she saw her friend she barely looked old enough to be a mother, let alone a grandmother.

Jenny went to the airport to collect her friend, but hardly recognised Michelle as she came through Passport control. She'd put on quite a lot of weight and her hair was beginning to grey. She was already beginning to look like a Grandma, Jenny thought.

Likewise Michelle hardly recognised Jenny. Her life in the sun obviously suited her, making her look much younger than when they'd last been together. Then, Jenny had looked drained and tired with the grief of losing John. As soon as they were able to, they ran to each other and hugged.

"My my Jenny, you look so well," Michelle said, giving her the once over. "If I didn't know otherwise, I'd say you had a new love in your life." Jenny felt herself redden as she thought of Yannis.

"Don't be silly, it's the sun and good living," she lied, but underneath she was disturbed by the feelings she had when thinking about the Greek man who'd entered her life.

Outside the airport, she ushered Michelle into the car to avoid any further talk of lovers. It would only take about fifteen minutes to get to the house and Jenny felt excited about the prospect of showing it to Michelle.

They were going to have two weeks together and she knew she was going to enjoy her company. However, she thought how guarded she'd have to be, lest the secret she was keeping would be carelessly revealed.

Jenny had always felt annoyed when people did not keep appointments. She was normally very punctual herself, always arriving early or telephoning ahead if she was going to be even a few minutes late. It was extremely bad mannered to let people down, yet she'd forgotten her meeting with Yiannis, and was now racked with guilt.

Having Michelle staying with her had filled her days and she'd not for a moment stopped to think about what had been said a week ago in the taverna at the beach. It was now too late. She'd missed the meeting and it wasn't as if she could telephone to apologise as she had no way of contacting him. The sad thing was that she'd been looking forward to meeting him again and getting to know him even better.

CHAPTER 22
STORMY WEATHER

She was unsure what had woken her from her dreams. She sat bolt upright in her bed and shivered. The room was pitch-black. Almost immediately it was lit with a brilliant white light, and then darkness returned, followed by a deep clap of thunder.

She'd taken to sleeping without drawing the curtains, since no one could see through the window and when she woke in the mornings she was met with the beautiful views of the bay. Within seconds the darkness in the room was split with white light and then came the thunder again.

She reached for her dressing gown. Putting it on, she fastened it tightly and walked to the window. She stood in awe of what met her. The sky was filled with white and purple light. Forked lightening savagely split the dark blue sky. Black clouds hurled themselves against each other. She was mesmerised by the spectacle of the black night, suddenly illuminated by the white and purple of the lightening.

Then the rain came. The heavens opened and the torrents fell. The wind blew the rain fiercely onto the patio doors and ran down in rivulets.

She looked at her watch. It was six-thirty in the morning. Dawn was beginning to break as the storm passed, with normal light returning. She wondered if the delicate blooms in the garden had survived the storm.

Grabbing a t-shirt and donning a pair of shorts, she ventured to the kitchen to make a coffee. Soon it would be light and then she'd go and check the devastation the storm had caused, if any. When she opened the front door she could see that the veranda was strewn with blossoms. It looked like the aftermath of a wedding, with rose petals everywhere like confetti. A heavy fragrance hung in the air as it often does after rainfall, as if the earth felt refreshed by the rain.

She ventured carefully down the slippery staircase and walked to the rear of the house, where she'd planted vegetables and fruit trees. Netting lay strewn about but not too much damage had been done to the plants, which was a relief. The ground under foot was soft and muddy, and her flat sandals had become more like platform shoes!

She walked to the basement area. As yet, this was still open to the elements, as she and John had intended to complete this once the move was completed. It still contained unopened boxes from England, placed in the corner.

A shallow river of water ran across the concrete floor, but luckily had not reached the storage area. Jenny took a brush and swept it outside, then wandered back to check that no water had got into the boxes. She noticed that one box appeared to be open and took a look to see what it contained. Right at the top of the contents was the book of poems she'd mysteriously received many years ago. She'd read it several times before, but took it from the box and placed it in her pocket. Having checked the rest of the basement and garden, she went back inside the house, made herself a coffee and settled in the lounge.

Taking out the book, she gently flicked through the pages. A tiny slip of paper marked one page and she opened it. She read the poem written there:-

A Lovers Lament

For woe is me that I have lost the love that gave me life
Alone now every waking hour, and every fear filled night
But when the storm has filled the skies
And earth is refreshed and sweet
Then shall I learn to love again
And a new sweetheart shall meet

Jenny thought of the storm the night before. Could this be the storm that would bring her love again, just as the poem promised? She put the book down on the table.

She decided to walk to the village to get fresh bread and could see from the streets just how much rain had fallen last night. A river of bright yellow water flowed down the side of the road, with the pathways beginning to steam. Soon there would be little trace of the storm.

So different from England, she thought, when the water would remain for days. Everything here now looked clean and bright. A new start, a fresh beginning for her too maybe, she thought to herself.

CHAPTER 23
CHANCE MEETING

She'd noticed that the sink in the basement was blocked, probably as a result of the storm. She walked to the ironmongers in the village to buy a sink plunger. She knew full well her limited Greek vocabulary did not include the word for sink plunger, so resorted to miming the actions needed, she tried in vain to get the confused shopkeeper to realise what she wanted. This caused tears of laughter to everyone inside the shop at the time.

Suddenly a voice behind her came out with a string of Greek, quite unintelligible to Jenny. Light dawned on the face of the shopkeeper and he hurried to the storeroom to find the much needed sink plunger. Jenny turned to see who'd come to her aid and there stood Yiannis.

She hadn't seen him in months, not since she'd failed to turn up that day when she'd forgotten about their arranged meeting when Michelle staying with her. She was very pleased to see him and hoped he felt the same. She'd opened her mouth to say something, when the shopkeeper returned sporting a bright yellow plunger. Jenny paid for her purchase and turned to tell Yiannis how sorry she was for missing their rendezvous, but he was gone.

"Oh not again," she wailed out loud. As she left the shop, she was so relieved to see him standing in wait for her.

"How are you?" he asked a little coldly.

"I'm fine," She replied.

"I'm sorry," they both said simultaneously and laughed.

Jenny explained the reason she'd not made the meeting, but then Yiannis told how he'd been called away at the very last minute to a family crisis, so also had not made the rendezvous and had no way of letting her know.

"Before we go any further," Yannis said, "Can we exchange addresses and phone numbers so this can never happen again? I don't want to lose you again."

"Me neither," Jenny smiled.

"Coffee?" suggested Yannis.

"Coffee," Jenny agreed.

Satisfied that he now had a means of contacting her he swiftly led her to the nearest coffee shop, clutching to her hand lest she vanished before him.

After making arrangements to meet the next day, Jenny went home. She thought deeply about the poem she'd read earlier -Was this a sign? Did it mean that she might have found "A new love?" She hoped so, because she liked Yiannis a lot and wondered what tomorrow would bring.

The next day would be here soon, and she was definitely not going to miss this meeting!

CHAPTER 24
LEARNING AGAIN

They were meeting almost daily now. People were noticing them together and beginning to speculate as to whether they would become an item. They certainly always seemed close when they were out together, yet there were no obvious signs of intimacy between them.

They walked close to each other, laughed a lot and sat talking for hours on end, yet no one had seen them hold hands or exchange kisses, other than the customary kiss on the cheek when greeting. They were a puzzle to the outside world. Even Jenny's children were unaware of the growing relationship between their mother and this handsome Greek.

They both lived for the company and comfort that the other offered, yet inside, both had a yearning to take their relationship further. One day Jenny made the decision to invite Yiannis to her home. She still didn't know exactly where he lived, but felt it was time to remove another of the barriers she'd created in an effort to distance her from the feelings she had for him, which seemed to betray the love she'd had for John.

It seemed that Yannis was a little reluctant to accept the invitation at first. Like Jenny, he was worried about taking their friendship further, feeling that in some way it could be seen as a betrayal to his deceased wife, Eleni, and to Jenny's husband, John. However, after a bit more persuasion and the offer by Jenny to cook him a traditional British roast beef dinner, the deal' as done.

She covered the dining table with the beautiful hand embroidered tablecloth bought in the village years ago and placed the blue and white candelabra in the centre. She carefully folded the linen napkins and put them into the blue and white napkin rings then lay them on the table. Taking a good look at her work, the setting looked ideal.

She admitted that the thought of bringing a man into her house had given her mixed feelings, being both excited and anxious at the same time. She'd been so meticulous in her preparations, wanting it to be perfect. But why was it so important when she was just having a friend round for dinner? Was she creating an environment for moving their relationship a step further? Oh lord, was she creating a seduction scene?

Beginning to panic, she ensured all the house lights were on and didn't light the fragranced candles as she'd planned, and no soppy, romantic music. It was just a special meal for a close friend, that's all, she told herself, but who was she trying to convince.

She'd bought a new cream dress for the occasion, sleeveless with a wide neck and a draped back, and just above knee length. She glanced at it now as it hung on her wardrobe door, wondering if it might be too sexy.

She remembered the new underwear she'd treated herself to. Why had she done that? She had perfectly good underwear already, and Yannis was not going to see it – was he? Her cheeks glowed a little at the thought of him seeing her in her new underwear.

'Don't be stupid. He's seen you many times in your bikini, so what's the difference?" she asked out loud.

She looked in the full length mirror. The dress fitted superbly and being silk it moved with her as she circled to try and see how she looked from the back. The strappy cream and diamante sandals, not too high healed, added a touch of elegance to the outfit.

His stomach churned as he drove up the hill to the outskirts of the village, to where Jenny told him she lived. He found the house and rang the bell to announce his arrival.

As the doorbell rang, Jenny struggled to breathe. She opened the door to see Yiannis waiting with a beautiful bouquet of flowers, dressed in a pale blue shirt and dark chinos. Unknown to her, his heart was also beating so hard and fast that he felt the whole world could hear it! Jenny thought he looked lovely today, if a little nervous.

"Kalispera, come in" Jenny managed to splutter. Yiannis didn't reply. He just couldn't speak. She looked more beautiful than he'd ever seen her before. He coughed to try and regain his composure and thrust the flowers at her.

"Welcome to my home," Jenny said, waving her arm in the air. Yiannis nodded in acknowledgement but still said nothing. "I'll show you round, if you like," Jenny said hesitantly, unsure of why Yiannis seemed to be rooted to the spot. After the guided tour, Yiannis followed Jenny as she returned to the lounge.

"You have a beautiful house," he finally managed to say, beginning to relax now. "I will show you mine soon…….my house I mean," he said.

"I'd like that," Jenny said smiling. "Are you ready now….. To eat I mean." They both laughed at their uneasiness.

As they sat together at the dining table they both wondered why they felt so awkward together this evening. Jenny shook her napkin and placed it on her lap. Yiannis did the same.

He picked up his glass of wine and raising it into the air, stretched across the table to chink his glass with Jenny's. Their fingers touched momentarily. They lowered their eyes, each feeling a little uncomfortable and not able to risk looking each other in the eye, lest their true feelings be shown.

Jenny presented the main meal, the traditional roast beef dinner and with it she opened a second bottle of wine, which helped them to relax a little and encouraged the conversation to flow more easily.

"Let's have coffee and brandy in the lounge," Jenny suggested. She'd thought of taking him outside to the terrace, but the evenings were getting a little cooler now. Yiannis sat on the couch with Jenny on the adjacent chair, their knees almost touching. He sipped his brandy, savouring the warm sensation in his throat. Yannis looked at Jenny and gazed straight into her eyes. She was held in the gaze.

"Jenny," he said, clearing his throat and obviously finding it difficult to speak. "When Eleni died," he paused. "A big part of me died too. I knew I could never love someone again in the same way I'd loved her. My life was so empty and meaningless without her and each day was the same, miserable and empty. But then I met you, and gradually life seemed to have a new meaning for me. I need to tell you something, Jenny."

"What?" Jenny questioned, feeling confused.

"I have to tell you that I'm falling in love with you," Yannis plucked up the courage to say. "I'm sorry, but I'm scared. I don't want to lose you by letting you know my true feelings. I know how much you loved and still love John, and I will understand if you want me to go." Jenny couldn't believe what she was hearing. It was exactly how she felt herself. She put her fingers to his lips

"Yannis, I feel the same way too," she confessed. She gazed into his eyes which were now moist with emotion. "I'm falling in love with you too" she managed to say before the tears began to slip down her cheeks.

Yannis took her hand gently and she sat beside him on the sofa. He put his arm around her and gently pulled her to him, her head resting on his chest. With his other hand he lifted her face upwards and slowly bowed his head towards hers and kissed her gently on the lips.

"You have no idea how long I've waited to do that," he smiled. "And it was every bit as wonderful as I'd dreamed it would be."

Jenny melted in his embrace. For a long time she'd longed to be kissed like this. Although the kiss only lasted only a few seconds, they both knew they'd taken an irrevocable step. They could no longer go back to being just friends! He kissed her again and she could feel her body responding, feelings and emotions dormant for so long now surfaced. She was afraid to open her eyes in case she was dreaming.

They sat in silence, wrapped in each other's arms for what seemed an eternity. Jenny was wondering what would happen next when Yiannis suddenly jumped to his feet.

"There is something I must do," he announced. "I must go now. I'll return for you in the morning at ten." He started walking towards the door and Jenny was flabbergasted. A moment ago she was wrapped in his arms, yet now he was running away as fast as possible. Reaching the door he turned to her.

"It was a lovely meal. I really enjoyed myself. Thank you," he said and was gone, not even waiting to kiss her goodbye.

She flopped down on the sofa, very upset, yet too shocked to cry. What had she done wrong? She was completely shocked!

She cleared away the debris of the meal, turned out the lights and went slowly and sadly to bed - on her own!

CHAPTER 25
HOME SWEET HOME

After a restless night pondering on what had gone wrong with what seemed a perfect evening, Jenny got up and showered. She picked up her discarded clothing from the night before and held her dress to her face. She could smell the aftershave Yiannis had worn last night. She wondered if he would turn up today as he had said he would, or had she frightened him away for good.

She dried her hair half-heartedly, thinking about the care she'd taken in preparing herself for last night. She left her hair hanging loose and put on a plain black sun top and shorts, along with her oldest, most comfortable flip-flops. She gazed out of the window, but saw nothing of the fantastic view before her.

Yiannis had said her would come at ten and it was now nine-forty-five. She picked up a magazine from the coffee table and flicked through without taking in any of it.

She watered her indoor plants – nine-fifty-five. She refilled the kettle but not knowing why – nine-fifty-nine. Was he coming or not? She wandered over to look out the front window.

Ten o'clock - A black Mercedes drove up the drive. It was him, but he didn't get out of the car. She walked slowly down the steps. He got out and opened the door for her. Saying nothing, he gave her the salutary kiss on both cheeks. He closed the door behind her, climbed back inside and drove off. Neither of them spoke but she soon realised where they were heading, the cove where they'd first met and where she'd rescued him from the sea. He stopped the car and opened the door for her. Jenny noted he was still polite, if nothing else!

"Follow me," he muttered and started to walk to the cliff top away from the beach. Jenny followed in silence, not sure if she should ask what this was all about.

Behind the gorse bushes that hid the cove was a flat area covered with sparse grasses and creepers. In the middle of this barren patch, Jenny noticed a large section of concrete. Yannis stopped close the concrete section and turned to her.

"This is my house," he said quietly. Jenny didn't understand what he meant. "I started to build it before Eleni became ill," he continued to explain. "It was to be a surprise for her." Jenny could see why he might have chosen this site, with its tremendous views of the cove, through the thicket of gorse bushes.

"It would have been lovely. Very secluded," Jenny commented.

"I want to start the building work again, Jenny," he said. "But there is something missing." As he said this, he handed Jenny the architect's plans and passed them to her. She laid them on the bonnet of the car and took a long, thoughtful look.

"Looks like it would be a beautiful home," Jenny revealed, "But the house looks complete to me."

"No," he said again. "There is something missing."

"Well I can't see anything," she confessed. "Tell me what it is that's missing?"

"You!" he said looking nervous. "You are missing from this house. I want to begin building again, but only if you will live here with me."

"I don't understand what you're saying," Jenny said, with a look of confusion etching her face.

"Jenny, I want to live with you in this house," he said, seeing her confused stare. "But I'm not asking you to live in sin. I want you to live here, with me, as my wife."

A stunned Jenny gazed at him, realising for the first time that she really did love the man standing before her. He looked anxious and upset.

"I'm sorry," he muttered." I shouldn't have asked. It's too soon after losing John, isn't it?"

"No," Jenny said firmly. "It's the right time, the right time for both of us. We have grieved long enough, and grief will never bring them back." She smiled at him and said, "Yannis, ask me again – properly."

He did not need to be asked a second time and swiftly went down on one knee.

"Jenny Peters," he smiled. "Would you do me the honour of becoming my wife? Will you marry me?"

"Yes!" she screamed, and as he stood up she leapt into his arms. "Yes I will marry you, you wonderful man," she happily confirmed.

The house was now almost completed and stood on three levels, complete with large windows and balconies taking full advantage of the fabulous views of the coastline to the front, and the hills and mountain to the rear. Standing several yards back from the cove, it was hidden behind the gorse bushes which were high enough to hide it from anyone walking along the pathway leading to the cove. The gardens extended all around the building and a road had been built at the rear, leading to the main road that led from the village to the coast. All in all, it looked spectacularly beautiful.

Although their future lives were now together neither ever forgot their previous partners, both insisting that the walls of the main reception area would be adorned by pictures of Jenny with first husband, John, and of Yannis with his beloved Eleni. However, there was a big space left empty in the middle of all the photos from the past.

"This is where we will put our own wedding photos," Yannis smiled.

"Agreed," Jenny said, kissing the new man of her dreams.

CHAPTER 26
FAMILY TIES

"Hi Mum, its Laura, how are you, or should I say, Te Kaneis? James told me you're practically Greek now."

"Yes darling," Jenny laughed. "I am fine thanks my love. How are you?"

"I have loads to tell you Mum, and something to ask you," Laura divulged.

'Me too,' Jenny thought, but she wanted to tell the whole family together, not individually over the phone.

Laura went on to tell Jenny that she'd passed her exams, "with honours" and with the highest marks in the entire year.

"What do you think of that, Mum?" Laura asked.

"I'm thrilled for you, you clever thing," Jenny replied proudly. "You must have inherited your brains from me," she laughed. Then getting very serious, she added, "Your dad would have been very proud."

"Thanks mum," she heard Laura say a little teary.

"Hey don't cry," Jenny offered. "Today is a happy day."

"Mum, I have to attend an award ceremony to be presented with a special award two weeks from now," Laura gushed. "Do you think you could come over for the ceremony?"

"Of course I'll be there," Jenny confirmed. "I wouldn't miss it for the world. But do you mind if I bring someone with me?"

"No problem, Mum, I can invite who I want. I thought I'd arrange a family meal afterwards. What do you think?"

"Sounds great, sweetheart," Jenny was pleased to say.

"Who are you bringing Mum," Laura queried.

"You wait and see," Jenny laughed out loud. She put down the receiver and instantly picked it up again, dialled Yiannis and explained the situation.

"We are going to England, my love," she announced. "That's if you're brave enough to meet my family."

"No problem," Yannis stated. "Anyway they're my family now and I'll be pleased to meet them."

The plane taxied across the tarmac at Manchester Airport. It had been a pleasant flight, but Jenny now agonised as to how the family would react when she introduced Yiannis to them, especially when telling of her intentions to marry him in around four months time. Would they accept him, or see him as an intruder, a betrayal of their father's memory?

Once through passport control, Jenny could feel her heart beating faster and faster. Only one more set of doors and then Laura would be there waiting for them. She took a deep breath in an attempt to calm herself, smiled at Yiannis and walked through as the double doors opened. Laura, upon seeing her mother leapt over the barrier and ran to her. They hugged for ages without saying a word.

"Laura, I have someone I want you to meet," Jenny finally said, breaking from the embrace and gesturing for Yannis to join them. "This is Yiannis, and Yiannis, this is my younger daughter, Laura." Yiannis extended his hand towards Laura and smiled.

"Pleased to meet you," she said, smiling back at him. "We guessed it must be a man our mum was bringing because of all the secrecy." Jenny could feel herself blushing. "Have we met before?" Laura asked. "I feel like I know you."

"I think not, but maybe," Yiannis replied with a shrug of his shoulders.

Laura released the boot of the car and then opened the door for Jenny.

"What a dish," she whispered to Jenny as she slid into the car. "Are there any more like him at home?"

Jenny winked at Laura. She said nothing, but was comforted by the fact that her daughter liked the look of him. Although there was no animosity from 'youngest daughter,' she wondered how the others would react. Forty-five minutes later, they were nearing the village where Laura now lived in a flat. As they pulled into the car park in front of the apartment block, a first floor window was flung open and a hand began frantically waving at the car.

"That's Suzie, my other daughter," Jenny informed Yiannis, as she waved just as frantically back towards the window.

They unloaded the car and Yiannis carried the heavy cases, whilst Jenny and Laura balanced the boxes between them. The door of the flat was flung open and Suzie emerged with a broad smile on her face. She tried to hug Jenny despite the boxes. Yiannis stood behind her smiling, as he witnessed the love and joy this family were sharing.

Before Jenny could introduce him to Suzie, Laura shouted out, "Just look what mum brought with her," pointing appreciatively towards Yiannis, who stepped forward to meet Suzie. Suzie looked him up and down and then smiled.

"You win, Laura," Suzie admitted. "He does have dark hair." Yiannis frowned. "We were taking bets about what you'd look like. I said fair, Laura said dark. I'm Suzie, pleased to meet you."

"I'm pleased to meet you too," Yannis said, his beautiful Greek accent shining through. "You look just like your mother," he proclaimed.

"Oh God, do I?" she laughed.

"Can we get inside please so I can put these parcels down?" Jenny pleaded, to which everyone laughed.

It was the first time Jenny had seen Laura's flat and she was impressed by what she saw, how tidy it was and how tastefully decorated and furnished. Jenny and Yiannis sat down on the pale grey leather sofa and began to relax. Just then the door opened and they were all surprised when Jamie and Caitlin entered.

"Managed to get away early," Jamie announced. "All quiet on the western front. Hi Mum, give us a hug."

Jenny stood and embraced her son. He was so tall now, even taller than when he'd visited that time, and handsome too, just like his father had been at that age.

"Jamie, I'd like you to meet Yiannis," Jenny said and Yiannis stood up. They were both about the same height. Jamie shook his hand firmly.

"I see Laura won the bet," he laughed, "Have we met before? Perhaps that time when I was in Kos. You seem very familiar."

"It seems everyone knows me," Yiannis smiled.

"Are you are from Kefalos?" Jamie questioned.

"Yes, I have lived there all my life," Yannis replied. He went on to give Jamie a brief story of his life, telling him about his life with Eleni, no, they'd never been blessed with children, and all about his hotel career.

"So many questions, Jamie," Jenny butted in to save Yannis. "What is this, a Spanish Inquisition?" The family laughed and Yannis looked relieved.

"Just like to know who's messing around with my mum," Jamie joked. Unfortunately, Yannis did not understand the humour.

"Messing around," he said looking worried. "I do not understand messing around." Jenny spoke in Greek, translating for him. He turned to face the expectant faces before him. "I do not mess with your mother. I love her." There was a deathly hush in the room.

"And just what are your intentions regarding our mum," Jamie asked a little aggressively.

"My intentions?" Yannis questioned. "My intention is to marry her and make her happy. That is if I have your permission."

"Well that's okay then," Jamie smiled. "You'll do for me." He put his hand out and Yannis shook it vigorously. "Welcome to the family," everyone cheered as Jamie welcomed his mum's new man to the nest.

Jenny looked across at Yiannis, who was chatting with Jamie and Caitlin. He seemed totally at ease with her family and she knew everything was going to be okay. She also knew that Yiannis was the right man for her.

The graduation ceremony went ahead and Jenny could not have been prouder. When Laura walked on the stage to receive her special award, she thought her heart would burst with the pride inside. She glanced at Yiannis, who was clapping enthusiastically. He also looked proud, as if it were his own daughter collecting the prize. He turned and grinned at her and she gulped back the tears. What a lovely, caring man he was.

After the ceremony they piled into the cars and drove the short distance to the restaurant where Laura had arranged the meal. Once they'd eaten, Jamie stood up to give a speech.

"This is a very special night for Laura and we all know how proud Dad would have been if he were here with us. He would have been standing here now, rather than me proposing a toast to his youngest offspring, so in his place, as the man of the household it falls on me to say a few words. Congratulations Laura, we are all thrilled and very proud of you and your achievements. Who would have thought that the baby would turn out to be such a genius? We love you." With this said, he raised his glass and everyone repeated the toast.

"Well done. We love you," they all said in unison. Jamie didn't sit down.

"Now before sitting down, I have a few more things to say," Jamie continued. "I would like to say, and I think I speak for the rest of us, when dad died we were all devastated, but mum especially. We were all so worried when she insisted she was still moving to Kos, as she and dad had planned. We couldn't understand why, until we visited the place and met her Greek friends living there. Then she met Yannis. Mum, we are pleased for you, and may I say that Dad would also be pleased that you have found someone to share your life with. Go for it, Mum, with all our blessings." He raised his glass. "Mum and Yiannis," he toasted.

"Mum and Yiannis," everyone echoed.

"Thank you," was all that Jenny managed to say before choking up. She looked around the room at all the smiling faces. She looked at her children with their prospective partners, knowing it must be hard for them, seeing their mum with a new man. It made her love them even more.

"May I say a few words?" Yiannis said standing. He hesitated but then everybody clapped in encouragement. "May I begin by offering my congratulations to Laura on her wonderful achievement, and Laura, thank you for letting me be a part of the celebration." He raised his glass towards Laura.

He went on to tell them all about his life in Kos, eventually reaching present day and of his meeting Jenny. He told this part of the story with an amazing smile on his face and everyone could see the genuine love he felt for her.

"I just want to say that I love your mother with all my heart, and want her to be happy. I know I can never replace your father and would never attempt to do so, but I will do everything possible to make her happy. I love her so much...."

He couldn't continue, as he was overcome with emotion. As he sat down, there was not a dry eye in the room. Suzie made the first move, walking to Yannis and kissing him on both cheeks.

"Welcome to the family," she whispered. Laura also gave him a big hug, which brought him to tears of happiness.

"Welcome to the family, Yannis. Hope you know what you are letting yourself in for," Jamie joked, lightening the mood.

Everyone seemed pleased for the happy couple.

"You are wonderful," Jenny whispered, squeezing Yiannis' hand.

"You too," he whispered in return, giving her a very public kiss.

CHAPTER 27
CONGRATULATIONS

All too soon, it was time to return to Kos. Suzie took them to the airport this time. Jenny had said her goodbyes to the rest of the family the night before. Not so tearful this time as she knew it would only be a few months until she saw them all again. Next time it would be in Kos for the wedding.

It was late afternoon when the plane touched down. They collected their luggage, which was considerably lighter on the return flight, collected Yiannis' car and drove the short distance to Kefalos.

"Your house or mine," Yiannis asked.

"Since yours is still a building site, I guess it will have to be mine," Jenny laughed.

Slipping the key in the lock, Jenny opened the front door and, followed by Yiannis carrying the luggage, went inside. She busied herself making coffee for the two, when she realised she was being watched.

"What?" she asked smiling.

"You are beautiful and I love you so much," Yannis beamed.

"You're not so bad yourself," she laughed, planting a kiss on the top of his head. "Mind if I take a quick shower? I feel really grubby after the journey. It won't take me long." Yiannis gave the Greek gesture for yes.

Whilst Jenny showered, he glanced around the room. The last time he'd been in here was when he came for the meal and had been too stressed to really notice anything. He admired the décor and the splendid views.

"The shower is free if you want it," Jenny offered, emerging from the shower wearing a white bathrobe with a towel on her head. He took her up on the offer. After a good long soak, he re-emerged from the bathroom with a bath towel draped around his waist.

"All my clean clothes are still in the suitcase," he divulged, looking at Jenny sitting in her bathrobe with a mop of half dried hair hanging loosely around her shoulders. He thought she looked amazing lazing there on the couch.

Jenny looked up from the book she was reading and saw Yiannis standing there. His olive shiny skin, his dark hair still damp and dressed only in a towel, he looked fantastic – Her Greek God!

"Come and sit down a minute," she beckoned, tapping the sofa beside her.

He sat next to jenny on the couch, noticing how the belt of her bathrobe had loosened, revealing the curves of her breasts. He felt a stirring in his loins! The excitement began to pulse through his veins and was becoming 'obvious!' He nervously looked around the room, trying to think of anything to take away the erotic feelings he was witnessing.

"Are you okay?" Jenny asked, puzzled by the way he was scanning the room.

"Yes, I'm okay," he replied.

"You don't look it to me," Jenny said laughing. She pulled her bathrobe a little tighter around her body, which was both a relief and a disappointment to Yiannis at the same time.

"So what are we going to do now?" she asked, to which Yiannis laughed, "What's the matter?" Jenny asked.

"You seem so relaxed," Yannis replied. "Here we are in a house on our own, both practically naked, and you don't seem to care."

Jenny realised she'd never even thought about it. It had seemed so natural to come home and have a shower and loaf around. Yiannis being there hadn't entered her mind.

"Scared I might seduce you?" she teased.

"Scared I might not be able to keep my hands off you," he replied. She smiled and moved closer to him, putting her head on his bare shoulder and ruffling the hair on his chest.

He tilted his head forward and kissed her on the nose. She arched her neck so she could reach his lips and kissed him long and hard. She felt his arms go round her and pull her tightly to him. It felt wonderful. The bathrobe slipped off Jenny's shoulder and Yiannis attempted to replace it.

"Spoilsport," she whispered, kissing him again.

"You're driving me crazy!" Yiannis admitted.

"Then do something about it," she smiled.

Yiannis took her in his arms and carried her to the bedroom. He laid her gently on the bed and then took his place next to her. She could feel her heart beating faster and faster.

Yiannis kissed her on her cheek and nose, brushed his lips gently across hers and then kissed her throat. Jenny sighed deeply, her entire body electrified by his touch. She felt his hand move slowly inside her bathrobe, until tantalisingly touching her breast. She moaned again.

"It's okay?" he asked, looking deep in her eyes.

"It's okay," she replied, as if giving him confirmation of her permission.

He pulled her to him and hugged her, as she ran her fingers up and down his spine. He shivered.

"Okay?" she asked.

"Okay?" was his reply.

Slowly, the two reluctant lovers began to explore each other's bodies. She knew what she wanted. He knew what he wanted.

"Should we not wait until we're married?" Yannis questioned.

"No," Jenny muttered. "We have waited too long already. I want you now!"

The lovemaking was wonderful, so sensual and tender. It was everything they'd wished for. When finished they collapsed into a satisfied heap, lay cradled in each other's arms, and drifted into a luxurious slumber.

When Jenny woke she lay watching Yiannis as he slept, just to see him breathe. She thought about how lucky she'd been to find the love of two good men in her life. Many women never feel love like she'd had with John, and here she was again, looking at Yannis and feeling so much love for him. She'd been truly blessed.

She slipped out from under the covers very carefully so as not to wake him, and ever so quietly opened the wardrobe door. There were two bathrobes hanging there and she took one of them, noticing that the label was still attached. It had never been worn since the day she brought them out to Greece. Putting it on, she pushed her hands into the deep pockets and could feel something in one of the pockets. She pulled out what was a small card and gagged as she read what was written on it:-

"CONGRATULATIONS - SO PLEASED YOU MADE IT AT LAST - HOPE YOU WILL BE REALLY HAPPY TOGETHER"

It was signed by John, and signed with a kiss. He must have written it when he knew he was about to leave her. She plonked back onto the bed forgetting Yiannis was still asleep. He woke to see her with her head in her hands and sobbing, wondering what was wrong. Had he done something to upset her? Did she regret sleeping with him? Had she suddenly thought it was all a mistake?

"Tell me Jenny, tell me," he pleaded, putting his arm around her. She showed him the card. "What does it mean?" he asked.

"It means its all okay. John has told me its okay. John has given us his blessing," she smiled, looking happier than he'd ever seen her before.

Still Yiannis frowned and Jenny began to explain to him about how John had made her promise to find someone to love her the way he did. He'd also joked that if she didn't, he would come back to haunt her until she did.

She explained to Yiannis that she fully believed that somehow this message had come from John, and he was giving his approval to their flourishing relationship.

"Do you see now?" Jenny said happily. "John is giving me his blessing to love another man, and that man is you." Yiannis put his arms around her and pulled her back under the sheets.

"Again?" he suggested.

"Again," she agreed, smiling.

This time they made love more slowly and less hungrily than before, each silently saying their goodbyes to their previous partners. It was their release, both comforted by the thought that John and Eleni had given their approval.

CHAPTER 28
VOWS

The horse drawn carriage was to pick her and James up from the house and take them down to the jetty in front of 'Captain Johns.' From there they would be ferried across to the tiny island of St Nicolas.

The carriage had been lovingly decorated with flowers and the grey horse pulling it had a plume of feathers on its head, with more flowers on its harness. Manolis, the driver and long time friend of Jenny's, wore his best suit and sported a red carnation in his buttonhole.

Jenny's nerves had been getting the better of her, so James had opened a bottle of champagne and handed her a glass. He looked so handsome in his white dinner jacket and black trousers. She hoped he wouldn't be too warm, as the weather had turned out magnificent in honour of the occasion.

"Are you ready Mum" James asked, gently touching her arm when almost time to leave. She nodded to him and smiled. "You look wonderful Mum," her son continued. "Dad would have loved you in that outfit." She smiled. "Of course, Mum, Yiannis will love you in that outfit too. The family all think he's is a fantastic guy and we all love him very much. We know he makes you happy and that's what we all want for you"

Jenny was really struggling now to keep her emotions in check. She knew today was the start of a new era of her life, and the first step to a new beginning, a promise of happiness in her life. She knew she had John's approval, and now she also had the approval of the family.

She left the house arm in arm with James, who was giving her away, closed the door on the past and walked confidently into the future – Her new life with Yannis.

Many of the locals were out in the streets to watch the bride on her journey through the village, down the steep hill and onto the coast road towards the jetty. The numerous bells on the horse harness jingled a merry tune throughout the journey.

Nearing the jetty, Jenny could see one boat waiting for her bobbing around in the water. Ten minutes earlier there'd been several boats moored at the jetty, but they'd already carried the guest to the island in readiness for the ceremony.

As they approached, Panos jumped from the boat to help them step aboard. Jenny hardly recognised him dressed in black trousers and a gleaming white shirt. She was so used to seeing him in his shorts and t-shirt, with his baseball cap pulled down over his sun glassed eyes. He smiled broadly as he greeted them. He was so happy that Jenny and Yiannis had found each other.

The trip to the island took only five minutes. As Jenny stepped from the boat she gazed at the fabulous view. The water was the deepest blue and crystal clear. With not a cloud in the sky, the day was picture perfect.

Jenny's daughters, Suzie and Laura, the bridesmaids, were waiting to met their mum and arrange her clothes to make sure she looked perfect. As they entered the church everyone turned to face her, all giving their seal of approval. Walking up the aisle with James by her side she could see Yiannis waiting for her, with a smile that could light up the entire building.

She looked incredibly beautiful as she reached her place next to Yannis at the altar. They exchanged smiles, no words were needed. They both knew they loved each other and were prepared to commit to each other and promise to be faithful. The look between them said it all, and the following ceremony was just words.

The bright sunlight dazzled them as they emerged from the church as 'Man and Wife.' Everyone came to congratulate them, each with their own message of love.

Eventually separated from Yannis by the crowd of well-wishers, Jenny wandered to the edge of the jetty for a brief moment of solitude, where she looked across the sweeping, horseshoe bay. Holidaymakers lay catching the afternoon sun, windsurfers whisked across the blue water, and someone in the far distance was water-skiing.

'Life goes on,' she thought. This was Kefalos as she'd first seen it all those years ago. This was the place she now called home.

CHAPTER 29
LIFE

Jenny sat in the rocking chair daydreaming, thinking over what cards life had dealt her. It had been a good life and she realised how lucky she'd been to have found real love, not once but twice.

She thought back to first meeting John at the fair, their brief courtship, splitting up, Michelle's short marriage, to having her life saved by Jamie and the beautiful friendship which emerged from it.

She thought about Sue's dreadful suicide following the horrific incident in Spain, and then finally meeting John again and the idyllic lifestyle they'd had in the house on the hills. But then John had become very ill and died, leaving her sad and lonely in her solitude.

She'd thought her life was over and resigned herself to an old age spent alone, albeit in Kos, as she'd promised John that she would fulfil their dreams, with or without him. Then she'd met the second love of her life, her wonderful Greek husband, Yannis. How could she be so lucky a second time?

It had been a good marriage, full of love and happy memories, but sadly, Yannis had passed away peacefully in his sleep more than three years ago, now leaving Jenny alone again in her old age. Still, she had her memories, which always put a smile on her face.

The children, all grown up now with children of their own, tried to persuade her to 'come home' to England,' but as she always told them, "This is my home. This is where I have lived for many years. This is where Yannis is buried in the cemetery overlooking the bay, and this is where I will eventually be buried with him, in the double plot we bought together."

As she sat rocking and enjoying the stillness of the early morning, inhaling the smells and taking in the sounds around her, she caught sight of a young couple hurrying hand in hand down to the beach below. They glanced around as they clambered down the steep cliff side, making sure that no one else was around. At this early hour of the day it was obvious to Jenny that they'd come to the beach to make love in the early morning sunshine, hidden from view in this cove just as she and John had done many times before, and she and Yannis had done in later years.

She could sense from the closeness of their bodies that their passion was already aroused. Their frantic undressing confirmed her suspicions.

She felt drawn to watch them, not as a voyeur with any sexual undertones, but as if given the chance to relive her own youthful experiences. Once undressed, the lovers hid themselves behind a large rock on the beach.

She watched as the young bodies entwined and rolled gently in the soft sand, their hands exploring each other, their lips caressing every part of each other's body. Then he laid her softly on the sand, as John had done, and covered her body with his. At this most intimate moment Jenny looked away, feeling a little guilty to have encroached on their secret lovemaking.

The young couple lay still now, their passions sated. They would take in the sunshine and experience the magic of the cove. It would be their secret place, just as it had been hers and Johns all those years ago, just as its magic had lead her to Yannis and helped her find love again.

She left the chair and walked to the cove. As she neared the top of the cliff, she saw the bronzed body of someone standing on the beach and looking out to sea.

Strangely she found she didn't have to struggle down the steep cliff face as she normally had to. Her decent was like that of an agile youngster, almost floating above the ground. She ran across the beach to where the waiting man beckoned to her, unsure whether it was John or Yannis. She couldn't quite make it out but it didn't matter, they had morphed together and were the same person as far as she was concerned. What puzzled her was how young and fit he looked standing there before her. She looked down at her own body and was mystified. Gone were the ravages of time. Her figure was once more that of a young woman.

She fell easily into his strong arms. They paused for a moment holding each other tightly and then, hand in hand, they walked slowly into the sea.

The Greek police found Jenny the next day. James had phoned them to say he was worried that his mum had not phoned him that morning as she normally did, and he'd not been able to contact her as she was not answering the phone.

They had to break the door down to gain entrance to the house, and that was when they found her. She'd died in her rocking chair on the balcony overlooking the bay. She'd passed with a massive smile on her face. No sign of pain, no sign of fear. She'd died happy.

Three days later, surrounded by her three children and five grandchildren, along with many of the Greek friends she'd made over the years, Jenny was laid to rest. She was laid next to her beloved Yannis, where they would stay together for all eternity. When they bought the plot all those years ago, they'd chosen this position as it over looked the cove, Jenny and John's cove before, then Jenny and Yannis' cove. It was the perfect place for them to be together.

Her family, although sad at her passing, also had tears of joy to think these two wonderful people who loved each other so unconditionally were finally reunited – back in each other's arms again. Their love story was finally complete.

THE END

Printed in Poland
by Amazon Fulfillment
Poland Sp. z o.o., Wrocław

61619957R00137